MW01281785

IDENTIFIABLE

IDENTIFIABLE

Dear Meg,
Thank you for
your
support!

Sincerely,
Julia Tvardovskaya

JULIA TVARDOVSKAYA

NEW DEGREE PRESS

COPYRIGHT © 2021 JULIA TVARDOVSKAYA

IDENTIFIABLE

ISBN   978-1-63730-702-1   *Paperback*
          978-1-63730-793-9   *Kindle Ebook*
          979-8-88504-013-6   *Ebook*

"The choice for mankind lies between freedom and happiness and for the great bulk of mankind, happiness is better."

—GEORGE ORWELL

For L, who inspired this thought experiment.

CONTENTS

———

AUTHOR'S NOTE

"I don't try to describe the future. I try to prevent it."

—RAY BRADBURY

Dear Readers,

As of late, I've been struggling with understanding the dichotomy of social technologies.

Social technologies, including social media, give us the opportunity to connect with others. On a daily, weekly, or monthly basis, I have the ability to update friends and family across the globe on my life and thoughts. I'm able to video call my family in Ukraine, direct message my friends in Canada, or send a disappearing video to my classmates in Washington, DC, on a whim, from anywhere in the world.

Particularly during a pandemic and in times of quarantine, these technologies have provided a link between us, saving us from solitude.

Does this make them good?

Social technologies are also addicting. Algorithms are created to monopolize our time and attention, sending us down rabbit holes and time-suckers, causing us to scroll for hours on end, polarizing and triggering us.

This tracking also depletes our privacy, telling the world and technology companies what we buy, where we live, where we are at any moment of any day, where our children go to school, and so much more. They commoditize our data, our children's data, with our children (and us, probably) unaware of the information being tracked that is sold to unknown buyers who sell it to other unknown buyers.

Does this make them bad?
This is usually where the public debate over social technologies ends. The need for connection versus the right to privacy and our time.

But for me, there is something this conversation is missing: identity.

While watching the documentary *The Social Dilemma* on Netflix for a class I was taking in the fall of 2020, a chart flashed across the screen showing how rates of self-harm had skyrocketed for children between the ages of ten and nineteen after 2009, which is the year that Facebook went mobile.

I remember thinking: *These are children who had a say in what was posted about them on social media because they were likely doing the posting. Their parents were likely not on social media. If these children were so affected by the responses to what they posted, how would children whose lives were posted without their input and consent be impacted?*

As kids, we all probably have memories of us at the age of ten or even sixteen of how mortified we felt when friends or our crushes saw our baby pictures around our houses. "Quick! Hide that!" was a knee-jerk reaction for me on multiple occasions. But today, with our generation, pictures and developmental milestones are no longer restricted to the safety of physical walls and scrapbooks. They are posted on accounts, public or private (although nothing on the internet is ever private), parading our pride and joy for the world to see, no longer just for our closest friends and family. There is no "Quick! Hide that!" on the internet. What we think is adorable and sweet may be humiliating to a developing child.

Even more than that, every picture we share, every post we write, is through our own lens, our own filtered version of perfection, implanting our vision through catchy captions like a highlight reel of a life we want *rather* than the one we may *have*. When we post information about others, it is always tainted by how we want others to see them, which many times may not be how they want to be seen. Wanting the best for someone is always our version of "the best," but it may not be theirs.

When we spend someone's entire childhood narrating their choices, we rob them from creating their own public identity and persona.

Psychologist Scott M. Stanley has provided research showing a correlation between wedding guests and marital quality (Stanley and Rhodes, 2014). Essentially, individuals who have larger guestlists are less likely to get divorced than those who have smaller celebrations. And this makes sense. When you make a promise, when you create a life as a partner in front of hundreds of people—although an impossible decision regardless of the size of the celebration—it is exceptionally hard to break when witnessed by hundreds of people; it's like breaking hundreds of individual promises.

Likewise, when someone posts an individual's entire life how they want it to be lived in front of thousands, potentially millions, of people, it becomes exceptionally hard to find one's own way and carve one's own identity that may fly in the face of what everyone has seen for years.

Revisiting Orwell's *1984*, which warns us of the consequences of totalitarianism, including repression and mass surveillance, I wondered if he warned us about the wrong people. Should we be scared of Big Brother? No. We are the ones inviting him into our homes, our pockets, and our lives. We give him all the information he would ever want about us on a silver platter, and we can't get mad at him for using that information. It's ourselves we should have been warned against.

So I came to the conclusion that social technologies are neither bad nor good. How we use them is what can make their impact positive or negative.

Every choice we make has consequences. Even done with the absolute best intentions, detrimental consequences are not inevitable.

The combination of studying Lifespan Development, watching *The Social Dilemma*, and having a child of my own made me want to explore the concept of given identities through social technologies and write about it.

Identifiable, a fictional dystopian novel that follows the life of one individual, Rory Walsh, navigating a world in which his identity has been forced upon him, explores this challenging link between social technologies and identity.

I hope that young adults, adults, and young parents who use social technologies are drawn to Rory's story and think about their own uses of social technologies and how their usage impacts others, particularly those too young to understand their consequences.

I'm excited you've decided to join me on this walk. See you on the other side.

Yours,

Julia J.T. Tvardovskaya

PROLOGUE: 2100

LEAH

Leah wrung out her hair and tried to shake off the wet as much as possible. She stopped counting the rainstorms that had fallen since making it to Central America. Pennsylvania weather may have sucked, but at least it was somewhat more predictable.

She reached into her pocket for a hair tie but found the locket instead. The inscription, *The light in my darkness—D,* had faded over the past year. It was the only memento she had taken from her parents' house, unless the $200 she stole out of her father's wallet on the night she left counted.

She thought about Daniel a lot. How could she not? His daughter was asleep on her back. His daughter was just as wet from the rain as Leah. Leah prayed she wouldn't get sick.

Did he ever end up going to college…?

Does he think of me at all anymore…?

Does he wonder if his daughter looks like him…?

She didn't, and that made Leah happy. If she had to suffer the past year while he was able to live his life exactly the way he had always planned, at least their daughter looked like her.

It was a small consolation as she walked through the jungle, working her way to the beach to start a new life with her daughter, blood dried on the back on her ankles from days of walking, hips sore from having her daughter perched on her back, and blisters on her hands from gripping the machete so tightly, swinging it across to clear her path but also at every single noise that startled her. The scurrying of collared peccaries and coatis made her jump, the literal howling of howler monkeys caused her heart to drop, and even one time a bat flew a foot or two above her head. She was terrified of the snakes and spiders the size of her hand, and although each passing day got easier, her motherly instincts made her pounce at everything within a three-foot radius.

Even the berries had upset her stomach, and she could feel her milk supply waning from the lack of food and water, not to mention seeing it in her daughter, as she stopped gaining weight.

She wanted to be angry with Daniel. Angry for not coming along with her when she told him she was leaving. Angry that he wasn't willing to spend his life with his girlfriend and soon-to-be-born daughter.

But she wasn't.

She couldn't blame him. Being woken up in the middle of the night by your seven-months pregnant girlfriend asking you to run away with her isn't exactly a decision that can be made spontaneously.

But they had been together for over a year. Didn't he love her? He had loved her enough to take her on a secret camping trip for her sixteenth birthday. He had loved her enough to share a tent and take a romantic walk in the moonlight to tell her that he loved her.

But he didn't just tell her, he showed her when he grabbed the nape in her back and brushed her hair off her neck, kissing it oh so tenderly that her knees began to tremble. Carefully peeling off his shirt, he stepped back and ran his eyes up and down Leah's body, licking his lips like a wolf about to attack his prey. And she had loved him too, running her fingers across his chest and inviting him to continue as she shook her head yes and stepped out of her panties, inching closer and closer until even air couldn't pass between them. He loved her enough to run his fingers across her thigh, slowly pulling her dress over her head, gently grazing her sides. To take her to the ground and lay her across a blanket to have sex under the stars, the first time for both of them. A little painful, a little awkward, a little short, but perfect for two teenagers madly in love.

Or maybe it wasn't love at all.

Because it didn't seem like love when she told him her period hadn't come when it was supposed to. There was no love in his eyes, only fear. "We need to get rid of it! I'll take you," he had said. "I'll pay. This cannot happen."

That wasn't love.

The little girl on her back was love. She was the only person in this whole world Leah truly had. Because when things got hard, when Leah mustered up the strength to call her parents into the kitchen around the table to tell them that she was pregnant, she wasn't met with love or support, she was abandoned—by everyone.

She proved her love for Daniel by protecting him. She didn't tell anyone he was the father, although Nora probably figured it out eventually.

Oh, Nora.

Thinking about her sister was hardest of all.

Leah's spirit was trampled upon for four months with the mandatory confession her parents forced upon her five times a week. The priest quickly became a fixture in the household. She felt worthless being punished with shame, suffering, and repentance. She almost would've preferred physical abuse over her parents avoiding her gaze at all costs, only treating her as an unworthy vessel for the miracle of God.

But what was truly hardest of all was losing her sister, her best friend. Seeing her every single day without being able to hear her voice or meet her gaze, or even just having to sit in silence in the same room together, destroyed her at a molecular level. Nora was her other half, and her sister had abandoned her.

Her daughter stirred. She hadn't cried as much in the past few days as she normally would. She was probably tired from traveling. Or hungry. Leah's breasts felt lighter, and her daughter was never fully satisfied after nursing. It was like her daughter knew they had nothing, no one, and she was trying to save her strength.

Her daughter barely moved. She was so active in Leah's belly; Leah remembered how it was her daughter's first kick that triggered her need to leave home.

She had been lying in bed and rolled to her left side. She remembered saying, "I hate you," out loud to the baby in the darkness. She began spiraling into a hole so deep that even light couldn't reach for miles and miles.

And then, *kick!* A little jab had startled her on the right side of her stomach.

That's when she had realized there was truly a little human inside.

"Oh," she had gasped and sat up in her bed. The movement of her unborn daughter sent a shock to her brain, a warmth enveloping her entire body. She had turned on the lamp by her bed and lifted her nightshirt, looking down at her twitching bump and said, "You're really in there." She wasn't alone; she wasn't abandoned. Not by everyone.

Leah touched her baby's dangling foot.

I still can't believe you're out here with me. I couldn't imagine my life without you. I'd still be trapped in that house.

She had never truly hated her daughter, not when she found out she was pregnant, not when she had to deal with the torture from her family, and not even now as she swung her machete in the jungle.

She had hated how she was being treated; she had hated that her family was making her resent her daughter. There was no way she could be a good mother to her daughter, no way she could truly love her daughter, while being held hostage by her parents, her congregation, her community.

And that kick, that little flutter of movement, changed everything. That was the night she decided to walk to her desk, grab a pen, rip out a sheet of notebook paper, and write a note to her sister.

The sister who she missed, who she would love no matter what, who would make her heart ache and cause her to forget about her hunger, the cold, and the fear of the deafening squawks in the jungle.

That night was the night she folded the note, walked into Nora's room, fought back tears, kissed her sister on the top of her head, and slowly left the house for the last time.

Leah was convinced she was a better mother to her daughter while trudging through the jungle than she ever could have been in that house.

But was she naive in thinking so?

No.

At home, Leah barely knew herself.

She was just a combination of the roles that were imposed on her. A sister… a daughter… a student… spending her life fitting into the boxes left open for her.

But for the first time, she made a choice, wholly her own, to take on this new role—mother—and this new adventure… all for that little girl on her back.

The jungle taught her that she was strong, that she was motivated, that she was passionate. That she would sacrifice the "comfort" of her parent's house for happiness, for fulfillment, for love.

Squish.

"Shit!" Literal shit.

This was an awful idea… How did I think I could do this?

The journey to where she ultimately found herself was hard, each leg more challenging and isolating than the last.

When Leah left Allentown, leaving her home, her family, and Daniel, she fled to New York. Her $200 didn't get her far; she spent all of it on some food and a train ticket to the city.

But New York was strange. It had a technology she had never heard of, something that hadn't made its way to Allentown yet. Some injection that was supposed to give an individual access to the internet in their own heads. It was called an AIP, and Leah just couldn't understand how it worked.

But somehow, everyone knew her. They would stare for a moment, and suddenly, a flash of recognition would appear across their faces. She had never met them, but they judged her as though they had grown up together… like neighbors.

With the AIPs, it seemed like there had come a new form of community separation too, called broods. These broods were like a classification system. Individuals who believed the same things, or had the same upbringing, or something, coexisted in a single brood, avoiding people from other broods. People would just look at one another and decide whether or not to talk to them. Walking through the streets of New York, people seemed to turn away from her. They quickly decided she was not worth talking to.

She just didn't fit in. A pregnant teenager from a family that shunned what the world stood for didn't receive a ton of sympathy. Too pregnant for the people who would normally like her, and too... intolerant... for the people who would normally help her.

So, she worked her way south... and then farther south... until the beaches of Central America sounded like the perfect place to find refuge from the world that shunned her.

But getting to those beaches with absolutely no money—well, that was the kind of thing only an invincible teenager was stupid enough to think she could do... with a baby that the sympathetic wife of a less-than-tolerant Mississippi preacher helped her deliver... in a stable, for that matter.

It was scary, but it was also invigorating. And Leah thrived. With each step and swing of the machete, her heart soared because if she had gotten that far, she could do anything.

And so, here she was, ears pointed to the noises of anything that could see her daughter as possible prey, eyes sharp to the world around her to find anything that could satiate even a fraction of the hunger she felt, and a nose that she thought was tricking her as roasting meat filled her nostrils.

She sniffed the air and wondered if the hunger made her hallucinate, but with every step, the smell became more potent. The rise of smoke stopped her in her tracks. The lack of movement caused her daughter to stir, so she started walking toward the smoke, quicker, until she was met with the crackle of a fire. She hid herself behind a tree and peeked over to see a man, possibly her father's age, standing over a rabbit rotating on the fire.

"*Caminas como un elefante,*" the man said without looking up.

Leah looked around but didn't see anyone.

Was he talking to me?

He grabbed the stick holding the rabbit and pointed it at her, meeting her gaze. "*¿Quieres conejo?*"

She hesitantly stepped out from behind the tree and said, "I'm sorry, I don't speak Spanish."

"Ah."

He turned away from her and reached for a large fork. He pulled the rabbit off its stick and split the meat into two. He walked into a small dwelling that looked like something he may have fashioned together and came out holding another plate and put half of the rabbit onto it. He held it out to her.

"You want to feed that baby, you need to feed yourself first."

She tentatively walked toward him. His eyes were gentle, meeting her gaze just enough not to intimidate her. Clothes, possibly out of burlap, gently hung off his body but didn't hide his lean muscles. The rabbit didn't stand a chance.

"I can hold your baby while you eat," he said, and she immediately stopped and put her arms behind her back, touching her daughter. "Okay," he said, putting her plate down on a small table and taking a step backward.

She inched toward the food and sat down, scooting the seat closer to the fire in an attempt to dry off. The man retreated to his dwelling with his half of the rabbit, and Leah ate hers so quickly it only aggravated her already upset stomach.

He came back out with a wooden cup and a bucket of water. "You can drink this; it's boiled," he said.

She dipped the cup and gulped the water, her stomach instantly settling.

"Why are you helping me?" she asked.

"Would you like me to tell you to leave?"

"No." She didn't know why, but she found comfort in his company.

"Okay." He sat next to her.

She slowly peeled her daughter off of her back and handed her to him.

He pulled her close to his chest. "*Niña perfecta,*" he said, smiling into her eyes.

"Her name is Nora." The only part of her old life she wanted to remember. Even though Nora may have disappeared when she needed her most, she still loved her sister, more than she could explain, and she missed her with her whole heart.

"And yours?"

"Leah."

"I am Amos."

"Thank you for showing me so much kindness."

"I have been here for a long time. Each day made me lonelier and lonelier. I am grateful you found my rabbit." He smiled at Leah.

"How long have you been here?"

"I lose count. Maybe twenty years? Maybe fifty years?" He pet Nora's cheek with his thumb.

"Why?"

"Do you know where we are?"

"Costa Rica," she responded.

"Yes," he laughed. "There used to be people all over the country, but the temperatures rose and with it brought disaster. It brought fire, it brought eruptions, it brought flood, and people started to leave. There are not many people across Costa Rica anymore. They either went up," he pointed north, "or down," he pointed south. "But I could not leave. We are standing in Monteverde, and this was my home, where I had everything and where I lost everything."

Nora started crying. Leah reached for the baby and lifted her shirt. Once Nora latched on, Leah said, "What do you mean?"

"My village used to be so big. There were so many people, so many families, so many children. But as I grew, the village shrank. Children became sick from the heat, so families left. By the time I was about eighteen years old, there were only a few families left, including mine, of course. It was a particularly hot evening. The sky crashed, and light illuminated our sky almost immediately. This was nothing new. Thunder and lightning happen all the time. Even without rain. My parents went to sleep, but I stayed out, listening to yowls of ocelots in heat."

He looked to the side and smiled.

"Have you ever heard the sound of an ocelot in heat?" he asked.

"No… I can't say I have." She shifted in her seat and darted her eyes to the jungle floor. She felt the heat behind her cheeks and couldn't help but let a little smile creep across one side of her mouth.

"It starts with a grumbling, like the engine of an old car. But when she's found her prey, her mate, it's a yowl that echoes through the night. To me, it's a beautiful sound, the sound of life being created. But the yowls were muffled by the thunder that night. And a crack shook the ground. I heard screams behind me, and when I turned, the house where my parents slept had leapt into flames. The door was blocked.

The roof was collapsing. I had no way inside. The damage was instant. We grabbed water and we poured… but the fire kept roaring."

Nora finished eating and gave a little burp, falling asleep in her mother's arms.

"And like that, my family was gone. Our home was gone. And within days, the rest of my village left. Some went up, and some went down. But they all left. But I couldn't leave. This land is my home."

Amos was unwavering during his telling of the story, as though he was merely regurgitating a fable rather than sharing his loss with her, but Leah would tell him her story in the exact same way. She would not relive the loss; she would not succumb to the pain. It was over, and there was nothing she could do to change that.

"This land has a lot to offer. You are welcome to share it for as long as you need," he told her.

Everywhere that Leah had stopped had an expiration: a few days, through labor and delivery, but his invitation had no end date. That comforted her. She could use somewhere to rest. Somewhere she didn't have to constantly worry about feeding herself and her daughter. Somewhere safe where she could truly sleep, not worried about protecting her daughter from the elements at every single moment.

But could she trust Amos?

He didn't judge her, he opened his home and his heart to her, he shared his rabbit with her and comforted her daughter. She may have only just met him, but he put her at ease.

She could see herself and Nora staying with him, almost like the father she never had. The father who would never hit her, never shame her, and would accept and love her for all she was.

Amos went back into his dwelling and retrieved a blanket, placing it over Leah and her sleeping daughter. She smiled up at him, thanking him with her eyes. He pulled his stool next to hers and joined her by the fire, both watching it crackle in silence. Maybe, just maybe, she could put down both her machete and her guard, at least for one night.

CHAPTER I

2110

NORA

Nora rolled away from her husband, gasping as her uterus contracted, sending a shooting pain across her abdomen. Finn watched Nora in agony for close to twenty-eight hours. She pleaded with him for an epidural while vomiting from pain.

"You don't need those toxins flowing through you," he gently lectured while wiping the sweat off her forehead. "God never gives us more than we can handle, and you'll regret not fully feeling the most natural of womanly processes and gifts, like you did with Maeve."

Labor with Maeve only took six hours.

How long did Leah's labor last? Did she even have the baby? He or she would be what, ten or so? Where were they now?

Maeve and Rory were three years apart, just like her and her sister.

No. She wouldn't let herself think of Leah. That part of her life had passed, had disappeared with her sister as she stole away in the dead of night.

Nora cycled through four shifts of nurses, not seeing the face of a single one during her entire stay at the hospital, either because of the pain or mask regulations, or a combination of both. She liked it that way. She preferred not knowing the identity or brood of the people taking care of her. Each of the nurses told Nora it was her choice to get an epidural or a cesarean section, not her husband's, clearly judging her as she turned to Finn.

But that wasn't true.

Nora had promised to be a wife, to be a mother, to be dutiful and loving, and to support Finn, no matter the circumstances. So, she labored.

When she felt the head pass through the birth canal, her tears were no longer those of pain but of relief. She pushed on hands and knees, grasping the sides of the hospital bed or digging her fingers into the sheets below her, immediately collapsing from exhaustion after the last push. Two nurses helped Nora get to her back, one joining the rest of the birthing team and the other trying to coax Rory to latch onto her chest. Rory wasn't interested in eating, and Nora was only interested in sleeping after a grueling labor.

"I need you to help her hand-express," Finn told the nurse while grabbing Rory from Nora's limp arms.

The other members of the birthing team were trying to stop her postpartum hemorrhaging and repair her third-degree vaginal tear.

"Excuse me?" the nurse said, watching Finn as he inspected Rory. "She's still bleeding pretty heavily and clearly needs some rest." The nurse turned to Nora, whose eyes were closed with tears still slowly running down her cheeks.

"We want her to breastfeed. Like God intended for his children to be fed," Finn said, his tone harsher with each word. "She's clearly tired, so I need you to help her."

Nora lifted her hand and reached out as the nurse slowly

pulled away the gown and cupped Nora's breast, squeezing out colostrum onto a spoon.

They finished stitching her tear before the nurse had finished hand-expressing for Nora, the rest of the birthing team taking their leave. The nurse put the colostrum into a syringe. "Are you ready for us to take measurements and get the baby all cleaned up for you?" the nurse asked as she gently placed Nora's gown back over her chest.

"Please," Finn responded, holding out Rory.

"Great. Let me drop off the baby with the rest of the team, and we'll get you guys over to recovery." She placed Rory in the warmer and wheeled him out of the delivery room.

Nora began to doze off. Finn watched the nurse wheel away Rory, seemingly in awe of the beautiful baby they just brought into the world. They hadn't said a word to each other in hours, Finn just holding Nora's shoulder during labor. Finally, just the two of them, Finn leaned over to kiss Nora on the head, petting her hair with a smile.

The recovery room, and recovery in general, had not changed with the rest of America. The government structure had changed. The concept of community had changed. Privacy no longer existed in a world where people could just look at you and learn everything about you. But the hospital beds were still hospital beds, and the couches new parents slept on hadn't gotten more comfortable. Mothers and babies were still monitored, and the hospital food was still not at all satisfying.

Nora didn't care as she drifted in and out of sleep. She didn't fall in love with Rory immediately like she had with Maeve.

It'll be better once it doesn't hurt so much, she thought when she felt him on her chest for the first time.

It'll be better once I'm not as tired, she thought when they wheeled him in fresh from his bath into the recovery room.

It'll be better once I eat something, she thought as they woke her from her first nap.

She'd been nauseous and unable to eat since early labor, approaching over thirty hours since her last meal. But she eventually ate, had taken some ibuprofen, and each time she was woken from a nap, she felt more distanced from the newborn.

They woke her every two hours, like clockwork. The nurses, lactation consultants, psychiatrists, nutritionists, what felt like every single hospital employee, staggered their visits.

"Why can't they all just come in at one time?" Nora pleaded into the stained hospital ceiling while clutching the sides of the bed after the nurse dropped off their required viewing materials.

Finn held Rory, the diapered baby sleeping on his bare chest.

"They're just making sure we have everything we need," Finn whispered, his attention fully on the baby now that Nora had served her purpose.

With Maeve, Nora wanted to spend every second after the birth snuggling with her daughter, Finn only taking over after seeing her head begin to bob and eyelids flutter. With Rory, she hadn't held him since the OB-GYN placed him on her chest after delivery.

Finn stood and put Rory back into the hospital crib, swaddling him like the nurses had. After walking over to the television, he plugged in the viewing materials.

"We've already had a baby," Nora said as Finn scrolled through the safe sleeping, baby cues, and other various baby 101 videos. "We watched these three years ago."

"They want to make sure we haven't forgotten any of the recommendations, or they might have new information about updates, especially for the AIPs," Finn said, picking the shortest video in the queue.

Nora liked going in order, but Finn watched videos shortest to longest.

Accessible Internet Products were an extraordinary technological feat when first created three decades ago—an injection into the forearm that traveled through the bloodstream to the brain where it would latch and expand. At full latch, thirty-six hours after injection, it looked like a mosquito perched on the Occipital Lobe.

Using a mechanism known as thoughtsearch, in which intentional thoughts would be responded to with results by the technology, AIPs gave the individual full access to recall anything that has ever been posted to the internet, providing an unparalleled opportunity for knowledge. Although the viewing happened directly in the brain, it read as though information was projected a few inches in front of one's eyes.

"Well, I don't understand why we can't just watch this over our AIPs," Nora said, forcing Finn to pause the video.

"You know they can't audit what we've watched through the AIPs. This television doesn't let us fast-forward or skip anything, so the staff can tell whether we've gone through all the materials before we get discharged."

Rory slept through every one of the videos. It wasn't until the pediatrician walked in that he began to stir.

"Perfect timing, it seems," the pediatrician said as he glided across to the hospital crib. "I'm assuming you'd like the baby to receive all his necessary vaccinations and an AIP before leaving the hospital?" he asked, not breaking eye contact with Rory.

"Has anyone ever said no?" Nora sarcastically grumbled from her bed.

"Nothing is mandated," the pediatrician casually said, "and, of course, everyone has a choice in the matter based on what is best for the individual family, but in my experience, no one has declined. Not only is it ill-advised to reject for the health of the individual and community, as well as would inhibit general opportunity, but it prevents an individual from basic existence in society."

Existing in society without vaccinations and an AIP was impossible. After numerous pandemics, having an authorized physical vaccination card to prevent digital fraud was mandatory for attending school, entering most places of business, and travel. Some individuals and business owners would allow a non-vaccinated individual to enter, but these were few and far between.

Originally facing pushback, misinformation, and a lack of willingness for injection, the AIPs were not expected to be successful. But twenty years prior, the United States had fully transitioned into a corporatocracy, and with that, a 100 percent injection rate with a global rate of close to 85 percent.

Before the transition to a corporatocracy, the world was transitioning into anarchy, with freedom of speech being limited across the globe by governments, censorship of media and information, and lack of access to the internet stunting development and prosperity. Informally known as the Holy Trinity, the three largest technology companies in the United States had explained that a change was needed.

People needed freedom. Freedom from weak governance. Freedom from censorship. Freedom to make decisions, regardless of how poor those decisions might be. Freedom to access the bottomless well of information to make individuals, businesses, countries, and the world more competitive.

The Holy Trinity had designated individuals from each state to run for congress, outspending any opponents and swiftly gaining majorities in both the House and the Senate. With large majorities, the Holy Trinity had unregulated and unparalleled access to the minds, and more importantly the attentions, of the American people as well as those around the globe.

The AIP was a joint innovation by the Holy Trinity and marketed as a social justice, or rather the lack of having one a social injustice. The Holy Trinity manipulated grassroots organizations across the globe to fight for equal access for every individual to an AIP. The population began to believe that it was a basic right, more important than housing or food. The Holy Trinity paid hospitals a stipend for each AIP injected to incentivize doctors to push the technology onto patients because every AIP injected increased consumerism and therefore their own profit.

The addictive technology captured countless hours of attention, filled with advertisements causing people to spend, spend, spend, which made the Holy Trinity more money than it could ever spend to disseminate the AIPs. With majorities in both houses of congress, the Holy Trinity formally created an alliance known as the Corporate Council. The Corporate Council questioned the formation of the US government, the intentions of the founders, and whether the way that the government functioned was a benefit or an impediment to the people.

Providing an alternative form of government where capitalism was no longer simply an economic framework but also a governing framework, the Corporate Council overturned the government of 1776 and created a new constitution, placing themselves and their caring, providing, and protecting hands at the center.

With that, America had lost big government but gained unlimited access to all of the information in the world, with the rest of the world on its heels.

Finn and Nora were injected as teenagers. They had seen how different life was before the AIP, and they could never imagine life without it now.

"No. Just enough to have an approved vaccine card. The fewer, the better," Finn said to the doctor.

"Whatever you wish, but I'll need to add the disclaimer to your file."

"That's fine. It's ridiculous that any of them are needed to begin with."

"You should know their impact on disease eradication, life expectancy, standard of living, health outcomes—"

"That's enough," Finn said, raising an arm in protest. "Take him away." Seeing his own father wither away under so much medical intervention, Finn's resistance was understandable to Nora.

"Of course," the pediatrician said, breaking his gaze with Finn and looking at Rory. She could tell from the way his eyes moved that he was smiling at the baby from under his mask, but they were filled not with joy but with pity.

Her fists clenched. *How dare he judge what we decide to put in our baby's body.* Rory was their child, and although they had only known him for a few hours, she was confident that no one would know better than them what was best for him.

"You can go now," she said closing her eyes, the rolling of the crib's wheels passing by her.

* * *

It had taken a few days after the hospital discharge for Nora to truly feel that spark of love for Rory.

Although the first few weeks with Rory were as difficult as any newborn, he had what psychologists called an "easy temperament." He was a good sleeper, a good eater, didn't cry much, and he enjoyed playing by himself for more than just a few minutes at a time. Nora called him her "convenient little companion."

The more perfect and convenient he became, the more imperfect Nora felt. No amount of love for him could fill the void of unworthiness.

She constantly questioned herself and her ability to be the perfect mother.

"He deserves more than me," Nora said to Finn while watching Rory sleep in his bassinet.

She couldn't find the validation she needed, the feeling that tells you, "Yes, this feels right. I'm doing something right here." With Maeve, she was confident. She didn't question her parenting style or the decisions she made. But with Rory, there wasn't a single decision she didn't question.

"You're exactly what he needs," Finn said, wrapping his arms around her shoulders. "I've run a bath for you, so go, relax, take some time to yourself." He was good to her after she provided him a child. But if the experience with Maeve was any precedent, he would become more distant as Rory aged.

His words of comfort weren't enough, and taking a bath was the last thing she wanted to do, but she didn't want to offend or anger him. She gave him a kiss on the cheek and threw on a robe, tossed a towel on the toilet, and shut the door behind her. The water, still steaming and swirling with flowers, enticed her. She brushed her hair into a ponytail and caught herself in the mirror.

"How could he ever need a mother like me? A mother who couldn't even love him the first time she saw him?" She gripped the sides of the bathroom vanity. For almost a full month, Nora couldn't bear to spend a moment alone. "Selfish. This is selfish. You are selfish."

She should be cleaning, washing diapers, or making dinner, not wasting precious minutes laying in a bathtub. The constant self-deprecation distracted her from her true fear of knowing that if she laid down in the bathtub, she didn't know whether she'd come back out.

He'd be better off without you, seduced a distant voice in the back of her head.

The voice was quieter when she wasn't alone. She could tune it out when she wasn't alone. But now she was alone, and with only the quiet humming of the bathroom fan, she couldn't silence it.

Nora dropped her robe and slowly lowered herself into the bathtub until each and every part of her was underwater.

What do you think hell looks like this time of year?

We found:
- -
Video: Preacher sermon on hell

Blog: The Fires of Hell Burn on Your Sinfulness

Buy Rosaries Here! Save Your Soul!

Images: Hell

Blog: Is Suicide a Sin? How the Bible
Tells Us So

Would you like to see more?
- -

Suicide was a sin, a selfish sin that would take her straight
to hell, and she didn't live her life to not end up in paradise.

Nora exploded out of the water, gasping for breath.

How long had she been under?

She was stuck on this earth until the good Lord decided
to take her from it, and she needed to reconcile that fact. Her
whole life, she was primed to be a mother, to be a wife, but
the constant failure and insufficiency forced her to question
herself. If she couldn't do this right, if she couldn't love every
moment and every flaw, then what was it all for? What was
her purpose?

Nora, as any mother, wanted to provide the best for Maeve
and Rory. But she also needed to hear that she was a good
mother. Fulfillment vibrated through her bones when other
mothers envied her. New life was breathed into her when
people commented on how sweet Rory was and what a great
job she was doing. If she couldn't create her own validation,
her broodmates could give her the satisfaction she needed.

By cultivating the most perfect, brood-compliant profiles
for her children, others would see how she raised them, what
she sacrificed for them, and how the profiles she curated for
them set them up for a lifetime of success and acceptance.
Her broodmates would admire her for her commitment to
her children. She would show the world that for her kids, she
would do everything.

What is more motherly than that?

When she stepped out of that bathtub, she made it her
mission to document every moment of her children's lives.

Someone would just look at her children and facial recognition would pull up every single picture and piece of personal information she would ever post of them.

She needed to make sure that every piece of information was in alignment with her brood's values because her brood was the best. It had the strongest values. It was morally superior to the other broods. So it was important that her children's profiles invited her broodmates to accept and love them while those same profiles repelled the other, sinful broods.

* * *

Over the next six months, she spent almost all of her time either documenting her children's every move, editing and crafting posts for their profiles, or scrolling through her AIP. Curating their profiles alone was a full-time job.

"Will you just sit still for one second and look at the freaking camera?" Nora screeched at Rory. By the end of the day, her patience wore thin, counting down the seconds until Finn would come home and they could put the kids down to bed.

It took him almost eight months, but he was crawling around the living room, not at all interested in this milestone picture.

Staring into the lens on Nora's device was a constant throughout the day, Rory recognizing the device more than his own mother's eyes.

"Finally," she breathed with a sigh of relief as she captured the sweetest picture of Rory crawling directly toward the lens. Most babies reach for their mothers when they need comfort, but Rory reached for the device.

"No, no, no. That's not for you, sweetie. We need to show our broodmates what a speedy little crawler you are," Nora parentesed as she placed him into a jumper. Putting the perfect filter on her picture and crafting a witty caption, she uploaded it to the internet while ignoring Rory's frustration to being contained.

I really should just buy him a baby barrier so he can roam around without me worrying, Nora thought, peeking over the top of her device at Rory and placing it on the couch next to her.

We found:

Newest Baby Barriers—Click Here!

Blog: How a Contained Baby Protects Mother's Sanity

List: Top Baby Barriers of the Year (with Photos!)

Quiz: What baby barrier works for your lifestyle?

Would you like to see more?

The AIP pulled up a list of baby barriers for Nora to look through, modifying her thoughtsearch recommendations based on thought feedback until she found the perfect one, updating her algorithms to provide her with similar searched for content.

Each AIP had a registration number. This registration number connected it to a device—a small, palm-sized rectangular computer, thin as a sheet of paper—that translated the viewing that occurred over the AIP into action. The AIPs themselves were still not advanced enough for anything more than viewing. Although they could store information, the actual "Buy Now!" button needed to be pressed on the device itself. Devices were attuned to the AIP's thoughtsearch mechanism, so when Nora found the perfect baby barrier, it automatically popped up on her device, taking longer for Nora to grab it off the couch cushion next to her than to actually purchase the baby barrier with same-hour arrival.

The click of the lock on the front door brought a smile to her face.

Throwing the door open a little too forcefully, Maeve ran to her as Finn's keys hit the floor.

"You need to be more careful!" Finn grunted, leaning over for his keys.

"Sowwy," Maeve whispered as she wrapped her arms around Nora's belly. "Mama, sweep?" she asked as she looked up into Nora's eyes.

"Of course I can do bedtime with you tonight," Nora said as she rested her head on Maeve's. "Are you okay to take Rory tonight?" she said to Finn.

"Let's go, little man!" he exclaimed as he hopped to Rory's jumper and lifted him in the air. Rory let out a squeal and laughed as his dad blew a raspberry on his belly.

Maeve climbed onto Nora's back and wrapped her arms around her neck. "Ewephant, Mama!" Maeve yelled, holding her mom tighter.

Nora hunched over and stood, one arm stabilizing her daughter and the other extended out, like an elephant trunk. "BVVVVVV"!" she yelled and stomped left foot, right foot, left, all the way to Maeve's room and plopped her daughter on the bed. "Jammies, brush, book, bed!" Nora said, reaching into Maeve's dresser and grabbing her daughter's favorite set of floral pajamas.

By the time she tidied up and turned down the bed, Maeve appeared right next to her, holding out *If Animals Kissed Goodnight.* Nora took the book and sat on the edge of the bed. Maeve crawled on all fours toward her pillow and weaseled under the covers.

Maeve placed her hand on Nora's arm as her mom opened the book and asked, "Mama wuv Maeve?"

Nora nuzzled in next to her daughter. Grabbing her face in both hands, Nora said, "More than the moon and the stars, and as much as the God who created them."

It didn't take long before Maeve leaned on Nora's chest and fell asleep as her mother finished reading. Sneaking out, she replaced herself with a pillow and watched in wonder as her precious daughter slept.

She turned off the light and walked out of the bedroom and stumbled into Finn walking out of the nursery, a bottle in his hand. The two smiled at one another, and he wrapped his arms around her.

"You're very affectionate this evening," she said pushing him away slightly.

"We just have some pretty great kids," he said and released himself from the hug.

"We do."

"I saw the notification for the baby barrier you purchased," he said and started walking toward the kitchen.

"I hope it's okay! I know it's a little more expensive than some of the others." Nora followed and opened the refrigerator. "How does leftover steak, peas, and potatoes sound? I don't want it to go to waste."

"Sounds fantastic! I'm starving. And of course it's okay. Plus, we can use it for all the other kids we have! It won't go to waste!" He beamed at her and grabbed a beer out of the fridge.

She froze and hid her face as she walked to get the dinner plates for them.

I need to tell him eventually.

Nora was told at her first and only postpartum appointment that she wouldn't be able to have any more children, but she knew how much Finn wanted to have a huge family. Telling him that Maeve and Rory would be their only children truly terrified her.

He's going to hate me. I'm supposed to be a wife and mother, and how will he see me as a perfect mother if I can't mother any more children for him?

"I saw that Rory's crawling too. I got the notification on my AIP when you tagged me in the post. How exciting. They're both just growing so quickly."

"I know! The time is just flying. What did you think of his profile? I feel like it's getting better every day."

"It is. They're really lucky to have you. With you continuing to work on their profiles, their brood affiliation will radiate from a mile away." Finn laughed and set the table. "People won't even *need* to scan them to know who they are."

Nora smiled and blushed, proud of herself for the work she was doing. "Just give me a few more years, and they won't be able to screw up their profiles at all! There will be too much data!" She put the plates down in front of them and sat around the table.

"You're right. There's no escaping the profile you created for them!" He smiled and joined her at the table, grabbing her hand and kissing it gently.

CHAPTER II

2113

————

FINN

Finn smiled as Nora moved the device to capture them at a different angle. The soccer game was lasting longer than Finn's patience, and Nora's charade of trying to capture the perfect photos of the most supporting parents only aggravated him further.

"Sit down. You're making a fool of yourself," he said as he grabbed her sleeve and pulled her into the chair next to him, a little too forcefully.

The week had been extraordinarily busy at work, and he hoped he would have had the Saturday to relax. Nora had other plans, dragging him out to the pitch to watch three-year-olds aimlessly chase each other more than the soccer ball.

"I want everyone to say 'Nora and Finn put their children first,'" Nora said. "That we will more than happily sit in these awful chairs on this groggy day for hours watching those little humans. Nothing is more important than family."

Nora leaned away from him to capture another photo, but he was finished. He lifted the hood of his parka over his head and crossed his arms, sinking into his folding chair.

"Goal!" the referee yelled as one of the children kicked a soccer ball through two posts.

Finn rolled his eyes. "He wasn't even running for the ball! He was chasing the girl with the braid across the field, and it bounced off his knee."

"They're just kids, Finn. Give them a break."

"Give *them* a break?" He straightened himself and shifted his weight toward Nora. "How about you give *me* a break? I've been at work all week, and I'd like a single day to myself. Is that too much to ask for?"

"You think I don't need breaks too? I spend all my time with these kids, creating their profiles. That's work too. You could spend a little more time with them!"

He couldn't continue arguing with her. His hands tensed, and it would only take a few more zingers for them to find themselves wrapping around her neck. But he promised himself he would never get there, would never lift a finger toward his wife or kids. He needed a subject change and fast.

"There aren't even teams. How can you score when no one is playing against anyone else? They're all wearing the same uniform and just running back and forth. Half the time they're on the opposite side of the field from the ball. The ref had to go pick it up and bring it to them, like, five minutes ago."

Nora didn't respond, just released a loud sigh and diverted her attention to her device.

His AIP dinged.

New! Photos of you.
- -

He scanned through the pictures she had posted, each one curated and flawlessly edited to radiate their devotion to Rory.

Finn admired her ability to tell stories, the pictures so full of life and happiness when all he wanted while taking them was to wring the life out of her.

He grabbed her device and shoved it in his pocket.

"Hey! What do you think you're doing?"

"If I have to watch this toddler train wreck, then so do you."

"Are you insane? How have you not figured out that we're not here to *be* here, but to show everyone else that we were here?" Her voice was a snake slithering from one of his ears to the other.

"Show everyone? There's no one else here! Look around, Nora. All the other parents obviously have better things going on."

"That's the point, Finn! *We* made the sacrifice. *We* are here for Rory while the other parents are prioritizing whatever the hell else they have to do. We are the good parents who love our kids, and why the hell should we not make everyone else feel bad that they don't love their kids as much as we do?" There was a cynicism to her voice he had never heard before. Maybe she needed a day in the woods too.

"So that's your ultimate goal?" he asked. "To make other parents feel bad?"

"No, it's for them to recognize how good we are. If they feel bad in the process, that's just an added benefit."

"Well, that's the first time I've ever heard you say that out loud."

Nora was the perfect wife and mother, but why was it so important for everyone else to see that? She was everything that he looked for in a partner. She listened to him, always looked her best, never questioned any of his decisions, could cook and clean, was always home with the children, and she occasionally dragged him out to be the perfect father and watch his son scrape up his knees after getting shoved by another three-year-old.

He always thought she loved doing it all. He never realized that she was doing it more to shape how other people saw her rather than out of pure enjoyment. This was another side to her.

"You may never tell me," she said, "but I'm a good parent. I'm a really good parent." The anger had faded from her and morphed into sadness as she reached for her device and grabbed it out of his pocket.

"What do you mean I never tell you that you're a good parent?"

"You always judge me, never thank me for anything I do, and honestly, I don't think you've ever told me I'm a good mom."

He didn't know whether her anger or sadness annoyed him more, but if he hadn't told her he admired her parenting, then he did feel a bit guilty.

"Well, I'm sorry. You're a very good parent."

She leaned over and rested her head on his arm. "I'm getting a lot better too."

"Better at parenting?" He was touched out, but he couldn't bring himself to push her off, so he scooted the rest of his body away from her while letting her keep his arm hostage.

"Creating their AIP personas," she said to clarify. "Did you notice how every post aligns perfectly with our brood expectations?"

"Don't all parents post about their children, though? I mean, scanning these kids, it seems like everything about them originates from their parents."

"Yes, but I do it better. I mean, think of Maeve, or go ahead and scan Rory. They have triple what other kids their age have on their profiles. There's no way anyone could question who they are or what brood they belong to, even at their young ages. Just think, once they hit thirteen and get access to their own profiles, they won't have to do anything at all to be accepted into the brood. They'll have so much data they'll be completely set up for the rest of their lives."

Finn shifted in his chair. "You're doing a great job, dear. They're lucky to have you as a mom."

"Think of how easy we're making this for them. Think of how much easier our lives would have been if our parents had been able to do this for us."

Bam!

A soccer ball smacked Finn straight in the head.

"That's it!" He stood and threw the ball back. "I'm sorry, but I'm done. I need to get out of here. I hate watching them play, I hate pretending that I'm enjoying it, and getting physically hit is where I draw the line." He folded up his chair.

"What are you going to do instead?" She glared at him through eyes no larger than slits, the new shape of her cheeks showing how hard she was grinding her teeth behind them. He didn't care enough to change his mind.

He just needed to get out to the woods, get away from everyone, and get lost in his head without any distractions.

"How does venison sound tonight?"

"I guess so." She looked away toward the running children.

"Do you want me to leave you and Rory the car?"

"Yes, please. Grab your chair, though." She crossed her legs and continued to avoid his gaze.

He kissed her on the top of the head. "Have fun. I'll see you later tonight."

She didn't respond and patted down her hair after his kiss as though she was trying to wipe it away.

He walked to the car and tossed the folded chair into the trunk.

All right. Let's go home.

I found: directions to home.

- -

Would you like to proceed?

- -

Yes.

The AIP allowed him to mindlessly walk to his house because it dictated every step he needed to take to get there. He could lose himself in his thoughts because the AIP would be right there to snap him out of it whenever a turn was approaching.

Walking by himself, it only took him about ten minutes to get home. He didn't have Rory trying to run in seven different directions, Nora stopping every three steps to take pictures of him—him with Rory, her with Rory, the three of them—every step from the pitch to their house documented.

He walked straight for the garage, opening it with the code, 0818.

They always warn you against using things like wedding anniversaries for codes and passwords, but they must not live around neighbors like these.

Finn was unworried about anyone walking into their home. They had a spare key behind the house, easy enough for his six-year-old daughter to find. His rifle was in the back of his truck, the fingerprint safety feature its only protection, but anyone motivated enough could probably override that. Someone could easily make their way into his garage, grab the fully loaded rifle in the back of his truck, use the key to his own house, and slaughter his whole family with his own weapon.

No one would ever do that. Not around here. Ever since his father passed, even though it was years ago, he was consumed with thoughts of death. *What if I get sick too? What if Rory falls a little too hard? What if Nora's vehicle malfunctions and doesn't warn her of oncoming traffic?*

His constant thoughts around death made his demeanor to it nonchalant because they were now so embedded. The death of his father combined with the patients he saw every day made it such an unavoidable reality.

He never thought hiding the gun would make a difference. People take all the right steps to protect themselves and their families, but they still die. Parents babyproof their homes, but kids override gates eventually. Hunters lock up their ammo but then can't protect themselves from home invasions. No matter how much someone prayed or went to church, or how many toxins they avoided, bodies still succumbed to cancer.

If it's in God's plan that we go, that we pass over, then no amount of safety measures or vaccines can truly save us.

Finn didn't trust modern medicine. He chose to work in a hospital, not to help people with medication and these absurd life lengthening techniques where doctors tried to play God, but solely to provide a good life for his family.

He was uncomfortable pumping toxins into the bodies of others, into the bodies of his kids, but he couldn't deprive them of the ability of living in modern society. That wouldn't be fair to them.

"We should just live the way we were intended to live," he said aloud as he loaded up his truck. "With nature. Letting God's plan take its course. Using the rivers and trees as our medication, letting death come and take our hand, lead us to our maker rather than running away from him while hooked up to machines, being pumped with steroids, telling God, 'I know better than you and I am not ready yet!' while God holds out his arms, ready to caress our heads and tell us, 'It's okay; it is your time to live in paradise. Let go of the materialistic, toxic purgatory you tether yourself to and join me.'"

Watching his father suffer had traumatized him, through his so-called "life-saving" treatments, attached to the tubes that pumped the alkylating agents through his body.

With the disease itself, he would've gotten sick, he would've made peace with his demise, and he would've left this world for another, better one.

But the drugs gave him false hope. They elongated his suffering. He still got sick and sicker and sicker. He just got sicker... slower. He still died; it just took him longer. God wanted to take him, God was ready to take him, and it was absolutely foolish to believe that they could change the will of God.

He got into his truck and made his way to the park where he and his father would hunt together.

Finn loved his dad, he respected his dad, but most of all, he missed him, especially when on his way to hunt. He wished his father was still here, in that passenger seat with his own rifle at his feet. But hoping for more time with his father was selfish because that would mean condemning him to more days in this wasteland of technology, drugs, and sinfulness rather than allowing him his peace in paradise.

Thinking about his dad, his AIP ran wild, bringing up every picture of the two of them, only breaking up his reminiscence with instructions on how to get to the park.

We found:

- -

Pictures of you and your father

Would you like to see more?

- -

He and his father were not always happy or on good terms, but when they hunted, when they tracked the animals together, their relationship was perfect. Nothing could come between the two of them.

The park was empty, taken over by his brood about a decade ago. There was a violent outburst between his brood and another who lived much closer to the Philadelphia area. The other brood was uncomfortable with the hunting. They wanted to preserve the environmental integrity of the park and keep it a safe place for them and their children to relax, explore, and play.

But what was safer than knowing how to protect yourself? Also, his brood had guns... so his brood now owned the park. There was even a sign his father had made from beautiful oak with an inscription that read "Hunting Parkway" with a rifle carved below.

Less and less of his broodmates hunted. He didn't know why. Maybe they got busy with their families or work. Maybe their wives really weren't as perfect as his and didn't let them take the time to themselves.

Whatever it was, the past few times he came, he had the entire park to himself.

He stepped out of the truck, grabbed his rifle, and started walking the old path he and his father would take.

He hoped he could have a relationship with Rory like the relationship he had with his father. Well, not completely like his father and him, more like the relationship his father and he had while they hunted. But he wanted that feeling of connection and closeness to permeate every aspect of that relationship, though he wasn't sure how to make that happen. Sometimes, Rory was a million miles away. Only three years old, but already such a strong personality and so different from his own.

Rory loved his sister, Finn could tell. When he wasn't at work and was at the house, Rory constantly chased after Maeve. "Come on, Rory! Let's go play!" Finn would say. But Rory ignored him, batting at the book his sister was reading or running into her room after bedtime and snuggling into her bed with his head by her feet because there wasn't enough room for them to lay side by side.

"Maeve's asleep. Why don't you come lay with me?" he would ask his son, but Rory wanted nothing to do with him and would snuggle his head further under the covers.

And now this stupid soccer.

We found:

New! Updates from soccer game

New! Photos of Rory with his team

Would you like to see more?

Finn may have been Irish way back when, but he was fully American now, and soccer was not the kind of football he wanted his son to play.

But he's just a kid. Maybe he'll hate it or grow out of it. Or maybe once he realizes how many other cool sports there are, he'll pick up those.

He didn't even really want Rory to play sports. He never played sports himself growing up, and he turned out perfectly fine and happy with his wonderful wife and his… small… family.

Plus, hunting was the first sport that ever existed. And, if he couldn't figure out how to start fostering that perfect relationship with his son, well, hunting was the perfect place to start. At least he could pull on the best times he had with his dad to create those same memories with his son. That was his in with Rory.

A snap of a twig brought him back to the woods. He crouched behind a tree and waited patiently.

A deer ran across the trail in front of him, but he must've spooked it because it didn't stop. He sighed and stood, realizing how much noise he must've been making while walking aimlessly through the park, thinking more about his son than providing dinner for the evening.

I guess it's not even really Rory's fault.

Seemingly out of nowhere, a second wave of anger overwhelmed him. He was mad at Nora for signing Rory up for soccer, for forcing him to sit in the cold to watch something that wasn't even soccer, let alone football. He didn't know soccer, but he knew that whatever those kids were doing, soccer wasn't it.

Does she even like doing any of this? Our entire lives, has she just been putting on a show for me, for everyone else? Has she been lying to me this entire time?

Her comment this morning continued to ring through his head.

"That's the point, Finn!" she had said. "We made the sacrifice. We are here for Rory while the other parents are prioritizing whatever the hell else they have to do. We are the good parents who love our kids, and why the hell should we not make everyone else feel bad that they don't love their kids as much as we do?"

Or even worse: "No, it's for them to recognize how good we are. If they feel bad in the process, that's just an added benefit."

Where did her newfound cynicism come from? Had it always been there, and was he completely oblivious to it? Did she even enjoy being a wife and a mother? Was she doing this out of love or a sense of obligation? Was she doing this for herself, for her husband, or for the rest of the world?

Why was it so important for her to be seen as a better mother than the Virgin Mary herself?

Shouldn't she want to clean the house for the comfort of living in a clean home? Shouldn't she want to make dinner, or all meals for that matter, so that the family could be full, both of good food and of love? Shouldn't she want to spend her days with the children, playing with them, teaching them, providing them with everything they need so they grow up happy, loved, fulfilled, and ready to tackle the world?

What if she actually hates our life?

Maybe she didn't hate it; maybe she just didn't love it. Maybe she just did all this because she felt like she was supposed to. But even if that was the reason, why didn't she talk to him about it? Was it his fault? Was he unapproachable?

He kept coming back to the question: Why was it so important to her that that was how she was seen by her broodmates?

What if she's not the best mom…what if she's been so good at proving to the world that she's actually something she's not that I've bought into it? What if she cared more about seeming like a good mom than actually being one?

He shook his head. He was spiraling, and he didn't like doubting his wife's intentions.

But why? That was the question he kept coming back to. And the answer was what his father made him feel every day, except when they were in this park together. *It's because of me. It's my fault. It has to be.*

Was he not a supportive partner?

He provided her with everything. He gave her everything he and his mom never had growing up. Stability. Income. A beautiful house filled with whatever the hell she wanted to fill it with. What more could she want?

The anger bubbled. *Ungrateful!* He took the butt of his rifle in both hands and raised it above his head, crashing it against the ground. He wanted to hit something. To smash something. *Is this how Dad felt?*

But he didn't want to turn into his father and take it out on the people around him. It was good he was in the park.

He also didn't want to break his gun. So he slid down onto his knees and started pummeling the ground with his fists, but it wasn't satisfying. His inability to satisfy his family made him powerless. Being so unappreciated decreased his worth, like what he was giving just wasn't enough.

He sat back and tried to push the anger away, but the more he pushed, the more persistent it was. He took his rifle and placed himself behind a bush. He would take his energy and guide his bullet with it.

It may have been five minutes, it may have been an hour, but eventually a deer tiptoed out, a doe, still illegal to hunt, but no one checked anymore. There was something satisfying to him about aiming at a doe and not letting her walk away unscathed. He was a good shot. He could kill it with one bullet, but he aimed for her back thigh.

Bam!

She tried to run. The doe was stunned but not completely incapacitated.

The thrill of chasing it erased his anger. He shot again. She fell over. No longer able to run.

He walked up to it, watching it breathe with the sharp up and down of its ribcage. He made his way to the deer's head and crouched. The eye of the doe stared up at him, and a smile crept across his lips. The laugh came from so deep inside of him that it shocked both him and the deer, the deer lifting its head.

Finn put his hand on the deer's shoulder, petting it gently. The deer, knowing it had lost, resigned and laid its head back down on the park floor.

He could've put it out of its misery, but still, too easy. He thrived on the power of looking down at the creature in front of him. What God must feel like.

He had the creature's life in his hands. But the creature wasn't human. It had no soul. Its only value was the taste it would provide on the plate Nora would hand him.

Finn's fingers danced across the rifle. He grabbed it in both hands and looked from the deer to the rifle, from the rifle to the deer. He lifted the rifle above his head again and brought it down, into the deer's skull.

Again.

Again.

Again.

After some time, the deer's head bore no resemblance to the head of any animal he'd ever seen. He dropped the rifle and pulled a knife out of his hunting boot. Methodically, with the precision he used while assisting during any hospital operation, he severed the head from the body and left it on the ground.

We never eat the head anyway.

He wiped off the knife and put it back into his boot. He tied the doe and hoisted it across a branch, watching the blood pour and then slowly trickle onto the ground below, petting its sides and letting the blood drip onto his hands. The anger had disappeared. The self-doubt, gone. The deer may have received the brunt of his emotional release, but his family wouldn't.

CHAPTER III

2115

___

NORA

"What a fun little party! I know the kids are loving it. Can you believe he's already five?" asked the parent of one of Rory's close friends, grabbing Nora by the arm as she walked past the extravagant refreshments table, catching her by surprise.

"Oh, thank you. Yeah, time's flying by so fast! We're so glad you could all make it. Rory is thrilled to have all his little friends here," she replied, less than genuinely.

It was three hours into the party, a perfect party, like all of Nora's. Everyone had eaten, Rory had cut his cake, and he had opened all his presents. After handing the parents party favors for the children, cleaning up the decorations, and packing Rory's gifts, Nora zigzagged through the park, the same large empty field hugged on three sides by trees used as a soccer pitch for her son's practices and games, avoiding the playing children. She scanned the gaggles of people, hoping to find Finn talking to the other dads.

He promised he'd be here. It would devastate Rory if his father didn't make it again, she thought.

A five-year-old girl bounced off her leg and fell over, laughing as a group of four other children jumped onto her, knocking Nora over.

Nora sprang to her feet and spun in a circle to see whether the grass had left a mark. She tugged at the sides of her blouse, patted out the wrinkles, and rubbed her hands together to get rid of the grass and dirt.

Ping!

New video of you.
- -

Her AIP interrupted her search for Finn and showed a video of herself spinning in a circle, posted by one of the parents just out of reach who had seen her tumble.

Great. I look like a dog chasing its tail, Nora thought and rolled her eyes. *At least my kids are immune for another few years.*

The proliferation of the AIP created heightened security for children, with mandatory parental controls until age thirteen. If anyone wanted to post a photo or information about Maeve and Rory, including the kids themselves, Nora or Finn had to approve.

Maeve sat on a bench on the far side of the park, reading a book. Nora walked over to her daughter and sat next to her, wrapping an arm around her shoulders.

"You don't want to play with the other kids, sweetie?"

"No," Maeve quickly responded, turning a page.

"Why not? There seem to be a few other eight-year-olds playing near the swings. You don't want to join your broodmates?"

"I'm okay." Maeve raised the book closer to her face. After a moment, she said, "Hey, Mom, can I ask you a question?"

She closed the book, *The Phantom Tollbooth*, and placed it on her lap, using her thumb and index finger as a bookmark.

"Of course. What's on your mind?"

"Why doesn't Dad come to our birthday parties?"

"He always stops by for a little bit," Nora responded, hugging her tighter.

Maeve shrugged off her mom's arm. "Only at the end."

Nora hoped her kids wouldn't notice Finn's pattern—he always made an appearance right as guests started packing up and leaving. For the past five years, for a combined ten birthday parties between Maeve and Rory, Finn conveniently got called into work and returned just in time to say goodbye to guests on their way out.

I guess they noticed.

"Your father is so hard-working, and the hospital needs him. He loves both of you so much and wants to make sure you have everything you could ever need. We need to be grateful that not only does he provide for us, but that he's still able to take a few minutes out of his busy day to come to your birthday parties and wish you a happy, happy birthday." Nora ran her thumb against her daughter's cheek and kissed her forehead.

Maeve opened her book and continued to read, turning her shoulders away from her mother.

I knew he'd be busy, but this is ridiculous. His own children's birthdays.

Nora crossed her arms and stared at the children running about the park. They used to be so madly in love, but each passing day made Finn more distant, his temper shorter, and his gaze more of contempt than anything else. What happened to them?

2105

She knew Finn would be a physician's assistant from the moment they first met in a class called Medicine and Ethics during Nora's sophomore year of college at St. Theresa's University, just a two-hour drive from Allentown. After her sister's disappearance, she focused all of her attention on school, skipping a year and attending college earlier than her peers.

On the first day of class, Nora had walked in and made eye contact with him, her AIP immediately scanning him, his brood affiliation dictated by a single yellow dot next to his name.

>>>>>>>>SCAN>>>>>>>>IN>>>>>>>>PROGRESS>>>>>>>>
- -

Name: Finn Walsh
- -

Born in: Allentown, Pennsylvania
- -

Most recently lived in: Alleghany, Pennsylvania
- -

Occupation: Student—St. Theresa's University
- -

Religion: Evangelical Christianity
- -

Photos:
- -

Finn Walsh at Hunting Parkway

Finn Walsh with broodmates

```
Finn Walsh at Mass

Finn Walsh working at Walsh Furniture
Store

Finn Walsh...

Finn Walsh...

Finn Walsh...
```

Would you like to see more?

Yes! We're in the same brood! He was from Allentown, just like her, and he knew the same people, attended the same church, and lived a few blocks away from her family. She couldn't believe they hadn't met yet.

The pictures came and went on her AIP: him at freedom rallies, on hunting trips with his father, a visit to Corporate Council Headquarters.

He is perfect.

Finn smiled at Nora and looked at the empty seat next to him. Hugging her books a little tighter, she glanced at her feet and blushed, slowly making her way to the open chair.

"Ironic that we both have two more years to go," Finn beamed.

Two more years... What year is Finn Walsh at STU?

We found:

```
Student Profile: Finn Walsh

Photos: Finn Walsh with acceptance
letter to STU Physician Assistant
program
```

Would you like to see more?

"Yeah, congratulations on being accepted into PA school!" Nora said while scooting herself closer to the table. "That's a wonderful accomplishment."

It was fate. Nora was a sophomore with two more years in college and Finn a senior with two years of PA school ahead of him.

"How did you like private school?" Finn asked.

"What?"

"I see that you attended a private all-girls school before college. Did you like it?"

Nora still struggled with navigating conversation in the AIP world. It had been about three years since she had even spoken her own name, conversations starting based on what scans provided.

Others could see everything about her: where she went to school, what church she attended, who her friends were, what her parents looked like. And she was also sure there were pictures of her and Leah that abruptly stopped after the age of thirteen.

They could hang onto whatever aspect of her life they found most intriguing, digging as deeply as the AIP would allow, all in a matter of seconds. Questions always caught her off-guard, being based on what others saw, not what she had told them.

"Oh, um, I liked it," she replied, always waiting for someone to ask her about Leah, but the questions never came.

"I found it challenging to be in the public school system, trying to find others like me, especially before the AIP," Finn explained. "I spent so much time trying to get to know people, only to be disappointed we were all so different. We had nothing in common."

Nora was distracted by the way his veins danced across his forearms as he clenched his fists and how his dark brown side-swept hair perfectly fell on his forehead while just missing those piercing emerald green eyes. If her AIP didn't tell her that he was Irish American, his face did—and almost everyone in her brood was Irish American.

He was strong in the traditional sense, his body built by years of helping his dad fashion furniture, and his facial hair rugged, as though he had come from an extended weekend camping trip. But his clothes were pressed, clean, his button up casually worn and untucked from his khaki pants as though he attended mass in the morning and then modified his clothes just enough for a university classroom.

"Nora?" Finn asked, cocking his head.

"Sorry?" Nora stuttered, embarrassed she had gotten so distracted.

"I was hoping you'd join me for some coffee after class."

Nora gasped. Eyes wide in excitement, she said, "Oh! I'd love to!"

Nora packed up her books in silence as Finn said, "Fill My Cup has an incredible latte if you haven't changed your mind."

Fill My Cup was next door to Fish & Loaves, the premier date destination for St. Theresa's students. Nora hoped their coffee date would progress to dinner.

"I'm ready if you are." She smiled and hugged her books.

Finn later told Nora that at that point he worried he had already lost her. Out of all the women and girls who had ever chased him, she was the one he wanted, the one who made him feel that immediate spark. The one who caused a shiver to run down his back the first time their eyes met.

He called her his Rebekah because from that first moment he knew she would be the perfect wife and mother to his children, and all he wanted was to get down on one knee and profess his love in front of God and the entire class. She loved knowing he was paralyzed with love for her.

Finn laughed over his latte as Nora asked him how many children he wanted.

"A huge family. More than four at least! I grew up as an only child, and it could get really lonely at times. I always imagined a house full of kids, always noisy, full of love and laughter."

"Me too! Well, I had a sister, but after I lost Leah, I couldn't find anyone to fill that space, and it was just... me," Nora said looking over Finn's shoulder and out the large window onto the street.

Finn grabbed her hand from across the table and gazed at her as though there was nothing more important in the world than sitting across from her at that moment.

Suffice it to say, the date went well. The two made their way over to Fish & Loaves, laughing and talking about their ideal future.

"Honestly, I really do love medicine, but being a mother is all I've ever been bred for and known," Nora said, breaking a breadstick over her plate. She was majoring in biology on a pre-med track and hoping that if she wasn't able to find a husband at St. Theresa's that she would find one in medical school.

"I couldn't imagine anything more fulfilling than working and providing the opportunity for my wife to be with our children," Finn said. "Teaching them, loving them, giving them everything they could ever need."

By the end of the evening, it seemed like Nora and Finn had planned out their entire lives together. It only took six months for the two to become engaged, getting married the August after they graduated and moving back to Allentown, Pennsylvania, where the two had spent their entire lives before college.

After getting married, they conceived Maeve in under two months. Getting pregnant with Maeve was easy, thrilling, and completely unexpected.

"We'll have four in no time!" Finn exclaimed, kissing Nora's stomach.

But it was work to conceive Rory. Nora faced secondary infertility, and for a while it seemed like no matter how hard they tried, they wouldn't be able to have another. But after two and a half years, Rory was their little miracle, and their last.

When they could no longer conceive, Finn dived into his work even more than he had before, pulling an extra eight-hour shift every week in addition to his four twelves. He was always working or sleeping with no time for her or the kids.

Nora took care of the house, cooked the meals, and created their brood-compliant profiles. Nora planned the parties and bought all the toys and gadgets the kids needed while Finn spent his days at the hospital. She worried that the only way he would get to know his kids was by scanning them, seeing all that she had compiled and created for them.

How had they gotten so broken? Their love started so pure; love for one another, love for their brood, love for their children. But the blows to their marriage kept coming. Finn's need for a large family made him neglect the ones he had. He pushed her away when she finally told him they couldn't have any more kids, his gazes of pity rather than love. Her presence a nuisance rather than a gift. She needed him, but he didn't need her. Not anymore.

CHAPTER IV

2115

FINN

Finn wrapped up at work. He took off his white coat and hung it in his locker, grabbing his son's present. Like every birthday party for the past five years, he dreaded attending but needed to make an appearance, both for his kids and for Nora's image.

He couldn't handle birthday parties. It broke his heart watching close to eighty brood children running around, playing, laughing, knowing that only two of them would ever be his. His house would never be full, and by extension, neither would his heart. He should have been grateful for his two beautiful and healthy children, but he was obsessed with loss.

Hiding in the hospital stitching up gunshot wounds or flushing out narcotics was easier than listening to broodmates corral countless kids.

He had wanted a house full of children, a house so different from the one in which he had grown up.

Driving to the park, Finn couldn't help but think back on his less than perfect childhood. He remembered the day he found his mother in the kitchen holding a positive pregnancy test. It was the first time, of many, that his father had hit him, and he couldn't stop himself from reliving it.

What was hardest on Finn was that his father wasn't always hurtful. Every day was rolling the dice on a high stakes game where the wins and losses were hugs or bruises. The uncertainty was worse than a beating.

He recalled the scene, his memories only interrupted by the AIP's directions to the birthday party.

"Mom! Please!" an eight-year-old Finn yelled,
running with his pamphlet for summer camp as
his father undid his belt.

"A waste of resources! Do you know how much we
gave up to support you?"

He had just lost his job at a manufacturing plant
that closed and spent what little money they had
drinking away his sorrows. There was no money
for summer camp.

"Mom!" Finn cried as his dad's belt whipped
across his back, a thousand wasp stings at once.

Finn ran to his mother, who sipped on a full glass
of wine in the kitchen, and he wrapped himself
around her legs.

He touched his lower back, a phantom sting lingering.

The feelings couldn't be reconciled. He respected and missed his father, but the image of his father's face made his scars and bruises throb. He regretted the way he last spoke to his mother, their parting words before she passed, but hated her for her sinfulness and the way she had destroyed their possible chances for happiness.

* * *

2108

The last day he spoke to his mother started off as the third happiest day of his life, trailing the birth of Maeve and his wedding day.

It was his first day of being a PA, and his excitement soared knowing that he could bring back a salary that would provide so much for Nora and Maeve.

Labor and delivery was his current rotation, and he took seeing the pregnant couples and newborn children as a sign from God that he and Nora would conceive again.

But in the back of his mind, he thought of his mother. How had that plus sign she held in her hand so many years ago never turned into a baby?

He snuck away and searched for his mother's records, trying to comprehend what could have happened.

What he found shook him to his core.

This must've been what God felt when he decided to flood the earth.

She was with his daughter. He needed to save his precious Maeve from that sinner's grasp.

He fumed and illegally printed the file, shoving it in his coat pocket. He drove straight to the house he grew up in, a house so empty since his father's passing.

"How could you?" he yelled at his mother as her frail arms opened the door.

He pushed his way in and threw the crumpled file at her.

She scanned the paper, and it seemed like she knew exactly what Finn was referring to. "Maeve, go to the kitchen, sweetie," his mother motioned to his newly walking daughter.

"No, Maeve. Get in the car." He grabbed her arm and pulled her out the door, her shrieking from a grasp a little too tight on her bicep.

"Wait, please," his mother begged. "You don't understand." She hid her face in her hands for a moment and composed herself. Taking a deep breath, she steadied herself and continued, "Your father, although I loved him without question, was a difficult man. Even at the best of times, he was erratic, forcing me into bed, slapping me across the face whenever I angered him, or finding other ways to put me in my place as subordinate to him in front of God as our witness."

"That was his right as the man, as the head of the family."

"Another child would not have been born out of love but punishment and desperation. For however sick your father was, he was a God-fearing man, so God-fearing he wouldn't let us use any forms of birth control, at one point flushing all the birth control pills he found hidden in my dresser and then punishing me by forcing himself on me."

"Laying with your husband is never a punishment," he said to his mother through gritted teeth.

"We couldn't afford a second child back then, and I could not mentally and emotionally mother another child with your father. I knew I could not protect us, or any other children, from your father. I could not condemn another child to the physical, emotional, and psychological abuse that we suffered. And I could not force us further into poverty, especially at a time when no income was being earned."

"There is no reason or excuse to murder my brother or sister." He put one arm on his hip and the other on his head as he paced the room.

"I was confident the choice was right for our family."

He stopped and stared at her. "It was *far* from right." He looked at Maeve sitting in the grass by the car, alone, and wished so badly he would have had someone to hold his hand, to shield the pain, to talk to. "I wouldn't have had to deal with him... his anger... all on my own," he whispered.

She walked up to him, her jaw firm and eyes unblinking. "So you would condemn your brothers or sisters to the same fate?"

"If that was God's will," he said.

"Well, clearly it wasn't, or they would still be here," she replied.

"Good-bye, Mother. I cannot let my family be around you. I must protect them from you and whatever forces working through you."

"Finn, you can't keep me from my granddaughter!" She reached out for him, tears in her eyes.

He snapped her hand away and slammed the door. He took a moment, knowing it would be the last time he would ever see the house or his mother. He could never forgive her. He almost wished he could've run to his father and told him so that she could be properly punished for her absolute sinfulness.

That was the right choice for *his* family.

* * *

2115

His mother had destroyed their family. He would never feel the love and safety of connecting with someone who understood exactly what he had gone through. Empty. Alone. And he had convinced himself that a house full of children was the only thing that would fill his void. But that dream would only ever be a dream now.

He pulled up to the park and took a deep breath before walking out into the mayhem.

Maeve and Nora sat on a bench, Maeve reading, of course, and Nora petting Rory's head in front of her.

He walked up behind Nora as she was saying, "Dad's doing the best he can, and he'll be here before you know it! Your friends are waiting for you, and you've got such a special day to celebrate."

"Dad!" Rory yelled, running around the bench.

"Little man!" Finn smiled, dropped Rory's gift, lifted his son into the air, and blew a raspberry on his tummy, their personal hello.

Finn put his son on the ground and handed him the gift off the ground. "Happy birthday."

"Thanks!" Rory ripped the gift open, a pair of hunting boots.

Finn crouched next to Rory and said, "I'm sorry I missed your party, pal. Let me make it up to you. How'd you like to go hunting with Dad next weekend? You're five years old now! Such a big guy! I think you're ready, if you're up for it." He tried so desperately to hold on to the only positive memories he had with his own father, trying to recreate them with Rory.

"You think that's a good idea?" Nora asked. She hadn't moved from her position on the bench or looked at him since he arrived.

"I think it's time we let Rory decide," Finn responded. "What do you say, little man?"

"Okay!" He dropped his present and ran to play with the other kids.

"Coming right at the end of the party as usual, I see," Nora said.

"I'm here. Now you don't need to worry about people posting that I missed it."

"Well, I didn't want to throw this incredible party for our son and then have the only thing people remember is that my husband, his own father, didn't even come."

"Seems like you don't need to worry about that," Finn said, walking around the bench and sitting next to Maeve, who still intently read her book. He kissed the side of her head. "Hey, kiddo."

Maeve stood and walked to a different bench, not looking up from her book.

"What was that about?" Finn asked.

"She's upset. You're not around anymore. You're always working, missing birthday parties."

"Jeez, Nora. I'm working for *us*. For *them*. Private school isn't cheap. St. Theresa's is getting more expensive by the minute. Imagine how much it'll cost when they're finally college-aged! I can't be everywhere."

"Okay," Nora said, grabbing her device to document the end of the party.

"And when I *am* here, you're just recording everything on that stupid device."

"I'm doing this for them. You know how much having a solid profile means for their brood acceptance," Nora said, not looking at him.

"You're right. Fine. We'll just sit here and keep not talking, like always." Finn leaned back on the bench and looked straight up at the sky, trying to tune out the sounds of the kids playing.

* * *

Finn counted down the days to their first hunting trip, the week passing by quickly.

Rory ran down the steps in his brand-new Irish Setter hunting boots, his camouflage coat, and his toy shotgun. "I'm ready!" he yelled, stomping on the floor after jumping the last two steps.

"We'll be safe and back in time for dinner, maybe even lunch," Finn told Nora, who was leaning against the doorframe in her robe and holding a coffee mug.

Rory ran past her into his truck, unable to hold his excitement, with Finn trailing after.

Turn left in one kilometer, the AIP directed Finn to Hunting Parkway.

Sitting in the passenger seat, his feet dangling, Rory played with his shotgun, flipping it around and inspecting it from every angle.

Finn smiled. This was the first time he and his son would be alone for more than a few minutes. No Nora. No Maeve. Just the two of them in the great outdoors. He was excited to share this part of his life with Rory, to be there with his son, and make lasting memories and traditions. If he could only have two children, only one son, he wanted to do it right and to share the best parts of himself.

You have arrived.

"Now, Rory, you need to stay by my side and make sure you keep quiet not to spook the turkeys. Got it, little man?" Finn asked as he parked the truck in the hunting grounds.

"Got it," Rory responded, waiting for his dad to walk around to his door.

He helped Rory out and tried to blow a raspberry on his tummy over the hunting clothes, bringing a squeal of joy to his son's lips.

They walked the woods, listening and searching for birds, Rory's excitement declining by the second.

"No more! Home," Rory said after an hour of walking, throwing his shotgun and plopping onto the dirt.

"Shh! Remember the rules, little man? We'll get one bird together, your first bird, and then we'll head back to Maeve and Mom."

Spotting a turkey in the distance, Finn crouched and pulled Rory's leg to shimmy his son behind him. "Shh..." he said, winking at Rory pulling at weeds and aiming his shotgun. He shifted the safety off and pulled the trigger, grazing the turkey.

Rory burst into tears when the turkey squawked, jumping up and smacking his father in the back.

"Daddy! No! He hurt!" Rory muffled through his wails as his dad grabbed his son's wrist and threw him into the ground next to him as he lifted his gun again.

"Shh, Rory," Finn said and took a second, fatal shot. "We did it! You got your first kill!"

Rory dived into the earth, his head hiding in his arms and his legs pounding at the ground, inconsolable after life left the turkey.

He would never have it. He would never have anything he wanted. No big family. No memories with his own son like those he had with his dad. His heart ached for everything he would never see in his lifetime.

But his son was still in front of him having some sort of mental breakdown, and he didn't know whether to smack it out of him or wrap him in a hug and tell him it would all be fine. What the hell was he so upset about, anyway?

Regardless, that would need to wait.

Nora couldn't see his failure. She may have been a bitch, but she was good with the kids. She couldn't know that he fucked up the one and only time he had a day with Rory.

He crawled over to his son and started to rub his back.

"It's okay. Look, we have dinner. We need to take a picture of you with your first kill." Pulling him off the ground, Finn wiped Rory's tears, shushing him to help him calm down. A handprint across his face probably wouldn't look best in the picture he was going for, so kindness over discipline would have to do. "We can't have you all sad for your pictures. We have to show your mom and broodmates how successful your first hunting trip was. Look, just take one picture for us, and then you can cry the whole way home. I promise."

Rory rubbed his eyes and cheeks, then cracked a smile just long enough for a picture of him with the turkey. Looking over at the turkey, he started to sob again.

"All right. Let's go," Finn said, both devastated and annoyed. He walked over to the turkey and placed it into his vest.

Rory hadn't budged. Finn walked back to his son and pointed toward the truck.

"Not again, Daddy," Rory said, shifting his gaze to the ground.

"Not again," his father sadly responded. "I promise."

CHAPTER V

2116

RORY

"Maeve, how they know me?" Rory asked after his sister's friends left the playground. He was playing with the mulch and reached his arms toward Maeve.

"Like you know them." She picked him up and put him on a swing. It was hot on his butt even though he was wearing pants. He grabbed the ropes tight, and his sister pushed him forward, the sun making his eyes water every time he reached the top.

"How I know them?" She walked to the front of the swing and grabbed his feet, shaking the swing side to side. He smiled but grabbed the ropes tighter.

She stopped the swing, placed her arms on his shoulders, and said, "The mosquito!"

"What?" He looked for the mosquito. Was it by his arms? By his head?

"The mosquito in your head."

He gasped and grabbed his head, shaking it and trying to get the mosquito to fall out through his ears. "No! Out!"

She laughed and put her hands on his, kissing him on the forehead. "It's okay! It's a good mosquito. It tells you about the other people, right?"

He pushed her hands off and jumped off the swing, walking to the stairs that led to a big green covered slide. "I see pictures and colors and names and—"

"Exactly! Everyone has a mosquito."

"Err-yone?" he asked as he walked up the steps to the slide. *One—two—three—four!* He took big steps, skipping the stairs in between until he got to the top.

"Everyone!" Maeve yelled back from the bottom of the slide. She held her arms out. She always caught him at the bottom so he wouldn't fall and hit his butt.

"Weeeeee!" he yelled as he slid down, hugging his sister when he got to the bottom. He looked at her and asked, "So they see pictures of them too?"

"They see pictures of everyone, just like you." She grabbed his hands and pulled him down, both of them sitting on the mulch.

"And me?"

"What?

"They see me?"

"Yep! They see your name, pictures of you, all your information." She laid down on the mulch, her head on her hands and eyes closed. She wasn't taking this seriously.

He leaned over and poked her cheek. "But how?"

"The mosquito!" She popped up and grabbed his head again.

"Maeve!" He didn't understand. He threw her hands away and grabbed some mulch, tossing it at her. She laughed and tossed some back. "But how the mosquito knows?"

"How does the mosquito know what?"

"Me!" He was getting frustrated that Maeve didn't understand what he was asking. He wanted to know everything, and she was telling him nothing! He threw some more mulch at her.

"The mosquito doesn't know you." She blocked his attack and smiled at him.

"Maeve!"

"Okay, okay!" she said and laughed. "So, the mosquito is like a piece of paper. And anyone can write on that paper."

"Mom?"

"Yes! Mom writes on the paper. And then everyone who has a mosquito can read that piece of paper. So anything that mom or anyone else writes, everyone can read."

"Can I write on mosquito paper?"

"No, we're too little."

"I'm not little!" He jumped up and stomped away from her. He was a big boy!

She stood up after him and ran around, kneeling in front of him. "You're right! But we just can't write on the paper yet."

"But if we no write, how people know me?"

"Because Mom writes about *us*."

"But how Mom knows what to write?"

"I don't know." Maeve stood and stepped back. He wasn't sure if he liked that his mom wrote about him. It was nice of her, but what if he wanted other people to see something she didn't write or not see something that she did? And how did she actually write? How was the mosquito like a paper, and where was the pen? It was too much for him.

"Hmph." He walked back to the swing, wanting to hop up, but couldn't lift his leg high enough. "Maeve!"

"Okay, okay." She laughed and placed him back on the swing. He kicked his legs but couldn't make the swing move.

"Maeve!"

She walked behind him and gently pushed him.

"I won't be able to push you always."

"What? No!"

"I just mean, you'll have your own friends, and you will need to learn how to push yourself when you play with them."

"You my best friend. I only play with you."

"You're my best friend too." She stopped the swing and hugged him from behind. He leaned his head on hers.

"Do you think someone wrote on mosquito that you my best friend?"

She kissed him on the top of the head. "Not yet, but maybe we can ask Mom."

"Okay. Everyone need to know."

"They sure do."

A picture of his mom holding a plate popped up in front of him. "Let's go!" Maeve said and pulled him off the swing.

"Did Mom come on you mosquito too?"

"Sure did! Mom must have set up notifications on our devices for dinner!"

"What?" What was a notification? Was the device another name for the mosquito? His head was spinning.

"It's okay. I know it's a lot, but I'm here to help you figure it all out." She grabbed his hand, and they walked back toward the house.

He counted seven trees from the park to their house.

"That one's an elm." Maeve knew all the trees. She knew everything. "Shh... You hear that?" He nodded. "That's the call of a mourning dove!"

"Can you teach me?" He wanted to know everything that she knew.

"Of course. But not right now. It seems like I need to help Mom set the table. Why don't you play out here with your truck, and we'll come get you when we're done?"

Maeve walked inside, and Rory walked over to the truck he had left in their front yard.

Across the street, a boy was drawing with chalk in his driveway. He looked up and waved at Rory.

I love chalk!

He looked both ways and ran across the street over to the boy.

>>>>>>>>SCAN>>>>>>>>IN>>>>>>>>PROGRESS>>>>>>>>

So many pictures of the boy!

"Can I draw?" Rory asked as he walked up to the boy.

The boy shook his head yes and handed Rory a piece of chalk. Green! Just like all the trees he and Maeve passed. He sat down and started drawing a mosquito, but it definitely looked more like a butterfly.

His mom holding a plate popped up again.

But he was almost done with his drawing! He wanted to finish it, so he didn't head back to the house and just kept on moving the chalk across the pavement.

"Rory!" his mother's voice thundered, startling him so much he dropped the chalk in his hand and jumped to his feet.

"M-m-m-ama?" he said, wiping his hands on his shorts and turning to face her. She wasn't running, but she was walking fast, her shoulders in front of the rest of her body. Her hands weren't open like usual—they were closed tight.

"What do you think you're doing?" She stormed up to him and grabbed his arm, pulling him toward the house.

She didn't even look both ways before crossing the street like she always told him to.

"You're hurting me!"

"Rory, you can't play with people from different broods!" Her nose was scrunched up and her eyes were wide, staring right at him.

"Mama!"

She dragged him to their front yard and extended out his toy firetruck to him. She leaned over to him and put her arms on her legs. She took a breath and closed her eyes. His arm still hurt from her grip. He massaged it with the other and plopped onto the grass in crisscross applesauce style.

She opened her eyes and shook her head. "Honey, there's something we need to talk about now that you're older." She placed the truck next to him and sat down. "When you look at someone, do you notice that a bunch of information comes up about them? Things like their name, some photos of them?"

"Uh-huh." He rubbed his arm. He just talked about this with Maeve!

"There's also something called a brood—do you know what that is?"

He shook his head no and started pulling at the grass. He didn't like the way she was looking at him.

"Okay. Do you know what a club is? Like a group of people who all like doing the same thing?"

"Like the Hornets?"

"Kind of like that. You all like playing soccer together, so you are on one team. That's right!" Her face changed. It wasn't as red as before. She smiled and lifted his chin. "Broods are more important than teams, though. They're like families."

He pushed her hand away and kept tugging at the grass.

"Rory, this is important, I need you to really listen to me."

He looked up at her.

"Okay."

"Every brood is given a color. Our color is yellow."

"I like yellow," he said trying to show his mom that he was listening. Yellow was the Hornets' color too!

"You do! Well, people in our brood have a yellow color next to their name. Do you know what colors are like yellow?"

"Uhm, orange?"

"If you look at someone and their color is close to yellow, that means their brood is similar to ours. The less the color is like yellow, the more different they are. Do you know colors that are not like yellow?"

"Green and blue!"

"Great job!" Nora raised her hand for a high-five, and he smacked it back. Her shoulders dropped, and she extended out her legs.

"Now, I know colors are still pretty hard for you, so we need to just stick to yellow, understand?"

"So I can only have yellow friends?"

"Exactly!"

"But why?"

"Because yellow means those people are just like us. They believe the same stuff that we do! The farther people are from yellow, the more different and wrong they are."

"So green people don't like soccer?"

"No, honey, I need you to listen to me." The smile began to go away again, and her eyes got smaller.

"I am!" He was the best listener! It hurt him that she didn't think he was listening.

"Right now, it's just important for you to know that we are yellow, we need to be around other yellows, and the farther from yellow that people are, the more evil they are."

"Evil?"

"Bad. They don't like you and want to hurt you and take your toys."

"But why?"

His dad's truck pulled into the driveway, and his mother stood and walked toward his tired dad. He followed along and wrapped himself around his dad's leg.

"Hey, little man," his dad said.

"Up!" He extended his arms, hoping for a tummy blow.

"Dad's tired right now. Maybe later."

"Everything all right?" his mom asked his dad and put her hand on his arm, but he turned away.

"It's getting so much worse. The interbrood violence is just flooding the emergency room. I'm exhausted."

"What's wrong, Daddy?"

His mom crouched and said, "Remember those bad people?"

"Uh-huh. Are they taking each other's toys?"

"Something like that, sweetie. That's why we need to be really careful." He looked back at his firetruck and then at his mom. What if the chalk boy took his truck? He was red, and that was kind of far from yellow!

"Remember when being in a different brood just meant quickly and easily finding people like us?" his dad said.

"It was wonderful… Who would've thought self-classification would make such tight-knit communities? Well, I guess it's not self-classification anymore, but placement based on content is probably more correct than that, anyway!" She laughed. His dad rolled his eyes.

"Not anymore. Now it's open season. Other broods are prey. It's 'I need to stay away from them or kill them.' Even our humanity isn't common ground anymore."

"What?" his mom asked.

"It's not enough to find like-minded people. It's attack—no, eradicate those not like us." He started walking toward the house, rubbing his hip.

Rory's mom kneeled and wrapped her arms around him. "It's so important to me that you understand what I told you."

He hugged her back. "Only yellow friends."

She laughed. "Only yellow friends."

"Maeve is yellow! You need to write on mosquito that Maeve and I best friends."

"What?"

"People need to know."

"That Maeve is your best friend?" She dropped her arms and pushed him in front of her.

He shook his head yes. She squinted her eyes and stood up, turning away from him. "Let's go inside. Dinner's cold by now, and we need to warm it up before your dad gets to it."

CHAPTER VI

2118

———

NORA

"You still think soccer is a waste of time for Rory?" Nora asked Finn as she led the way into the Corporate Council Headquarters.

Finn rolled his eyes.

"Listen, I know you're upset that he's taken to it so well, but why can't you just be happy he has something he enjoys doing?"

"What do you mean, 'taken to it so well'? He's a kid. It's still just luck at this point."

"Why can't you bond with him over this? You barely spend any time with him."

"That's not true. I see him almost every day."

"Yes, okay, you're right. You physically see him. But you never talk to him. You've taken one hunting trip with him. You don't sit with him or play with him or read with him—"

"I'm here, aren't I? I took two days off of work so I could drive you, Rory, and Maeve down to Washington to spend a whole afternoon at CCHQ."

"If this trip was anywhere else, would you have even come? You just wanted to see CCHQ again. Sometimes I swear that the CC is the only thing you believe in." She turned and yelled for her children, "Rory! Maeve!"

The children had started to run around the huge, empty room, and Nora wanted to keep them close and make sure they were being respectful, and so she sped up to corral them, leaving Finn lagging behind.

Finn had visited CCHQ one time right before he received his Accessible Internet Product. He was extremely cautious and did not like the idea of anything being put into his body, "the temple that God created," or so he called it. The CC had created an opportunity for all that had been originally opposed to the AIP to come down to HQ and see how it was created, how it was injected, and to watch their own AIP from creation to injection to assuage fears of this new technology. He, himself, was injected here.

CCHQ was in the old Capitol building in Washington, DC. It was one of the few federal buildings that remained, as many were destroyed in various protests and insurrections prior to the rise of the corporatocracy.

This one, however, was reinforced, redesigned, and repurposed. It housed the representatives of the Corporate Council, and it was where AIPs were designed and manufactured.

Nora always wondered how the Holy Trinity managed to be the only worldwide manufacturer of AIPs. Seeing the extent of security around this particular building answered that question automatically. No uninvited guests would be able to overcome the gates, walls, tunnels, cameras, guards, and whatever else the Corporate Council had installed or implemented that couldn't be seen by visitors. And those were just the physical precautions to protect the structure itself. She couldn't even imagine the type of security they had to protect their virtual systems.

To get inside the building, they were scanned by three different sets of guards in all black. However, once in the building, it was empty. She was surprised there hadn't been anyone to greet them or monitor them once inside.

"Hello! You must be the Walsh family!" a man in a white coat greeted them from behind.

>>>>>>>>SCAN>>>>>>>>IN>>>>>>>>PROGRESS>>>>>>>>
- -
Name: Joseph Ridders
- -
Information Classified due to Corporate Council Representation
- -

"Hello, yes," Finn responded.

"I'm sorry, but where did you even come from?" Nora asked. She didn't see a single door except for the main entrance. The room was a huge, white box with only the ceiling supporting the original architectural integrity of the building.

Joseph pointed around the room. "I'll let you in on a little secret! This room is full of covert doors with installed scanners. Each individual who works here has various levels of clearance, and each door is programmed to open only for individuals who have been cleared. Only those with the highest levels of clearance even know where all of the doors are located." He looked at each family member in turn, scanning them. "I see that you all have been given second level clearance as invited visitors, which means I can give you a general tour as well as access to the AIP facilities and a lunch with mid-level representatives to the Corporate Council."

"Cool!" Rory yelled and clapped.

"Very much so," Joseph responded. "We can take questions during the tour, but do you have any before we start? Let's start with you, Finn, since you've already been here."

"Has anything changed since I was last here?"

"No, but it looks like you only had a level one clearance, so you didn't have access to mid-level representatives."

"Then I don't have any questions yet. Thank you for asking."

"I'm sorry," Nora said sheepishly. "I have a question, if you don't mind."

"Of course. What can I illuminate for you?"

"Well, I'm sure you know, but my son's soccer team won the interbrood league this year for the eight-to-twelve-year-old division," Nora said and wrapped her arms around Rory, beaming with pride.

Joseph nodded.

"Yes, well, I talked to some of the other parents, and only a few kids from the team were invited. Well, I was just wondering, where are those other children?"

"In order to prevent disruption, as well as to promote the safety of those who work for the Corporate Council, we only allow a maximum of five visitors into the building per day."

Well, that makes sense why it's so impossible to ever get a tour, Nora thought.

"Okay, so the other children's families will be visiting on different days?" she asked.

"Correct. But not all of them. Although we have invited them to visit, we understand that there are certain broods who do not support everything the Corporate Council does or stands for, and therefore they have declined our invitations."

"Like who?" Maeve said.

"Maeve!" Finn scolded.

"What?"

"It's all right," Joseph said. "There are some people, very, very few, of course, who prefer the world the way it used to be, with censorship, anti-capitalist policies, violence, and a select group of officials who would tell them what to do, how to think, and how to live. The Corporate Council believes all people should have the freedom to express themselves, to not live in a world full of fear that their words will be hidden from others, that economic success is important and is only possible with a completely free market, and more. We support the liberty and self-determination of all people."

Finn smiled and leaned down to his daughter and said, "Maeve, the individuals who do not support the CC are full of hate. They'll take the AIP and get the benefits from it, but then turn around and judge the CC for the way it runs the country. They hate you for who you are, what you have, what you believe, what you stand for, and for who your family is. They want you to be silent. To live in fear. To apologize for things you didn't do. And most importantly, to take away your freedoms."

"They sound scary," Maeve said and hugged her father. Nora grabbed Rory's hand as he started to wander away from the group. She couldn't blame someone his age for his short attention span.

"They are scary," Finn responded. "That's why the AIPs are so wonderful. They make sure we never have to talk to or see those people. They protect us by allowing us to scan everyone we meet, to avoid *those* people. Best of all, before the AIPs and the CC taking control of this country, our liberties and freedoms were disappearing. We were unable to find information because it was being hidden, destroyed, removed. But now, everything is available. We can see everything. We can learn everything. We are not only shown what certain individuals want us to see, and this is beautiful. That is freedom. Freedom from others. Freedom for ourselves."

"That is well-put, Mr. Walsh. You are right. The Corporate Council provides opportunity, safety, liberty, but it does not impose any of these things. It allows individuals to make fully-informed decisions. Although it was not the intention, the AIP allowed for broods to arise. Broods, which are like families. Which have recreated communities. Which have created bonds stronger than family. With the increase in broods, we have seen a decrease in violence reported to the Corporate Council, which has allowed us to reallocate resources because individuals are now protecting and taking care of one another. It's… a wonderful thing."

"I don't think we have any more questions," Finn said without looking at or consulting Nora.

"Wonderful. Let's begin the tour. Please follow me." Rory tugged Nora's hand and pulled her toward Joseph. She grabbed Maeve, and the group followed their guide to a blank white wall.

Joseph stood perfectly still. "Scan complete," a voice behind the wall said. *Click!* A door-sized section of the wall pulled itself in and slid away, creating an opening. They walked through, and the door immediately slid back into place. *Puff!* Smoke covered the opening for a moment and then disappeared.

"Cool!" Rory said smiling at Nora and squeezing her hand.

"What was that?" Nora asked.

"The smoke acts as a sealant, heating the door and causing it to expand. This expansion ensures the door fits the opening so tightly that all cracks or gaps remain hidden from view of the naked eye."

"How do you know where the door is?" Maeve asked.

"Maeve!" Finn said again.

"It's quite all right, Mr. Walsh." Joseph looked at Maeve. "You know how when you look at other people, you can scan them and it brings up all of the information about them?"

"Not you," she said.

Joseph chuckled. "That's true. That's to protect me because I work for the Corporate Council. Those people your father and I told you about, remember? Well, sometimes they can get so mad that they want to hurt us, the people who work here. So by hiding information about us, the Corporate Council is protecting us."

"Oh," Maeve responded.

"But when I scan that room, something really similar happens. My AIP provides me outlines of the doors I have access to, and it tells me where those doors lead. It's pretty remarkable. Now, I can only show you a few rooms on the general tour because of your clearance level, but the AIP portion is definitely the most exciting, and you have full access to that."

"What about before the AIPs?" Maeve asked. "How did you find the doors then?"

"Well, we would need to use our devices. But that was pretty dangerous because if someone ever stole the device, and if they were motivated, they could potentially hack in and find this information."

"Are we allowed to take pictures?" Nora asked.

"Come on, Nora," Finn said with an edge to his voice.

She ignored him and pulled out her device.

"Of course! Let me let you in on another secret." Joseph motioned for the family to get closer to him. "Everyone in the entire country has first level clearance. We believe in full and complete transparency, particularly around AIPs, so anyone who wants to see anything on the general tour or the AIP process is completely welcome to do so."

"If they can get an appointment, right?" Nora said.

"Yes. We realize how hard it is for individuals to come to headquarters, so we make this information accessible. You'll notice that the information you receive on your AIP if you think about headquarters is exactly what you will see on this tour. So go ahead and snap away."

"Would you mind?" She handed Joseph the device.

"Not at all." He snapped a few pictures and returned it to Nora.

"Now, look around. What do you see here?"

"Another blank room," Maeve said. "But it's longer. Like a hallway. Are there doors in here too?"

"Yes! This hallway actually has many doors, all of which I have access to, and I can show you the first three. Let's start here." Joseph stood in front of the wall. "Scan complete," the wall said, and a chunk pulled in and slid away like the first.

"This is the Brood Reconciliation Unit."

Walking through the opening, they ended up on a balcony encased in glass overlooking a large chamber. There was a judge sitting at the front dressed in a white coat, a gavel in his hand, too far away for Nora to scan. Across from him were two men on opposing sides of the chamber.

A voice came over a speaker on the balcony. "What was your intent in assaulting this man?" The judge leaned back in his chair, looking at his hands rather than the men in front of him. He tapped his fingers as he waited for a response.

"Your Honor, he started it!" another voice exclaimed. "His brood took over the land that my brood lived on. They ran us out with weapons and took our homes!"

The reverberating voice must've shaken Rory, who was shivering and sliding closer to Nora.

"That is upsetting, but that is not the case at hand. Did this man attack you in any way?"

How is that not important to the case? Nora wondered. *Wasn't the reason people did something usually in direct response to something that was done to them? Why would the attack be relevant but not the reason for it? Had there already been a prior case that dealt with the stolen land?*

"No, but…"

"There are no buts here. You walked up to a man on the street, you scanned him, and rather than walking away and not engaging, you attacked him. That is unacceptable and inappropriate. I am sorry, but you are found guilty."

"Of what? Protecting my people?" The man slammed his fist on a table. Rory scurried behind Nora's legs and rubbed his face in the back of her thigh. She pet his head with the hand he dropped while squeezing Maeve's with her other.

"Adjourned. You are sentenced to life in labor. We cannot have you on our streets."

She had heard of the labor camps that replaced traditional prisons but never personally knew anyone who was sent to them. They were supposed to be more humane and economically beneficial forms of rehabilitation, but she wasn't sure how a lifetime sentence counted as humane.

Although not many people could afford to retire anymore, so wasn't everyone technically "sentenced to life in labor"?

Finn had probably known how the system worked. He was versed in the CC and its policies… but it wasn't her place to research things like that. How could she when she spent all her time making profiles and taking care of the kids?

The man found guilty began to pound on the table and cry. He yelled, and Nora pushed Maeve behind her to join Rory. She turned and hugged them both, trying to cover their ears.

"Okay children, face me now," Joseph said, coaxing the children to look away from the chamber. Nora forced her shoulders into their faces to block their view. Neither fought back, hugging her and looking at each other rather than the scene behind her.

Two large men in black walked into the chamber, grabbed the yelling man, and carried him away. The chamber emptied, and Nora peeled her children off her, kissing the tops of their heads in turn.

Joseph smiled and clasped his hands together. "How exciting! It's not common that our tours actually stumble upon the unit being utilized!"

"Is this how all cases are tried?" Nora asked. She had never known anyone who had entered the justice system.

"Only for disputes between broods, not within them."

"What about disputes within broods?"

"The Corporate Council believes that disputes between brood members are successfully and efficiently solved by the brood. Additionally, broods do not like when outsiders dictate how their issues should be resolved. Therefore, the Corporate Council does not get involved in these disputes."

"I fully support that," Finn said. "No need to have people who do not know you tell you how to live your life and solve your problems."

What if someone kills someone else in my brood? Nora wondered. Do they face no repercussions if the rest of the brood votes on it? What happens if there are larger disagreements between multiple brood members? Does the brood split off into smaller broods?

Joseph opened the door, and the kids followed him off the balcony. She could tell Finn's anger with her kept rising. It was not her place to keep asking Joseph questions, so she followed the rest of the group out of the BRU and into the hallway.

"All right, up next is the Representative Voting Unit. They are currently in session, and therefore it is important we keep our voices down. Please save your questions for after we exit."

They followed him through the door onto a second glass balcony.

There was another chamber below them, similar to the first, but this one was full of people in white coats in the middle of a conversation, also too far away to scan.

"Listen, I understand that everyone votes because it's convenient, but I want to know how many people actually know what they're voting about."

"That's what I've been trying to say for the past twenty minutes. How many people just vote on their device to get rid of the pop-up on their AIP? What if they just click on the option that's most convenient for their finger instead of what's in their actual self-interest? Do we trust the people to be informed on these issues?"

"What do you propose? People writing an essay justifying their vote?"

"I'm just saying. Look at this data." A chart appeared at the far end of the chamber across the wall. Nora looked around but couldn't figure out where the projection was coming from. "For the past three issue votes that we've proposed, the top most option has won. That seems like an odd coincidence to me. Are people voting for that because it's the best option?"

"You're explaining the problem again. I think we all agree it's an issue. But you're not proposing any solutions."

"Well, what if we create an informational packet or a video or something about the issue? And then we send that out over the AIP with the vote. Then people who haven't seen the video or read whatever won't be able to access the vote."

"I think that's a bad idea."

"Why?"

"Because it'll decrease the amount of people who vote!"

"Okay, but why does voter turnout matter more than ensuring that those who are voting are actually aware of what they're voting on?"

Joseph tapped Nora and Finn on the shoulders and beckoned for them to follow him out of the Unit.

Puff!

"Wasn't that riveting? You guys have had such a treat that both units were in session today."

"What were they talking about?" Nora asked. "Are they actually going to do that with the voting function?"

She had been one of the convenience voters the representatives in the unit mentioned. When voting first moved to the AIP as a notification, she simply ignored it, but once it became more persistent, the notification not disappearing until a vote was cast, she would simply vote for the option that appeared first.

"Only time will tell," Joseph said. "Personally, I believe requiring individuals to view certain materials may stand against the CC's principles of freedom of information, questioning why certain materials were chosen, but I am not a Voting Representative and therefore only speculate."

"That makes sense," Finn responded.

"Well, if you have no other questions, let's head on over to the most exciting part of the tour."

"Oh, we're going to see how the AIPs are made, aren't we?" Nora nudged the back of her children's heads for them to follow the guide as Joseph led them to another blank section on the white wall. "Scan complete." *Click!*

This time they didn't walk onto a glass balcony but directly onto a factory floor. There was an aisle ahead of them with red rope on either end.

"What's the rope for?" Nora asked.

"Although you have full access here, we stay on this aisle for your safety. There is some heavy and impressive machinery, and we wouldn't want anyone to get hurt."

"Also, they probably don't want us getting in the way and ruining their processes," Finn said and laughed.

Joseph returned a smile and a wink. "We are starting backward, unfortunately. This is where the physical AIP is created." He reached out, and a woman in a matching white coat from the other side of the rope dropped a vial in his hand. "Gather around. This is the vial that feeds into the syringe that goes into you, everyone. If you look closely, it almost looks like a tiny little ant."

"Ew!" Maeve yelled and backed away. "There's an ant inside of me?"

"I guess it's not a mosquito!" Rory laughed and poked his sister in the side.

"Shh!" Finn smacked the back of Rory's head. Nora clenched her fists from smacking him right back in front of a CC representative.

"It's not a real ant. This is why it stinks that we start at the end. It's a wonderful piece of constructed technology that just so happens to look like an ant in this little vial."

Maeve looked at her mother, and Nora wrapped her arm around her shoulder.

"Okay, let's move on." Joseph had a little hesitancy to his voice. They walked a few steps and stopped in front of a huge machine with twenty protruding arms.

"Cool!" Rory yelled.

"Dear Lord," Finn muttered next to Nora as he pulled Rory back. "Settle my soul and teach this child another word."

"This is the amazing piece of technology that delicately puts the pieces of the AIP together. It takes the tiny components and essentially welds them together. This machine—it removes all human error. Since its inception, we have never, not a single time, had a malfunction with an AIP anywhere in the entire world.

Nora never questioned the AIP or its benefits, but after seeing this incredible technology in front of her, she could never even imagine doubting it. She understood why Finn could be so willing to implant himself after seeing this while not letting a single other toxin voluntarily into his system. He even told her that if his parents didn't vaccinate him as a child that he wouldn't have done it himself.

They followed Joseph to the end of the factory floor. He walked up to the white wall at the end. "Scan complete." *Click!*

A group of white-coated individuals inside sat around a table looking at plans projected on the far wall.

"And this is the Brain. This is where the design of the AIP happens, along with updates and troubleshooting. It looks like they're trying to enhance a specific aspect of the algorithm." Joseph led them through the office space until they stopped at a big conference room. "After you," he said and pointed them inside.

Two mid-level representatives sat behind a table.

>>>>>>>SCAN>>>>>>>IN>>>>>>>PROGRESS>>>>>>>

Name: Rachel Bennett

Information Classified due to Corporate Council
Representation

>>>>>>>SCAN>>>>>>>IN>>>>>>>PROGRESS>>>>>>>

Name: Thomas Vanis

Information Classified due to Corporate Council
Representation

Nora and the children joined the representatives at the table where lunch was already plated for them while Finn walked up to the representatives and shook their hands. He said, "Thank you so much for spending your time having lunch with us today. It really is such an honor to meet you both," and joined the rest of his family.

"What can we answer for you?" Thomas said. "I assume you have questions."

"I actually do not," Finn answered. "But it was so wonderful getting to visit again."

"Oh." Rachel looked at Thomas awkwardly and said, "If you do not have any questions, then we should go. Let you enjoy your lunch in peace," while rising from her chair.

"Please, wait," Nora appreciated Finn taking the reins, but sometimes he could drown out her voice, and when she actually had something to say, it hurt. He may have been here before, but she had not. Most importantly, she wanted to get some more pictures. Pictures with some mid-level representatives that couldn't even be scanned? The rest of the brood would be so incredibly jealous!

"Yes?" Rachel said.

"I actually have some questions, if you don't mind."

Nora could feel Finn's eyes burrowing into her side, but she paid no attention because she was excited to meet with these representatives and use her new, albeit temporary, clearance.

"Why the AIP?" she asked. "I mean, of course there's so much speculation online, but why did the Holy Trinity really create the AIP?"

"Well, it's right in the name," Thomas responded. "To make the internet accessible to everyone." Nora was completely unsatisfied with his answer, and he must have noticed because he continued. "Times were tough before the Corporate Council was democratically elected to change the way this country functioned. The Corporate Council did not at all believe in the silencing of anyone, regardless of what they had to say. I'm sure you've noticed this. There is much information against the Corporate Council, almost all of it false or based in falsehoods, but the Corporate Council removes none of it because it believes people should have the freedom to say anything they would like to say."

"I'd like to add," Rachel began after Thomas seemed to finish his statement, "the Corporate Council believes in equality for everyone. It wants to ensure that all individuals, regardless of where they are or where they come from, have access to all the information in the world. Knowledge breeds opportunity, and if everyone has access to that knowledge, then everyone has access to opportunity, and what is more equal than that?" She sat back and smiled.

Knowledge does create opportunity! That makes so much sense.

"But what I've always really wondered is, why? How does it make sense for the Corporate Council to provide this technology to everyone in the world for free? Walking through what we just saw, it must cost a fortune to design and make these."

"Actually," Thomas explained, "we've become so efficient that it no longer is that extraordinarily expensive to make them. Yes, there are costs associated, of course, but they aren't as large as you may think."

Rachel continued, "Also, the AIPs are the largest revenue stream for the Corporate Council. That is why taxes continue to decrease year over year. So much of our attention is dedicated to the AIP that advertisers fight to capture that attention, increasing their sales and profits, therefore making that advertising space more competitive. So, it makes sense for the Corporate Council to want proliferation of the AIPs, not only as a great equalizer, but to support its financial health as well so it can successfully support the growth of the United States and its economic development without burdening its citizens."

"Thank you so much for that explanation," Nora said.

"I'm so glad we could help answer your questions," Thomas said.

"Can I ask one last question?"

"That's why we're here," Thomas said.

"How does the algorithm work?"

The representatives looked at each other. "The algorithm makes sure that you get to see what you want to see," Thomas responded hesitantly.

"Does that mean that other information gets hidden?"

"It means your profile curates your results," Thomas said. "You can see other information, but it would take a little longer and some creative hunting. What you want to see based on your profile is what will come up first, and that will continue to lead you to results similar to the ones that resonate with what you spend most time looking at. Does that answer your question?"

"I think so," Nora responded, though she wasn't completely sure.

"Thank you so much for your time and willingness to answer my wife's questions," Finn said to the representatives, and he stood and shook each of their hands.

"Oh! Could we grab a picture together with you first?" Nora asked.

The representatives beckoned for the family to join them as Nora handed her device to Joseph to capture a few pictures. Walking to a final door, he thanked them for their trip, wished them well, and hoped they would share their experiences of their time at CCHQ. After their parting words, he ushered them to the exit, which spit them out onto the street.

The door returned to its spot in the wall and a *puff* made it disappear.

"What were you thinking, Nora?" Finn looked at her with squinted eyes.

"What?" she asked, unsure of where his hostility was coming from.

"You made us look like complete fools with your questions! What a poor representation of our brood and our support for the CC. Did you not read a single press conference or statement before you came? All those questions could have been answered with just a second of research!" He turned away from her and grabbed his children. "Let's go. I want to get home before it gets dark."

She watched her husband and kids walk to the car, them somehow getting bigger with each step rather than smaller, she the one shrinking instead.

CHAPTER VII

2119

———

NORA

Maeve read to Rory in the back of the car. Her most recent obsession was the Harry Potter series, and it seemed like she was on the third book. It was sweet that she started reading the series with Rory and would only pick it up when they were together, but Nora hated that her daughter wouldn't pick something more sensible, like the Bible.

Nora remembered when she and Maeve would read together, how they would snuggle up on the couch or in Maeve's bed, Nora holding her daughter and reading a book Maeve picked out for them.

But she and Maeve hadn't spent much time together lately, Maeve's attention fully on Rory.

She should be happy her children got along so well, but she couldn't help missing the time she spent with her daughter, finding herself quietly resenting Rory in the rearview mirror for his imposition on their relationship.

"Sweetie, we're almost there. Can we put the book away, please? Make sure that you and your brother look nice for the other kids." Nora shifted her gaze to Maeve.

"But we're just going to run around. Why does it matter?"

Nora sighed. She didn't want the other moms judging her for the way her children looked unless they were perfectly put together, unless that judgment was pure jealousy.

"Because, Maeve, I don't want the other parents to think I let you out of the house without providing for you, without making sure you have everything you need, without checking you are both absolutely perfect."

Nora pulled down her visor and lifted the flap of the small mirror. The bags under her eyes showed even through her flawlessly applied makeup. She patted her cheeks, hoping to bring down the redness, unsuccessfully.

She hadn't seen Finn in three days. There was no way he was scheduled for three twelve-hour days in a row. He had to be picking up shifts, and he wasn't telling her why. Were they having money troubles? Was he upset with her? Was he having an affair?

No way. He was much too religious to believe in affairs. He couldn't even comprehend the concept of divorce, let alone the capability to commit adultery.

Worst of all, she was singlehandedly doing everything. She didn't have time to clean the house, take the kids to their playdates, drive them to school, drive Rory to soccer, cook all the meals—which included preparing Finn's for the work day—and do the laundry, cultivate the kids' profiles, help with their homework… on and on the to-do list went.

Drained.

But she couldn't let anyone else see that.

She may not be doing it all very well, but she was doing it all. And it only took the right angle, the perfect filter to show the brood that she was handling everything with grace and ease. She needed that.

She needed everyone to think she was handling it so they could convince her because she couldn't fully trust that she was doing the right things or she was doing a good job.

"Maeve, will you finish the story tonight?" Rory asked her.

"Maeve has a project she needs to finish this evening, Rory," Nora snapped.

Her daughter whispered something to him, but she didn't care. She checked the mirror on the visor one last time to run a finger under her eyes and brush back her hair as they approached the house hosting the day's playdate.

She closed the visor and snuck a peek into the backseat. *Beautiful. They look great. The car is clean. I look alright. They have their little snack goodie-bags. All homemade, of course. I can do this.*

The house continued to grow until they arrived directly in front of it. A huge Georgian, with French doors facading as a large arched window opened onto a beautiful Juliet balcony directly above the portico pillars that framed the front door. The bricks recently repainted white provided a luxurious feel. Nothing like their quaint two-story Tudor.

The driveway was short, particularly in comparison to the grandness of the house, but filled with three cars. Nora parked on the street, last to arrive.

The car door opened onto a beautiful spring day, the skies clear, the air sweet, smelling of lilacs. She shepherded her kids across the street and put their snacks in her purse. They ran into the backyard before she even had time to lock the car.

"Maeve! Rory!" she called as she tried to elegantly chase after them.

Four other kids were playing there. The backyard was impressive: a swing set, a sandbox, a trampoline, and a pool. She tried to think of the home, find a recent listing, but nothing popped up on her AIP. She wondered how large their backyard really was. The far back was lined with trees, protecting the kids from getting to the creek behind it.

Did they own the creek too?

The grass had been recently cut in a diagonal formation. The landscaping was nothing like their own, either. The back of the home had three sets of French doors that were open, white curtains fluttering in the gentle breeze. The doors led out onto a rectangular stone terrace surrounded by concrete planters and housed a large, round glass table with six chairs.

Why can't we afford any of this? We should have more for Maeve and Rory to play with. What do they do again?

Her AIP provided results on the family, including the salary of Abigail's husband, a surgeon. Nora, originally admiring her husband's career as a PA, now disappointed that he hadn't made the commitment to go to medical school to provide a better life for them.

Her thoughts were interrupted. "Hi, Nora!" Abigail called. "Come, join us!" Her, along with two other mothers, were sitting around a glass table, sipping drinks while Abigail held the pitcher. "Sangria?"

She made her way to join the women at the table, taking a seat next to their gracious host.

"No thanks! I don't love drinking while I have the kids. I want to make sure all of my attention is with them," she said with a smile.

Was that an eyeroll? Are they judging me for my decision not to drink with them in the middle of the afternoon? She was the one being responsible with every right to question the decisions they made in a backyard full of kids. She hoped they felt guilty for even asking, realizing she was the better parent among the group.

"So, Nora, how are you doing?" Abigail asked as she topped off the other mothers' drinks.

"Fantastic! Rory is really thriving at soccer, and Maeve is doing so well in school."

"Seems like he'd rather not play with other kids, though," one of the other mothers said while taking a huge gulp of her sangria and waving the glass.

"Excuse me?"

She pointed to the children. Rory and Maeve were on the far side of the yard, away from the other kids.

You've got to be joking me.

"Oh, he just *loves* listening to her read!" Nora said and laughed. "I'm definitely blessed they're such good friends. Can't pry one from the other."

"Seems like it. I'm so excited to share, but Mary is going to have someone to spend her time with too!" Abigail said, smiling at the rest of the group and patting her stomach.

A chorus of congratulations showered Abigail from the other two women.

"That's wonderful," Nora said, not nearly as enthusiastically as the others. She immediately looked to Abigail's glass and noticed that although she was the one pouring from the pitcher, the liquid in her own glass was completely clear.

"Finn always said he wanted a *huge* family, right?" Abigail asked her. "When are you going to bring more joy into this world?" She scanned Nora and winked at the glass on the table, clinking the two water-filled glasses together by herself.

"Oh, we thought about it, but we're just going to let God tell us when we're ready for another. We're not particularly trying, but we'll be thrilled when it happens!" She tried to muster up enthusiasm but wasn't sure if she hid her relief at not being able to have more children.

She could feel her temperature rising. She didn't want any more kids. She loved Maeve and Rory, but she couldn't imagine adding more to-dos to her list. She was exhausted, and if she was honest with herself, she missed how much time she and Maeve used to spend together. She wasn't willing to give up any more of that attention.

"Oh! I forgot, I have Maeve and Rory's snacks in my purse. Let me go take those to them!" She needed to leave the conversation before they saw right through her. Hopefully they'd be on a different one by the time she came back.

Nora walked over to her kids. She had been at the playdate for fifteen minutes and was already ready to go home. She bent over in front of Maeve, handing her the snacks. She made sure her back was to the women.

"Maeve, what are you doing?" she asked with frustration. She couldn't believe how her children were making her look in front of the others.

"We're reading. Rory wanted to know what happened next."

Of course, this would be his fault.

"First, I hate that you have that book. Magic is what you receive in turn for a deal with the devil. This is nothing to be filling your heads with." She didn't care if it was true, but the pleasure she received from ruining the book they were bonding over was surprisingly gratifying. "Second, you have plenty of time to read at home. We are here, with other kids. Go play with them."

"But Rory doesn't like the other kids."

"Is that true?"

Rory shook his head yes and started pulling grass.

"Quite honestly, I do not care. I will not have the other parents thinking you are unfriendly, rude, or oddly obsessed with one another. Do you know how that looks if they think

I raised you this way? Give me that book, go play for an hour, and then we will go home. Okay?"

Maeve slowly handed her mother the book and grabbed her brother's hand. "Okay. Let's go play. I'll play with you while you play with the other kids if you want!"

Rory smiled at his sister and stood up.

"Wonderful," Nora said, standing up and rolling her eyes as her children joined the others.

Maybe I should've said yes to that drink.

She tucked the book under her arm and returned to the rest of the moms.

"I'm sure they loved that," one of them snickered as Nora approached the table.

"Shh..." Abigail said and elbowed her in the side. "Looks like they're having so much fun."

"Absolutely. They're a little shy, but they do so much love having these playdates!"

They're sitting here drinking wine and judging me because my children like to spend time together and read? That's rich!

Was the mask she wore beginning to crack? Was everyone beginning to see her for the fraud she was? If even her best posts and the few moments that she spent with others couldn't convince them of her talent as a parent, then her worst nightmare had come alive. She wasn't a good parent.

And if no one thought she was from the highlight reel she was showing then she really had no hope in convincing herself. As the other moms laughed and peeked at her from above their sangrias, she felt herself evaporating. She couldn't stand here...or sit here... and have them poke holes in her story.

"You know, I just realized, I completely forgot I told Finn we would meet him at work for his dinner break. I'm so sorry that we need to leave so early, but we so appreciate you inviting us." Nora grabbed her purse. "Maeve! Rory!"

The two came running up to her.

"We really should get going, kids."

The children looked relieved, like this is what they wanted all along, and they rushed off toward the car.

Abigail stood and gave Nora a hug. "Oh, it was so wonderful you stopped by. Shame you need to leave so early."

"Yes, but thank you again. I love seeing you all. Next time, I'd love to have you all over to our place." Nora turned away and followed her children, hoping she didn't give anyone time to consider her offer. She would be too embarrassed having them see her cottage after spending the afternoon in Abigail's mansion.

"Mom! It's locked," Rory said.

"I know it's locked. I locked it," she snapped, trying to keep her voice down. "What were you guys thinking? Running off by yourselves like that and sneaking this garbage with you?" She threw the book on the ground. "I expected this from Rory, but Maeve, sweetie. You know how important it is that you play with other children. You two can't just get caught up in one another." She unlocked the car and ushered her children inside.

"I'm sorry, Mom. We just really like spending time together. Rory is my best friend."

The words stung. Nora's eyes began to water. The punches just kept coming.

He *is your best friend?*

Maeve was always Nora's best friend. Rory had stolen her daughter from her, and it broke her heart.

Maeve never wanted to read together anymore or be put in bed, snuggling under the covers like they used to. She only ever wanted to read to Rory, holding his hand like she used to hold hers. Her daughter never played with her or talked to her, only perpetually focused on Rory.

She should be excited her children were so close and love one another so much, but it was hard to swallow that she was not the most important person in their lives. She gave up everything for them, did everything for them, worked so hard to cultivate the perfect profiles for them, spending every moment she could on her device for them, but they were ungrateful. But what could she do?

Being their mother was her job—no, it was her calling. A job is a choice, but this, this is something she was primed for, not something she chose, but something that was in her DNA. It shouldn't matter if they didn't love her as much or appreciate her; it was still in her to do all that was best for them. And what was best? Making sure they had the most perfectly curated profiles. It would ensure their futures would be provided for. What more could they possibly want or ask for?

She pulled up to the house and scrunched her face in disgust. The tiny Tudor with the old windows, the cracked stones, in desperate need of updates that probably couldn't be afforded. In the driveway, she pulled up next to Finn's truck.

That doesn't make sense. He should've still been at the hospital. His shift wouldn't end for a few hours.

She turned off the car and coaxed her kids out.

"Go inside, kids. Dinner will be in a few hours. Do your homework." Maeve and Rory ran inside, Nora slowly following. "Finn?" she said when she walked into the house.

"In here," he said from the kitchen. He had a sandwich in one hand and his device in the other. "I see Maeve and Rory didn't go to their playdate?"

"What do you mean?"

"Abigail shared a picture, and I don't see our children in it." He nonchalantly leaned on the counter and took a bite of his sandwich.

"We went. But we only stayed for a little while."

Finn put his sandwich on the counter and looked at her. With every word, the anger was more potent in his voice. "Nora, what could you possibly have to do that's more important than socializing our children?" He reached into his pocket and slammed his device on the kitchen counter.

"Excuse me?" Nora couldn't close her mouth no matter how hard she tried.

"You heard me. I'm at the hospital almost every day, working to provide for you, for this family. You are supposed to take care of these kids, and you can't even make it to some of their basic obligations?"

"Abigail's husband is at the hospital too, so why is it that their wants can be provided for while we only get needs?" She hoped he would connect the dots.

"Excuse me?" For the first time ever, he raised his arm above his head and slapped it across her face.

CHAPTER VIII

2120

———

NORA

The music filled the auditorium with a mediocrity that only a parent could appreciate. The talent show was about three-fourths of the way through, Maeve's "Clair de Lune" wrapping up her three-song set.

Nora appreciated Maeve's position near the end of the program. She could patiently sit through the beginning of the talent show, the excitement of watching Maeve keeping her present, but after her daughter's performance, she would be watching the clock, waiting for the seconds until she could wrap her arms around Maeve, showering her with compliments and the flowers she picked up on the way.

Nora had signed her up for piano lessons a little over two years ago, realizing she was shaping into a beautiful preteen, becoming recognized by the boys in her classes. She couldn't let her daughter realize how breathtaking she was, how many hearts she would break. Nora needed to fill up Maeve's time to protect her from the boys who would chase her and not give her any opportunity to even think about falling into sin.

Debussy serenading Nora, she couldn't help but see Leah's face on that stage. *My God, carbon copy*, she thought. "Thirteen," she sighed.

Nora was just thirteen when Leah ran away.

Thirteen years old when her life had changed, when her best friend had left, taking a chunk of Nora's heart with her.

She rarely thought about Leah after the first few years following her disappearance. But in that auditorium, seeing Maeve on that stage, Leah was all she could think about.

* * *

2099

"You slut! You unworthy, disgusting, ungrateful sinner!" Nora's father shouted all those years ago, with a slap so loud she was convinced it could've pushed Leah's soul straight out of her body.

"I'm sorry!" Leah whimpered through tears.

Nora couldn't see Leah from the steps, but she could imagine her sister cowering by the kitchen island, her eyes pleading with their father.

"How could you do this to us? To your family? To God Himself?" His tone was steady and deep, followed by what sounded like the cracking of a whip.

"Stop!" cried their mother, still sitting at the kitchen table and restraining herself from running to their father to avoid being collateral damage in his rage. "You'll hurt the baby! Leah's sin did bring us a miracle, and we must respect that!"

Nora watched their father lean over to Leah, and gripping her bicep, he raised her from the floor and pushed her toward the steps. "Get upstairs. Pray. Thank God for your mother's sensibilities."

Leah, eyes red from crying and face red from their father, ran past Nora and into her room, Nora running after her.

"Are you okay?" Nora asked, quietly shutting the door behind her. Her best friend was hurt, and she wanted to hold her to try and make it better.

Lying on her bed, sobbing into her pillow, Leah didn't answer.

"Leah. Please," Nora said, inching closer.

They had told each other everything. Always. Leah was exactly three years older than her, to the date, and from Nora's birth, Leah told her that she instantly fell in love. Nora was not an obligation, but a gift to treasure. She had been gifted a best friend.

They were inseparable. The private, Catholic, all-girls school they attended was so small they would spend each year in the same building until Leah went off to college. They walked to school together, ate lunch together, only separating for their volleyball practices that Leah said was because of their age, but was really due to Leah's incredible talent and Nora's lack of it.

Leah seemed to have it all. She was extraordinarily talented, being contacted by universities all across the country even as a sophomore in high school.

"We aren't allowed to recruit you yet or give you an offer, but we'll pay for you to come to California and meet some of our girls," the volleyball coach from UCLA had said over the phone while Nora and Leah huddled around it. But UCLA could be swapped out for any top performing volleyball program in the country.

Both Nora and Leah were pretty, but Leah was truly hypnotizing.

Boys and men would stop them on the street and berate Leah with proposals and compliments.

"Come on, just one date!"

"I'm going to marry you someday."

"That smile could make a blind man see, gorgeous!"

"No one in this whole town is good enough for you, but let me at least try!"

Leah would smile gently, run her fingers over her hair, place a hand over her heart, or for the truly lucky ones, would reach out and pet their hand or even run her lips across their cheeks. But her response was usually the same. "I'm so flattered, and you're going to make some woman extraordinarily lucky someday, but the stars just don't align for us."

Her sister would grab her hand and walk past them, sometimes patting them on the shoulder as if saying, *It's all right, sport. Better luck next time.*

Nora always looked back, but Leah never did. And every single time, she was met with an open jaw, eyes wide and unblinking. Leah left each one completely intoxicated. She would never be able to do that.

And Leah's laugh. Oh, that laugh. It was infectious. She could make a widow at a funeral chuckle with just a single giggle. But what truly amazed Nora was the way Leah could radiate a sense of belonging with a single smile. That look in her eyes was more inviting than a siren's song, but instead of luring to shipwreck, she lured to hidden treasure.

Witty.

Well-read.

Intelligent.

What Nora wouldn't give to have even a fraction of it all, hoping her sister would rub off on her at least as well as the perfume samples they would steal from their mother's boudoir and then dilute with water so she wouldn't notice. So it was no surprise when the first boy from the brother school started attending Leah's volleyball games. And it was even less shocking when one turned into five and five turned into eleven because news of the enticing volleyball player on a team of women in spandex no doubt spread faster than a wildfire.

Most of the boys rotated, and some volleyball games had more cheering spectators than others, of course. But there was always the same group of four who would sit directly opposite Nora in the bleachers.

What did surprise Nora was Leah finally accepting a date with one of her loyal fans. He was sweet, determined, and one of the few unintimidated by her sister.

"I'll prove it to you, I will give you everything I possibly can in this big, wonderful world. Just take a chance on me!" he had said after one of Leah's volleyball games.

Nora and Leah would traditionally grab ice cream after each of Leah's games, so Nora was always there when this poor boy would grovel for a moment of her sister's attention. Nora expected the same kiss on the cheek and pat on the back he always received, so when Leah had accepted, it was Nora's jaw that dropped.

With months of sneaking around, Nora was both excited that she was her sister's secret keeper but also a bit dejected that she was losing pieces of her sister's heart to a complete stranger. She no longer got to experience the most exhilarating moments of her sister's life but was forced to hang on every detail of the less-than-satisfying reenactment.

But Nora didn't realize that her sister, her best friend, her most trusted confidante, had begun to hide things from her. She began to shield a piece of her life and build a wall between them.

And so now, Nora, looking upon her crying sister, wanted to want to show compassion. She wanted to want to wrap her arms around her and tell her everything would be all right and she would never leave her side. But she couldn't push down the betrayal, the hurt from being excluded. The pain from being ignorantly and slowly pushed out of her sister's life consumed her more than the responsibility she knew that she had to be her sister's crutch.

She looked at her sobbing sister on the bed, grabbed the doorknob, and shut the door on their relationship.

For four months, she avoided Leah. She let her sister be tormented by their parents. She knew she was hurting her sister, and Leah was utterly alone in the absolute suffering that was imparted on her. Her friends were like ships in the night because of the constant supervision by her appointed chaperone from the church who would walk her to mass each day before school, accompany her to classes, and ensure her return home every afternoon.

Her sister's nights consisted of confession, constant reminders of the shame she had brought to their family, chaperoned praying, forced-feeding, abuse, and who knows what else Nora wasn't privy to.

She shouldn't have been surprised that her sister needed to escape. But the morning she had realized her pregnant sister was gone chilled her to her core. She awoke with nothing seeming amiss until swinging her legs over the side of her bed and stepping onto a note folded in thirds that must have fallen off the bedside table.

I can't do this. I can't be here. I'm so sorry. Please know that I love you, that I will always love you, that there will not be a day that I don't think of you.

Clutching the note, she peeked in every single room, searching for her sister and feeling her chest tighten with each empty room.

What have I done? she thought, the last four months replaying in her mind like a slideshow. The unreciprocated glances. The unanswered calls for help. She had pushed her sister away. And she couldn't take any of it back. She couldn't apologize, and the regret washed over her.

Unable to catch her breath, she walked to the kitchen and stood outside, watching her mother cooking breakfast and her father reading the paper.

"Morning, Nora," her father said without looking up.

Silence.

"I said, 'good morning.' It's rude not to respond," he said, putting his paper on the table. "What's wrong?"

Silence.

"What's in your hand?" he asked as her mother turned to her.

The letter was an extension of her hand, as though she had absorbed it, forgetting she was even holding it. Nora slowly lifted her arm, waiting for her father to come retrieve the letter because she couldn't move. If she tried, she was convinced she would collapse.

He uncurled Nora's fingers, pulling out the letter. "Satan must've called his sinner back," he said, crumbling and throwing it onto the floor. "Seems like you're cooking for three from now on," he said, grabbing his keys and coat.

Nora's mother picked up the letter and skimmed it, composing herself after letting a few tears slip. "This is for the best," she said. "In a way, our prayers have been answered."

And just like that, Leah was gone, not just physically, but in every trace. The pictures of her cut or burned. Her stuff given away. They didn't even talk about Leah after that. It was as though she had never existed.

* * *

Nora may have lost her first best friend, but her most important, her everything, was on the stage in front of her. She held onto her daughter for dear life because keeping a distance only allows for someone to slip away through it, and she couldn't let Maeve make the same mistakes her sister had.

2120

Maeve didn't know what she hated more: playing the piano or being on stage in front of hundreds of people.

Her fingers shook rather than glided across the keys, making each note sound a little too staccato.

Would anyone notice if I just sped this up? Maeve thought as she wished for her set to be over.

She scanned the crowd to gauge whether anyone was even paying attention, catching his gaze. Nick. She could not stop thinking about him, the way he smiled out of one corner of his mouth, the confidence he had when speaking to the seventh-grade teachers, how funny he was in a crowd, and how he was never without a book, just like her.

* * *

Maeve had first noticed him on a swing reading *The Giver* a few weeks ago after school while waiting for her mom to pick her up. She loved *The Giver*.

He was in a different brood, but it was a golden yellow, similar enough that she hoped he wouldn't notice too much.

"Hi," she said, wrapping her hair behind her ear.

"Oh, hi," Nick said looking up at her. The way he had said it wasn't as though he was excited or surprised to see her but disappointed, as though he wished she'd never interrupted his thoughts. They had never spoken before, so she wondered what he was seeing through his AIP that made him dislike her.

"Um. That's a really good book," Maeve said hesitantly, doubting whether she should've even approached him and wondering whether it was too late to turn around and walk away. Her friends were the characters in her books, not other kids, and she liked it that way. The characters never judged her. They took her on adventures and told her their most intimate secrets.

People, though, were scary. People would stare and scan their AIPs, finding her flaws and insecurities. She didn't know what to say to people. What were they thinking? What were they seeing? Were they going to hate her the second they recognized her face? It was always too much, so hiding in a book with her true friends was her refuge.

But maybe she could let Nick into her world. He was walking with Jonas, like she was, learning the same secrets, exploring the same worlds, and maybe, just maybe, they could walk together. She couldn't talk about much, but books… books she could talk about.

"Yeah, that's why I'm reading it," Nick responded, his mouth starting to form into that corner smile but then snapping back into a straight line as he immediately looked down at his shoes, a transition so fast it gave Maeve emotional whiplash.

"I..." Maeve started, wishing she could melt on the spot like the wicked witch of the west, never allowing Nick to see her face or scan her again.

"Cool. My mom's waiting so I better go. She doesn't want me talking to other broods," Nick said, hopping off the swing, rushing past her without a second glance.

"Oh, yeah, okay," Maeve responded, holding back tears and wrapping her arms around her stomach.

What did he see? What did I do? How could he already hate me so much?

The thoughts raced through Maeve's brain like a high-speed train, gaining traction with each word.

Her mother waited for her across the lot. She had seen Nick walk past her and had seen her clutch her stomach. The embarrassment hit a new level, knowing her mother had seen it all.

Another thing she could post about and humiliate me with.

She ran past her mother and straight to the car, her mind unable to stop replaying what she had just gone through, each time making Nick a little bit more judgmental.

The thoughts were all-consuming. Each day made her smaller, quieter, a little more distant than usual, with no one noticing her silent cries.

She wanted to hide, blend in with the scenery, disappear, but no one could hide. Everywhere she went, she was identifiable. Every person knowing her most intimate details with a simple scan, her most embarrassing moments from birth to puberty and everything in between because her mother had shared it all, and she could never take it back. She couldn't stop anyone from seeing or make them un-see.

It was only two weeks since she had approached Nick. She had thought she had successfully made herself smaller, just a little more unnoticeable, until her mother shattered her attempts.

"No! I'm not doing it!" Maeve yelled at her mother for the first time in her life, the day Nora had told her she signed her up for the talent show.

They had never fought before.

"Just a few songs, Maeve. You've worked so hard; don't you want to show it off for the world?" Nora calmly replied.

"No! I don't want to show anything off. Ever! I don't want the world to know me. I don't want any of this!" she responded, choking back tears.

"Well, I've already signed you up. Pick your set and practice. You'll thank me when you're older," Nora said leaving Maeve standing in the foyer.

How could she hide now? Hundreds of eyes, of AIPs would be watching her on a stage. Any inkling of hope was gone.

* * *

At that moment, when Maeve's eyes locked with Nick's in the crowded auditorium, thanking her mother was the last thing she wanted to do. She wanted to cry, to scream, to rip her hair out and use it as a mask, a shield protecting her face from the AIPs and devices around her.

But she couldn't do any of that. There would be hundreds of different angles of her meltdown, and she was ashamed enough without every single person in the world seeing her crying on a stage when scanning her.

Nick smiled that corner smile of his, nudging his two friends sitting next to him. He pointed at Maeve, and the three started laughing so loudly she swore it drowned out the sound of her playing. A moment of terror passed through her, panic from the silence of the piano and crippling anxiety from whatever Nick and his friends had seen. Maeve stiffened and hunched over the piano, flying through the rest of "Clair de Lune" and running backstage without even waiting for the applause after her set.

She didn't meet her mom after the performance. She didn't even wait for the talent show to end before running home. The pavement stung her feet in her too-tight ballet flats, her purple dress snapping against her thighs in the wind, but the pain wasn't strong enough to distract her mind from the image of Nick and his friends pointing and laughing at her.

What did they see? kept repeating in Maeve's head the entire way home.

The auditorium was only a few blocks away, so she arrived home before the next act had even finished.

The anxiety drove her mad. It was one thing if she knew what he was seeing, if she could laugh with him. The uncertainty of not knowing pounded against her skull, mortified her, not knowing which embarrassing photo he had seen, what offensive post her mother could have shared about her.

What was it?

Maeve ran around to the back door and grabbed the hidden key in a planter next to the door.

What was it? I hate this!

She fumbled with the key, but her momentum wasn't slowing. She flung the door open and ran up to her room.

I can't do this! I can't feel this way anymore!

The weight of the world crashing down, she melted onto the floor, shoulders shaking. She wrapped herself into a ball, arms around her knees.

Everything about her, visible to the world. Her mom posted about her "becoming a woman." Was that what they laughed at? Or maybe she was ugly, so ugly they couldn't stop themselves from pointing.

Zooming into pictures of her, maybe they saw her abnormally large head as a baby.

Or maybe she was sweating during her performance—*Oh god, did I have sweat stains that* hundreds *of people could see?*

Or maybe...

Or maybe...

She smacked her head trying to turn off her brain, but the "what-ifs" only got louder... and there would only be more and more of them as there would be more information about her in the world.

And now her parental controls would be gone... anyone anywhere could post anything about her...

Pulling out a box from under her bed, she grabbed the pills her mom had hidden in her room. Antidepressants she used to take shortly after Rory's first birthday.

"Don't tell your father about these," she'd said. "They're just vitamins, but you know how your dad is about us taking medicine."

She knew they weren't vitamins.

Maeve just wanted the pain, the anxiety, the fear to all go away. She wanted the pounding to stop. She didn't want to live the rest of her life seen by every single person, them knowing every detail of her life and past, judging her every photo and post. She couldn't take it.

She opened the half-empty bottle and dumped the pills into her hand.

It's too much. Everything is too much.

Closing her eyes, she lifted her hand to her mouth and swallowed.

CHAPTER IX

2120

LEAH

"We're so grateful for this incredible community, but we need to go back," Jonathan said looking at his wife. "We know it's gotten worse, but we need to see our families, our parents." The two were holding the same large backpacks that they arrived with at the colony just a few years ago.

"We've been so lucky to get to know you and are indebted to you for the skills you've been able to provide and teach. We'd be squeezing in a dozen people in Amos's hut if it wasn't for the both of you," Leah said reaching out for the two and kissing their hands. "Just know that you always have a home here with us, and we will all miss you so dearly."

With a smile, the couple turned and walked away, stopping after a few feet and waving before disappearing into the jungle.

Leah lost count of the years. Her daughter looked twenty, maybe twenty-five? Had they really been with Amos that long? It seemed like it. The age was taking its toll on him. She could see it in the way he moved, the way his eyes fell.

It was just the three of them at the beginning, but their size had slowly grown four-fold, individuals running from a past life and stumbling upon their little oasis, just like she and Nora had.

Jonathan and his wife were a blessing, she an architect and he a civil engineer, joining their community and turning their primitive sanctuary in the jungle into a true settlement or colony of sorts. Leah marveled at the original designs, the pair working together to model a little neighborhood for optimum security and efficiency, creating a large clearing in the jungle and erecting three sides of dwellings looking onto a central square. One that would protect them, provide for them, and allow for growth if their numbers continued to increase.

More impressive was watching them work, fashioning materials and constructing their plans, their new home as though plucked off the page and placed inside of Monteverde.

The other members of their new family assisted in any way they could, providing support and learning the techniques necessary to carry on if needed. And it was lucky they did.

But Leah didn't fashion herself a construction worker. Her skills laid elsewhere. Never would she have imagined it as a teenager, but after becoming a mother, she thrived in the role of provider. Jonathan had made her tiny, private garden, which she began to cultivate with Nora on her back, the focal point in the direct center of the square, and it was large enough to provide for a growing community.

Nora grew up in the garden. The two began foraging in the jungle, finding edible berries and plants that could be brought back and grown more conveniently closer to their home. Slowly, as more travelers arrived, they brought with them food from all over the Americas, some invasive to the jungle, some easy to tend, and others withering in the climate.

"Bueno para ellos," Amos said from behind her, draping his hand on her shoulder.

"I hope they find what they're looking for. I really will miss them," she said resting her head on his hand.

"I'm going to take a few out to the river. Do you need anything before we go?"

"I don't think so. I know Nora's at the garden, so I'm going to go help her a little bit and then get started on dinner. Sad to think I'll only be cooking for ten tonight."

"Maybe just tonight. I remember when I used to cook for three," he said with a wink and kissed her on the forehead.

"*Estás a salvo papá.*"

"*Te amo.*" He started for the jungle, motioning for the rest of his group to follow.

She stood hugging her elbows, waiting for the group to disappear from view. Every person to have joined them was so different from the others, some coming together, some alone, some from the North, some from the South, some speaking English, some speaking Spanish, some speaking Portuguese, some older, some younger than she was when she found Amos. Each escaping someone or something, searching for a new life. Oh, how surprised they all were to find that they weren't alone, all of them at different stages of the same journey.

Nora waved to her from the garden.

"Hi, sweetie," she said walking over and giving her daughter a kiss. "It's looking great. I was worried the rain last night would flood it out a bit, but it seems to be just what these guys needed." She inspected a tomato plant.

"Jonathan actually created a little run-off in that corner last night once it picked up. He was out here for a few hours; I'm surprised you didn't see him." Nora wiped the sweat off her forehead with her arm.

"They really built this place, didn't they?"

"They may have built the physical place, but you and Amos built this community. You guys made it a home."

Leah smiled. "How are the yams? You think we've got enough for me to boil them for everyone?"

Nora nodded and grabbed her mother's hands, leading her out of the garden and closing the fence behind them.

They sat on a patch of ground, and Nora pulled a granadilla out of her apron. She cut it in half and gave a portion to her mother.

"Do you think we'd ever go back?" Nora asked.

"We don't have anything to go back to," she replied, taking a bite out of her fruit. She wondered where her sister was. Was Nora still in Allentown? Did she have a family of her own? How would she react if the two of them just showed up at her doorstep after all this time? Would her sister still hate her?

"You haven't told me anything about life back there. I've learned more from the travelers who have joined."

"They probably know better. We left a long time ago; a lot has changed."

"I mean about your... our... family. Your life... What was it like?"

"I don't like talking about it."

"I know, but it was mine too."

She pulled Nora in for a hug and sighed.

"Life was a lot easier without the AIPs. Honestly, I think we were lucky we left when we did. That's why Amos and I are so set on having people start over here in whichever way they wish. People not having to talk about their past if they don't want to—"

"No last names, no nothing, I get it."

She gently pushed her daughter off of her and met her gaze directly.

"Are you happy here?"

Nora looked away and whispered, "Yes."

"Amos is more of a father… grandfather… than mine ever was. I left with you because I felt I had no choice. We weren't safe in that house with those people."

"Who were they?"

"They had very set beliefs. That things should happen a certain way. And when life challenged those beliefs, they refused to bend their worldview. I'm sure they would've loved you very much, but every time they looked at me, I saw nothing more than disdain. I couldn't be a good mother, or a mother at all, under that roof. Honestly, once I told them I was pregnant with you, even human dignity disappeared."

"And my dad?"

"He was a nice boy, but he was just a boy. He wasn't ready to be a father. We—you were so incredibly lucky to have Amos to guide and teach you. I know, that's probably an unsatisfying answer."

"No, no. It actually isn't. I just… always want to know more about you."

"Knowing me here, in this place, with these people, is knowing me more completely. I'm a better person, a more perfect version of myself, than I ever was back with my parents." She grabbed her daughter's hands. "I hope that you only ever know me and see me this way."

"I love you, Mom."

"I love you too. I remember bringing you here. You used to be so little, strapped to my back. And now, look at you."

"Did you ever think that when you left you'd find or create something like this?"

She shook her head no. "Every time someone stumbles upon us, I just see so much of myself in them. I couldn't imagine how different our life together would be if Amos didn't open himself up and share his meal with a malnourished teenager who had a baby strapped to her back." She laughed. "It must've been the hunger that made me delusional, trusting a strange man in the middle of the jungle."

"Are we not supposed to trust people?" Nora asked confused.

"Back where we come from, no, and most certainly not that quickly."

"Well, I'm glad you trusted him too, then." Her daughter reached for her canteen and poured a little water over her hands to wash off the fruit. "What's wrong?"

"What? Nothing."

"You look... perplexed."

"I was just thinking about Davina and her parents." Davina was the first child to be born into the colony a few years ago. Her parents had been from different broods and fallen in love.

"Why?"

"Well, they were the last people to join, and although it makes me so happy that they found us, a family, someone to share their lives with, it also makes me so incredibly sad that they found us."

"Sad?"

"Because that means they were so lost, so unhappy, so shunned for loving one another, finding happiness in the other, that they had to leave their entire worlds behind. It breaks my heart that we live in a world that is so full of people willing to destroy one another and each other's happiness because they don't fit into a particular mold or expectation."

"I do feel lucky that I'll never have to experience that."

"Never?"

"I've definitely thought about leaving, even as recently as yesterday when Jonathan told me they were going back, seeing what it's like. Sometimes this place can feel a little... small. I know that sounds silly since we have the whole jungle to explore, but I mean... there are only twelve... well, ten of us..." She paused a moment and looked to the path that Jonathan and his wife took. "But then hearing about what you went through and what everyone else has run from, I get pulled back. Our world may be small, but it's so full of acceptance, unconditional love, and support, and I wouldn't want to trade that."

"Every day I look at you and your unrelenting optimism, and any doubts I had of leaving and taking you with me just disappear."

"It's easy to be optimistic growing up here. Seeing how this community rallied around Davina's birth, making baby clothes, taking shifts when she woke, sharing meals... I just can't wrap my head around what you went through. That pain has never existed in my world."

"And I hope it never will." She laid back and smiled up at the sky, the tree canopies above smiling back.

CHAPTER X

2127

RORY

It always started the same way.

The driveway greeted them, Rory still pulling at his jersey as his dad's truck inched closer to the garage. It stuck to him after playing another scrimmage in the unbearable humidity.

His father was careful pulling into the driveway, the truck moving at a speed slower than if Rory had tied it to himself and pulled it toward the house. The salt from the sweat that dripped down his face lingered on his tongue, his mouth thankfully dry, because another drop of water down his throat and his bladder would burst.

The entire drive was silent, his father never caring enough to ask about how his scrimmage, practice, game, or whatever went. And he, discouraged to share, hoping to avoid his father's silent disappointment. The *pluck* of Rory's jersey was the only soundtrack from the pitch to the Walsh house that evening.

The truck finally puttered to a stop, and he jumped out and sprinted to the door, waiting for Finn to catch up.

"Hold up, little man," his dad said, a hammer crashing on the silence between them. He dropped the keys getting out of the truck and then struggled to find the right one for the front door.

"But I really gotta go!" Rory said, shifting his weight back and forth. His composure had disappeared. He grabbed his crotch, a mental pep-talk to his penis to hold on just a little bit longer.

Finn walked up to the door, turned the key, and flung the door open. He stepped aside with an arm extended, gesturing through the foyer. "Don't forget to change and wash up! You're not eating dinner all grass-stained and sweaty!" Finn yelled as Rory flew past him and straight up the steps with his soccer bag trailing behind him.

Don't forget to change and wash up... psh... like he didn't just spend fifteen minutes watching me want nothing but to get out of this thing. He tried to think of anything but the need to go to the bathroom.

Just a few feet further. The bathroom was wedged right in between his and Maeve's rooms with his room on the far side of the hallway. But racing past Maeve's room, he caught a glimpse of something on the floor that made him double back. A hand laid across the ground, glittered by the sunset through the partially opened door.

She's not supposed to be home yet.

He gently pushed open the door. "Maeve," he whispered, almost as though it was a question. He dropped his bag outside the door and slowly crept into her room. She laid on the floor, facing away from him as though she'd fallen asleep on her arm. "Maeve," he said more confidently, crouching down and reaching out his arm, touching her shoulder.

No answer.

"Maeve!" he yelled, shaking her to wake her up. The momentum rolled her onto her back, and he made direct eye contact with her open, glazed-over eyes.

He screamed and fell back onto his butt, unable to look away from her hypnotizing stare. A warm rush of urine flooded him and surrounded him in a puddle next to his dead sister.

Those eyes haunted him. That exact chain of events seared into his brain, always stopping with Maeve's eyes peering directly into his soul.

The nightmare never continued long enough for him to relive his dad coming upstairs and performing CPR on his sister and grabbing the empty pill bottle next to her, cursing at the sky. Or his father yelling at him to call the police, the hospital, anyone who could help, him unable to move, or breathe, or even fully comprehend what was or what had happened. Or his mom coming home with a police escort to an ambulance in the driveway and him wrapped in a blanket on the front lawn because she had already called the police when she couldn't find Maeve after the talent show. No, none of that haunted him.

Just Maeve's piercing dead eyes.

Seven years later and the nightmare just as clear as the day he found her.

He sat up and swung his legs over the side of the bed, resting his head on his hands. He wasn't ready to start school again. He had spent the entire summer playing soccer, reaching for his way out: out of Allentown, out of the brood, just out. But now he would have to go back to the school that housed the people he had been trying to mentally run away from all summer, and he just didn't want to face them.

But he could keep his head down. He could focus on soccer, on getting a scholarship, on using that as his drive to make it through.

Senior year. His last chance. He had to be serious, do well enough in his classes, and truly excel on the pitch.

He'd be damned if he was trapped in his parents' lives, going to St. Theresa's with his brood a constant branding iron chasing him, corralling him toward decisions that weren't truly his. He wouldn't do it. He wanted more for himself. He deserved more.

But the only way he could escape this cycle was if someone would take a chance on him. University was too expensive, a rich man's game, and his parents were those rich men.

But their money came with restrictions, and it would go nowhere except the brood school: St. Theresa's, of course. So finding someone who would be willing to give him money—that would mean everything. Very few things transcended broods, but sports could be his answer.

He got out of bed and dragged his feet to the bathroom, stopping at the entrance. He took a few steps and placed his hand on Maeve's closed door. If he opened it, nothing would be different. Her bed draped in the same sheets, her books in a stack next to her bedside table, even her dresser drawers half closed with her clothes partly hanging out.

But he imagined her laying on her bed, reading her book like she used to. Looking up at him, smiling, and waving him inside. He reached for the doorknob, but the piece of him that haunted him, that was terrified he would be met with those eyes again, snapped his hand back.

But the only thing that was different about that room was that Maeve wouldn't be in it.

"Rory! Let's go!" his father called up the steps.

He whipped his neck toward the sound and backed away from his sister's door.

"Why do you give a shit if I'm late? You don't drive me anymore," he muttered under his breath and walked back to the bathroom, dropping his clothes and hopping into the lukewarm shower. *Oh good, I'm glad we never fixed that hot water tank,* he thought as he raced through washing himself.

Nothing ever seemed quite right about living in that house. Something was always off or broken, Rory himself the karmic puzzle piece that never fit. Maybe everything would come together if he wasn't there.

Getting out of the shower and wrapping the towel around his waist, he caught a glimpse of himself in the mirror. *That's a nasty one.* He touched the bruise on the right side of his rib cage. Rory's teammate tackled him in practice the day before, and the bruise was already starting to turn purple. He put his hand on the bruise, with purple and yellow peeking out from every angle between his fingers.

He wasn't a masochist, but he admired his bruises, sometimes wishing his mother was the one to cause them instead of his teammates. *At least then she'd know that I'm a real person, not just a profile to scan.*

"Rory!" his dad yelled again.

Rory rolled his eyes. He caressed his bruise one more time before strolling back to his room. He threw his towel on the pile of clothes in his closet, trading it for his pressed school uniform. He grabbed his backpack and soccer bag and worked his way toward his screeching father.

Woof. That's pain. His ribs contracted on every stair as he walked down to the kitchen, the bruise reminding him of its presence.

"I'm not even running late," Rory said as he threw his bags on the floor and walked toward his dad.

"I know, but this is the first year I won't be driving you to school. I'd like to at least eat breakfast with you… getting a little of that time back that I'll be losing," his dad said with a half-smile, putting his device on the counter and looking up at his son.

Rory didn't exactly consider their car rides together as "quality time." They consisted of his father yelling at him for almost being late in the morning… therefore almost making him late for work… but of course he never was because they were never actually late. The conversation would find its way to Rory being unappreciative of his father's hard work and what he provided for the family. And on and on… He couldn't be more excited to avoid the scripted rerun of the Rory and Finn morning debacle.

"I made eggs," his dad said, putting a plate down on the table.

Rory nestled himself in the chair and started picking at his breakfast.

"So, are you excited for your first day of senior year?"

"Yeah, I'm super thrilled for people to constantly look at me like I'm broken or something," he responded, passing the fork between his fingers and avoiding his father's gaze.

"What?"

"Maeve." Rory slammed the fork down and looked up at his dad. He almost wished for the conversation about "being ungrateful" to return so they didn't have to talk about this.

"It was seven years ago. I doubt people even see it through the AIP anymore," his father responded, not confidently.

"Dad, I swear the news is the first thing they see about someone. Probably the pictures of me sitting in that blanket on the front lawn, covered in my own piss. Every year, I'm the boy who found his dead sister. People don't know how to act around me."

"I'm sure they're just intimidated."

"Intimidated of what?" Rory said. He crossed his arms and leaned back in his chair. "I'm not a scary person. I do my homework, I play some soccer, and that's it. All I want is someone, just one person, to talk to, to hang out with. But I can't run away from what people are seeing. And I don't even have a single say over what they see." Rory raised his voice with the last line, darting his eyes across the living room at his mother at the far end, sitting by the window with her device.

Maeve's death changed her. She never passed the fourth stage of grief: depression.

First, denial. How long his mother tried to hide that Maeve was dead, he couldn't remember. Refusing him the courtesy of seeing a therapist after finding her, continuing to post on her account after she was gone, and telling her friends that Maeve "wasn't feeling well," which is why she couldn't go to playdates, lasted at least a few weeks.

But everyone knew. The news cameras and the neighbors had picked up the videos of Maeve on a covered stretcher, him on the ground in complete shock, and their mother running toward the stretcher, inconsolable and pulling off her dead daughter into her arms.

Second, anger. That came in full force. Although with his mother, it was more like irritability. Toward everyone and everything. Particularly him for being the one to live… it seemed.

And third, bargaining. Whose fault was it that Maeve died? Was it hers for losing track of Maeve at the talent show?

Was it his father's for not being successful at CPR? Was it his for who knows what reason? She came to the conclusion that it was the expiring parental controls.

That *had* to be why Maeve took her life. She was overwhelmed by the new opportunity to shape her own profile. It was too much. Or at least that's what he assumed when his mother began to hover over him much more than she ever had.

After Maeve died, his mother became extraordinarily protective of his device usage, forcing every post and picture to acquire her approval until his eighteenth birthday. His posts would never get her approval so he stopped trying altogether, with his mother continuing to curate his persona for him. He didn't know whether it was because she somehow felt guilty for Maeve's death or because she wanted to ensure at least one of her children would be unquestionably portrayed in her image, the image of their brood, but he knew he hated it.

He hated her creating his identity for him, but even more than that, he hated how much time she spent doing it. He didn't know his mother, never had. And she never knew *him*, just the persona of him.

And finally, the stage she couldn't seem to let go of: depression. Sitting in the chair by the window as though placed there by Caspar David Friedrich himself. Her words became few and far between. Her face constantly in her device. A smile… nowhere to be seen.

"It's just to keep you safe. Your mother loves you," his father said.

"Oh yeah? Then how come she hasn't been able to look at me for as long as I can remember? How come she can't be in a room alone with me? That can't be about Maeve. You said it yourself, it was seven years ago," Rory said leaning across the table toward his father.

How can she love me if she doesn't even know me?

"She's busy creating a good life for you. She's making sure you continue to get the brood's acceptance. She spends every day curating the posts and photos that people are going to see when they see you to make sure that they know you, that they know your values."

"But she's not! She's making sure they know *her* and *her* values," Rory said standing up from the table. "I don't even know who I am! I don't know what I believe or who I want to be or what I care about or anything!"

"Enough!" His father slammed his fist on the table, sending Rory's fork flying onto the floor. "You know who you are. You are who we raised you to be."

Rory turned toward the door and grabbed his bags. "I gotta go. Don't want to be late for my first day. Glad we did breakfast together. Really fun. Great start to my morning," he said, walking out the door and grabbing the keys off the hook.

* * *

Samantha stood at her locker grabbing her books when Rory walked in through the main double doors.

He looked a bit disheveled and frustrated, walking with purpose to the office, probably to get his locker combination for the year or something, making contact with no one on the way.

Samantha smiled to herself.

"Volkova and Walsh sitting in a tree," her best friend, Mila, whispered in her ear. Samantha was so busy salivating, watching Rory, that she hadn't noticed Mila walk up behind her.

"No idea what you're talking about," Samantha replied, turning up the corner of her mouth and raising an eyebrow.

"Oh, come on, you can lie to a lot of people, but I know you better than you know yourself," Mila replied, putting her hand on her hip.

"I won't deny he's yummy for sure," Samantha said and blushed.

"Sam, we on for tonight?" Pavel said, leaning on the locker next to her, blocking her view of Rory through the office window.

"It's Samantha, Pav. It's always been Samantha. Thanks."

"Is that a yes?" he asked.

"Absolutely not. We broke up, remember?"

Rory walked out of the office and headed straight for her. She straightened and watched him come up behind Pavel.

"Oh, you weren't kidding?" Pavel said, genuinely surprised.

"Hey, Pavel," Rory said. "I'm sorry, but you're in front of my locker."

Pavel jumped but didn't budge. "So?" he said, reaching for Samantha's hair.

She smacked his hand away.

"Can you give me just a second to throw my backpack in and then you can go back to harassing the girls?" Rory said without a hint of sarcasm in his voice.

Pavel turned and scowled at him.

"It's fine. He was just leaving," Samantha said through laughter.

Pavel pushed himself off Rory's locker, not breaking eye contact with her until running into a water fountain. His face bright red, he shuffled his feet and disappeared into the closest classroom.

"Thanks, Rory. I thought he'd never leave," Samantha said, smiling.

"I do what I can," Rory said, shutting his locker and walking in the direction of his first class. Those words hung in the air as he made his way inside.

"No," Mila said to Samantha.

"What?"

"You can't."

"Can't what?"

"There are so many problems with this," Mila said, stepping in front of Samantha and grabbing her face. "One: He's not in our brood. Two: He's damaged goods. Three: Literally every and *any* guy in this school would date you, so can't you chase after one of them?"

"Okay, so I hear you," Samantha said. "But I don't see any of that to be a problem."

"But how?" Mila said, dropping her hands.

"Just because he's not in our brood doesn't mean we're not compatible. Literally, the only thing that differentiates our broods is heritage. Hear me out," Samantha said, stopping Mila from interrupting her. "We are exactly alike. Our political stances are identical. Have you not seen the pictures of him at Corporate Council Headquarters? Our values, also identical. I mean, just look through how conservative he and his family are. Really, the biggest thing is religion, but our religions are so tangential. Like, Catholicism and Orthodoxy are pretty much the same. Besides some married priests and different calendars, we could totally figure it out." She winked at Mila.

"You're making this sound way less complicated than it is," Mila said and stepped back, appearing to try to convince herself of what Samantha said. "I guess I could give it to you. You're right, our broods are pretty similar. It's not like you're trying to jump an anti-CC idealist or something."

"Second, it's not the worst thing in the world that he's damaged goods."

"I'm sorry... come again?"

"If you think about it, that means I'll have, like, no competition. No one else is going to want to take on some guy who literally found his dead sister when he was a kid. Like, that is some hard shit. He's one hundred percent got some problems going on up there," Samantha said, pointing to her head. "But also, that means I've got a project."

"Stop..." Mila said, her mouth hanging open. "A project?"

"Yeah! Like, I've got something... someone to fix. If I can help him get over his dead sister shit then there's really nothing I can't do," Samantha said, beaming.

Mila just shook her head, eyes wide.

"Look, my ultimate goal is to be a mom and a wife. That's kind of what our brood breeds us for, right?"

"I mean, you're not wrong," Mila said.

"Well, if I can take a man like that and make him a little less damaged... then there's no doubt I can raise perfect little babies, which kind of seems super in line with his brood too," Samantha said dreamily, imagining little kids running around her legs. "Plus, I've already dated everyone uninteresting. I'm ready to go for the interesting ones."

"I just feel like this is an absolute disaster waiting to happen. How are you even going to get him to talk to you? Your locker has been assigned next to his for three years, and I swear today is the most you've ever talked to him."

"I mean, come on. It can't be that hard," Samantha said. "Like you said, pretty much every guy here wants to date me. I'm perfect wife and mom material."

She was right. Almost every guy in the school wanted to take a chance with her. They'd all tried. Why wouldn't they? She was petite and thin, but her breasts were round and maybe even bordering on a little too big for her small body. It was hard not to imagine a perfect little baby, or even grown men, hanging off of them, sucking for dear life, as she had imagined more times than she could count.

"He is yummy, though," Mila said, agreeing. "And the summer was definitely good to him."

Samantha nodded. Rory always had the potential to be attractive, but he was a little lanky and awkward, not quite filling out the almost six feet of height his dad had passed onto him. He was so unlike his dad who made every girl swoon and dream of being wrapped in those strong arms. The two may have only seen his dad through scans of Rory or in the stands during the few soccer games they went to, but she and Mila were not immune from those dreams.

But Rory walked in on that first day of senior year fully transitioned from lanky little kid into a grown man. His legs easily carried his weight, and he no longer tripped over his feet. His facial hair started to cover the youth in his face, coming in with a tint of red in contrast to his darker hair. His chest was the perfect size and his shoulders strong for Samantha to lay her head on, like they could finally carry the weight of the pain she assumed he had. His arms reminded her of the dreams she had about his father, thinking that if she could never have Finn, that Rory would be an absolutely decent replacement.

"We would make some good-looking babies, for sure," Samantha said, more to herself than to Mila.

"I just hope you know what you're getting yourself into."

With the ring of the first period bell, Mila and Samantha smiled to one another and turned away, walking to their respective classrooms.

CHAPTER XI

2127

——

SAMANTHA

"Are you sure about it?" Samantha's mother asked her as she lingered outside her bedroom. She was nothing if not a professional dater, her nerves never calmer than before a date, but there was something about Rory. Whether it was the way he analyzed her with his eyes, the way he questioned her, or the way he was completely comfortable in silence. Probably all of the above. Whatever it was, she had a hard time quelling the flips her stomach was doing.

"What?" Samantha responded. She prepared herself for another lecture about her mistakes, how ineligible he was. Their broods were similar enough to mingle, but dating was a completely different story. Her mother couldn't imagine her with someone… like him.

"Your hair. Your features will stand out too much if it's pulled back like that. You should leave it down."

"Rory likes it up," Samantha said with her hands in her hair, molding a ponytail, dropping the bobby pin she held between her teeth. She wasn't expecting that. Her mother never took an interest in her dates with Rory before. If anything, her mom wanted her to look a little flawed, just enough to repel him.

Granted, Rory had only ever seen her hair up once when he dropped in on a gymnastics practice unannounced, driving her anxiety through the roof of him seeing her less than perfect and completely sweaty. He had said, "You look cute like that."

"Then he is dumb. Why are you dating dumb boys?" her mother scolded. Just another reason for her to hate him.

"He's not dumb, Mom. What, a boy can't think I'm pretty unless my whole face is hidden behind my hair?"

"Your whole face doesn't need to be hidden, but your scar. It's less visible when all attention isn't just on your face," her mother said and walked in, pulling the ponytail out and framing Samantha's face with her hair. "See? Much better. You are perfectly imperfect, and I love you, but not everyone needs to see your flaws."

"What's so bad about having flaws? Everyone has flaws," Samantha said to her mother's reflection in the mirror. Her mother was right. She couldn't draw attention to the scar above her lip.

"You think boys will want to marry girls who have such visible flaws? No. They will think, *If she has flaws in the places I can see, then what about the places I can't see?* And you want a husband, yes?"

Samantha could see the thoughts written on her mother's face. *Oh, but please not this boy.*

"And you want to be a mother? Yes? Who will put a baby in you if they think the baby will come out just as flawed?"

Her mother and father never told anyone she was born with a cleft palate, completely shielding her from the world until she was able to receive her corrective surgery. Not their broodmates or even Samantha's grandparents knew.

Samantha's entire life, she was told her worth was based on her ability to get married and mother children. Her mother was even more primal, though, convinced that the only quality that mattered to men, particularly men in her brood, was beauty. And worse, Samantha thought in order to be beautiful she had to look like a doll, no creases or crevices, no wrinkles or scars. The embodiment of youth and perfection. It was exhausting.

Her mom never failed to mention all the ways Samantha could and should improve, buying her makeup before textbooks, paying for gymnastics lessons before school tuition. Eventually, Samantha became just as obsessed as her mother with showing the world how absolutely breathtaking she could be, a perfect vessel for growing and bringing new life into this world. All the while trying to hide how ugly she truly thought she was.

Samantha constantly bounced back and forth between binge eating and starving herself, practiced her makeup daily, and spent hours to ensure her hair fell at just the right angle. But no matter how much she changed herself, she never felt "just right." She exuded overconfidence and vanity to hide from her insecurities and the fear that someone, anyone, would see that she may not be as beautiful as she felt like she needed to be.

"Thank you," she said. She grabbed her mom's hands and pet them before reaching for the brush to touch up her makeup.

Her mom walked in front of her and bent down. She grabbed the brush out of Samantha's hand and ran it across her daughter's cheekbones. "I only want what's best for you." Her mom still had a youthful beauty about her. Her eyes still sparkled, and there wasn't a single wrinkle to be seen. Samantha couldn't figure out how she could manage it. Samantha worked so hard to look her best, but it just came naturally for her mom.

Time had been good to her. *It must be so hard being so perfect and then seeing someone like me come out after nine months.*

"I know." She looked up at the ceiling as her mom ran the brush under her eyes. *She is always so much better at blending than me.*

"This boy... Are you sure about him? Do you like him?"

"Honestly, I don't know. He's... different. I feel like I don't know anything about him."

"How is that possible? It's all on the AIP."

"I know, and it's weird. I mean, this will only be our third date, but I feel like the person over the AIP and the person sitting in front of me aren't exactly the same. I don't know, maybe I'm just overthinking it because I've never dated someone outside our brood." Her mother's nose twitched when she said the phrase "outside our brood."

The doorbell rang, startling the both of them.

"He's here!" Samantha said. "Shoot! I'm not dressed!" She jumped up out of her chair, knocking the brush right out of her mom's hand. She ran to her dresser, throwing clothes on the floor like a cartoon character, unable to find anything at all to wear.

Her mother calmly straightened herself up and walked over to the closet. She moved a few garments to the side and grabbed a dress, mid-thigh, halter, in a light blush color. She stepped back and admired it, placing it on the bed. "This one. This one makes your breasts look the right size. Not too big and not too small," she said casually. "I'll greet him."

How does she do that?

Samantha pulled the dress carefully over her head, trying not to move a single strand of hair out of place. She walked back over to the mirror, turning left and right. *I do look good.*

The light hit the scar in a way that Samantha couldn't stop staring at it in the mirror. She walked back up to the vanity and lifted a finger to it.

I'm never going to be perfect. No matter how hard I try.

Her fingers reached for the brush. The brush, dipped in more concealer, ran across the scar.

"Hello, Rory," her mom said from the living room.

Samantha dropped the brush and tilted her head every which direction to make sure the scar was fully hidden from sight.

"Hi," Rory responded.

Why does he sound scared?

Backing away, she took one last look and headed out the door. She didn't want to leave Rory alone with her mom for too long.

"Where are you going tonight?" her mother asked Rory.

Rory hadn't come inside and seemed to be avoiding eye contact with her mother.

That's odd.

"I think Samantha wanted to go to a restaurant, so we're going to do that," Rory responded.

He was right. They hadn't had a formal dinner date yet. On the first date, they went to a movie, one of those weird choose-your-own-adventure types where you could vote in the theater on your device for what you wanted to happen next.

The second date, they just went out to get milkshakes after one of Rory's soccer games; that one maybe lasted about thirty minutes. It started out fine and well, but then he had asked her, "Well, what do you want to do after high school?" and she had responded, "I'm not sure, but I know I want to be a wife and mother," hoping he would say something like, "That's great! I want to be a husband and father." But he didn't. Instead, he'd said, "Is that what you want, or what your parents want?"

What a peculiar question. She hadn't known how to respond. Lucky for her, her mother had called, telling her she needed to come home. *So lucky!*

But she was curious. She wanted to try and figure him out, and she needed to actually spend some time talking to him to do that. She looked at the man standing in the doorframe. *That is one nice suit, and it hugs him in all the right places.* She ran her tongue across her front teeth. The shirt seemed a little too tight, the buttons pulling across his chest.

I remember him taller, though. Avoiding her mom's eyes, he was hunched. Her mom was petite, like her, but Rory was the one who looked small. The lack of confidence was not sexy. Good thing the shirt was doing its job.

He turned to the side, shifting his weight so that his backside was in full view to her. Samantha shivered. The pants were working harder than the shirt, and she just wanted to walk right up behind him and pull him into her, running her hands up and down his chest, down into his pockets.

"Hi, Rory!" she said a little too eagerly.

Ew. Well, if that tone doesn't scream desperation...

"You ready?" he responded, turning back to the door.

He barely even looked at me. No "hello"... no "wow!"... no jaw on the floor... no "you look nice"? She was disappointed. She and her mom spent so much time getting her ready, and he wouldn't even make eye contact with her.

"Bye, Mom," she said. "I'll be home soon."

Rory was already waiting out by the car by the time she finished saying goodbye. *Jeez, what's his rush?*

She walked over to the car and let herself inside. *Thanks for holding the door open for me*, she thought sarcastically and rolled her eyes.

"Where to?" Rory said, buckling his seatbelt.

"I thought we could go to *Vanya*. It's a great Russian place about ten minutes from here." She knew everyone at *Vanya*. It was her favorite restaurant. Maybe going somewhere familiar would calm her nerves.

"Sure." He was so steady, one hand on the gear shift and the other just resting on the steering wheel. He still hadn't looked at her.

Biting her lip, she hoped her eyes would burn a hole in his side, forcing him to look over, to notice her. But after a few minutes, he still hadn't averted his eyes from the road. She sighed and began to scan him on her AIP.

She had no idea how to start a conversation. Usually, the boys she went out with would do the heavy lifting. She just had to sit there and look beautiful. But Rory wasn't making this easy.

Soccer... dead sister... church... more soccer... hunting... CCHQ... So much soccer...

"You ready?" he asked. She was so busy scanning him, trying to find a way to break the silence, that she hadn't realized they already pulled into the Vanya parking lot.

She smiled and shook her head yes. He stepped out of the car and began to walk toward the restaurant, but she hadn't budged. *No way. He's not getting off like that.* She crossed her legs and arms and waited to see how long it would take him to notice she wasn't right behind him.

It only took him a few steps. He looked back and walked to her side of the car. *There we go.* She smirked. He opened the door and waited for her to shimmy out.

They walked to the door in silence, pulling out their vaccine cards for the host.

"Two, please," Rory said, an edge to his voice.

Why is he so irritable? Why won't he say anything to me? Rory had taken off after the host, and Samantha trailed behind. *So much for ladies first.*

"Here we are." The host seated them and asked, "Would you like paper menus?"

"That's okay. We can just scan," Rory said. He grabbed a piece of bread from the table and took a bite.

The host walked away, and Rory looked directly at her.

* * *

Shit, a Russian place. Don't they put meat or, like, animal fat in literally everything?

He struggled to find anything on the menu.

Seriously, even the pierogis? No plain potato or something?

"Is there anything without meat?" he asked Samantha.

"I'm sorry?" she responded with a combination of surprise and an air of judgment. *Man, I wish I would've told her at milkshakes that I was a vegetarian.*

"I'm a vegetarian. It seems like everything on this menu has meat." Her lips pursed together.

"Oh. I thought you hunted?"

Got it. So anytime I don't align with what you've seen or your expectations then I'm just a disappointment?

"That was just one time with my dad." He wanted to open himself up to her. To tell her about how gut-wrenching the squawk of the turkey was when the bullet pierced her. How he couldn't keep his legs from shaking and how he could've sworn that he watched her soul leave her body after the second shot. He wished she knew his smile wasn't real and it was through tears that the picture was snapped. He longed to say he knew he disappointed his father and how he didn't think he could ever find something to connect over with his dad after that. He remembered the sadness in his dad's eyes and how it was almost as powerful as the sadness he felt while holding that limp bird in his hand.

But she had interrupted him before he could continue. The moment was over.

He would start smaller. Maybe a joke? *Who doesn't love a good Jesus comparison? And that would be a good segue to talk about our families! Our parents, maybe.*

"Yeah, my mom didn't want people to know. Said if Jesus was fine with eating meat then who was I thinking I was morally superior?" he said with a chuckle.

She didn't take the bait.

He wanted her to say something like, *Yeah! My mom also doesn't share some stuff about me. I also feel like there are pieces of myself that I need to hide.* But she said nothing. A moment of silence passed.

"I found a side of potato pancakes. I'll get that."

"Sorry I wore my hair down like this." She started twisting her hair in her hands.

"What?" he responded.

"You said you liked it the way I had it at practice last week when you stopped by."

The conversation shifted so quickly, he couldn't understand how she managed to bring up herself. *Her hair, really? So much for talking about anything real.*

"Oh, I don't care either way."

He couldn't even name the emotion that flowed through him at that moment—annoyance? Frustration? Anger?

Disappointment? Sadness? Was it possible they all existed at the same moment?

"What do you mean?" she asked, dropping her eyes and hands.

Her vanity knew no ends. *Why is it that all you care about is how you look? Why can't you have a real conversation about anything other than your stupid. Physical. Appearance?*

"I think you look fine either way." Searching for something, anything that would take them away from this superficial topic, his AIP scanned her. Something he could use as an entrance to learn about her, her desires, her fears, anything he couldn't get from just scanning her face. "So, you said you want to be a mom?" popped out of his mouth before his brain could even fully process that he had asked her the question.

"Yes!" Her answer was a little too enthusiastic. *Shit, please don't think this is, like, me planning a proposal or something.* "I don't think anything could be more meaningful than being a wife and a mother. It would be absolutely magical," she said.

Christ, maybe this really is all that she is.

He wasn't ready to give up on her just yet. Maybe there was more to her story. A moment. Something that made her truly want this. "How long have you known that's what you wanted?" he asked. She tilted her head to the side and squinted her eyes at him. "Well, was there a specific moment that you thought, *Yes! That's what I want to do!?* I don't know, maybe watching a movie, or seeing a mom in a park with her kids or something?"

But her answers continued to disappoint. "Oh, um, I don't think so. I think I've just wanted it as long as I can remember." She was a puppet. Controlled by the broods and forced into a narrative.

He had to find an escape. He couldn't take sitting at a table with someone who was exactly like everyone else, molded by their broods rather than finding themselves in a deeper place.

But wasn't he just like everyone else too? He sat here, on this date, living out his brood's expectations too. He was a coward, and he hated her for making him feel that way.

"Well, we should get the bill. I think it's about time I took you home," he said after his last bite.

The car ride home flew by. The neighborhood was so similar to his own. The same little white boxes in a row. Planters in the windows. Street dividers with fancy dogwood trees. Whether it was his own brood, or a brood similar to his like Samantha's, he didn't belong. He just didn't want this. It was fine for the people who did, but he just wasn't one of them.

Who am I? What do I want?

Is there more to life than my stupid brood?

Am I trapped?

How someone from a different brood even approached me blows my mind. There's no way that's happening again.

We all hate each other.

We were bred to hate each other.

Do I hate them? Do I hate myself?

What even is "myself" when myself is only what Nora made myself to be? How do I find myself?

How can I find someone who has made a choice for themselves rather than let their choices be made?

He pulled in her driveway, not able to stop his mind from racing.

"Listen, I'll see you at school tomorrow," he said, waiting for her to get out of the car.

"Okay. Should we do this again sometime?"

She has to be kidding. No fucking way! he wanted to shout, but all he could say was, "I don't think so."

He couldn't go home. He was too confused with himself and too angry with Nora, the system, everything, and he needed to cool down. He didn't know where to go, but he just drove for hours until he realized the one thing he knew he couldn't do.

He could not make his parents feel the pain of losing another child, at least not yet.

But hadn't they already lost him, anyway? They didn't know him. He was a stranger under their roof, unable to fit the mold Nora created for him.

He turned the car back in the direction of his parents' house. His parents' *house*, because *home* didn't feel like the right word to use.

CHAPTER XII

2127

———

RORY

By the time Rory arrived at his house, his parents were well asleep. The light on the front porch was the only one still on. He steadied his hands as he turned the knob on the front door, slowly peeling it open, stopping every few seconds and listening for footsteps or restless sounds. The old Tudor door, heavy against his hand, wasn't doing him any favors. Each inch it opened, the hinges became more angered and strained, whining against the silence.

He shimmied through the gap he created, perfectly spaced to fit nothing more than his sideways body.

Like a Band-Aid, just do it, he thought as he quickly shut the door behind him. His ears perked toward the steps as he quietly whispered, "One... two... three," waiting for the stirring of his parents. Hearing nothing but the grumbling of his stomach, he breathed a sigh of relief.

He made his way into the kitchen, not sure if he was still hungry or hungry again. The potato pancakes were less than satisfying.

The house showed its age with each step, the hardwoods having separated, creaking as he made his way across the floor. Tiptoeing and hopping like a ballerina pirouetting across a stage, spotting his final destination, he avoided the noisiest spots he had memorized through years of sneaking midnight snacks, dancing his way into the kitchen.

He knew he looked silly, exaggerating his movements in the darkness, but he couldn't bear the thought of waking his dad. Rory was quite surprised with how even-tempered his dad actually was in general, never angry with him. But in the middle of the night, that was a different story.

The last time he had woken his dad, he stomped down the steps, brows furrowed and fists clenched, yelling so loudly Rory swore the house shook. He ran straight for Rory, grabbed the collar of his shirt, lifting him up off of his feet, and wound up his arm. "No! Dad!" Rory had yelled, bringing his hands up to his face and hiding behind them.

He never hit him. He said he thought Rory was an intruder, but Rory never bought it. His dad looked directly into his eyes before grabbing him and wound his arm back well after realizing he was holding his son. Lying or not, he never wanted to see that side of him again, so if he needed to chassé into the kitchen, he had no problems at all doing so.

The light of the refrigerator illuminated a slip of paper on the counter with his name on it. Ignoring it, he grabbed some jelly and left the fridge door open to spread light into the pantry for some bread and peanut butter.

After licking the peanut butter off of his knife, he tossed it into the sink where it hit a plate, sending a shiver down his spine. *Shit*, he thought as his body froze, sending his eyes to the ceiling and waiting for his dad's feet to hit the floor.

Nothing.

He grabbed the note and slid down onto the ground as close to the light as he could get, sandwich in one hand and the note in the other.

I hope you had a wonderful time! Seems like a sweet girl. We love you.

—MOM

He crumbled the note and tossed it toward the trash can on the other side of the kitchen.

Not even close, he thought.

He didn't want to think about his date. He didn't want to think about Samantha. He didn't want to think about marriage, or broods, or AIPs, or the Corporate Council... All he wanted was to focus on the stickiness of the jelly as it dripped in his hand with every bite, the peanuts stuck in his teeth, and how much he wanted another sandwich but was too lazy to make it.

But he couldn't switch off his brain or the AIP latched to it. He washed his hands, closed the fridge, and made his way upstairs, hoping sleep would be a refuge.

Shifting his weight, he couldn't find a place on the mattress where it didn't feel like the springs were trying to jab him. He turned from side to side, punching the bed as though trying to force the springs to recoil. But if it wasn't the mattress keeping him awake, it was the sheets, like boa constrictors wrapping themselves around his legs. Pulling the sheets this way and that, unable to get free, his frustration was his momentum, rolling him off the bed with a *thud!*

"Shit," he said as he lay on his back, staring at the ceiling. "Maybe they're not as light of sleepers as I thought..."

He lifted himself onto his butt and was greeted with shades of orange and purple creeping through his window. Unraveling himself from the mess of fabric, he reached across the floor and grabbed the clothes he wore the prior night.

He wasn't ready to face his parents, and they would be awake in just a few hours. His mom, making eye contact for the first time in years, would be asking about Samantha, their date, and probably coaxing him to never see her again and find a nice girl in their own brood before retreating to her chair by the window. His dad would be smirking at his mom and telling him to focus on college and his St. Theresa's application so that he could provide the same standard of living for his future family.

All of this to show their broodmates what great parents they were, how successfully they had raised their child without ever truly asking what he himself wanted.

But did he even know what he wanted?

What was he allowed to want?

Was it realistic for him to want something he wasn't bred for?

He left just enough evidence to show he had made it home the last night before heading back out toward his car. His device buzzed.

"Okay, no, thank you," he said and walked back inside, leaving his device in a drawer by the front door. Not wanting his parents to worry (or more accurately, to bother him), he left a note that read, *Out—R.*

Maybe I should've checked who it was, he thought behind the wheel driving to Cedar Creek State Park. His fingers tapped, anxious to be so far from his device. The thought caused his email to pop up across his AIP and push the directions to Cedar Creek out of sight.

He couldn't get away, not really. The thought algorithm constantly pulled up something, anything it deemed relevant. *No matter where I go or what I do, there's no escape.*

He tightened his grip on the steering wheel. With every thought of the date, the AIP always had a response.

Shit, a Russian place. Don't they put meat or, like, animal fat in literally everything?

We found:

- -

Russians eating animal fat

Russians eating meat

Buy Russian Meat

Russian farmer

Russian farm

Tickets to Russia! Book Now!

Russian slaughterhouse

Russian slaughtering animals

Would you like to see more?

- -

Man, I wish I would've told her at milkshakes that I was a vegetarian.

We found:

- -

Vegetarian—definition

PETA Riot Destroys Stores

Blog: Why You Need Meat to Live

```
Vegetarians Are the Anti-Christ

Order a Milkshake—We Deliver!
```

Would you like to see more?
- -

Got it. So anytime I don't align with what you've seen or your expectations then I'm just a disappointment?

We found:
- -

```
Disappointment—definition

Depression

Therapist

Call Now for a Free Consultation!
```

Would you like to see more?
- -

"That was just one time with my dad."

We found:
- -

```
That picture of you with a dead bird
```

Would you like to continue to relive that experience?
- -

"Said if Jesus was fine with eating meat then who was I thinking I was morally superior?"

We found:
- -

```
Jesus
```

```
Jesus is coming

Blog: Non-Believers Are Going to Hell

Hell

Church

Churches Near You

Save Your Soul Today—Donate Now

Video: Pastor Explains Why Your Brood
Will Be the Only to Enter Heaven

Pictures: Your Broodmates at Church

Morality
```

Let me show you more.

Why are you so vain? Why is it that all you care about is how you look? Why can you not have a real conversation about anything other than your stupid. Physical. Appearance?

We found:

```
Purchase vanity—mirror included!

Every. Single. Fucking. Picture. Of.
Samantha. Ever.
```

Would you like to see more?

Shit, please don't think this is like me planning a proposal or something.

We found:

Proposal pictures

Beautiful Engagement Rings—Buy Here

Wedding ideas

Blog: Marriage Is Between a Man and a Woman

Proposal photographers

Blog: Why You Will Go to Hell If You Aren't Married in the Church

Wedding venues

Would you like to see more?

- -

Who am I?

We found:

- -

Rory Walsh

Every. Single. Fucking. Thing. ~~Anyone.~~ Pretty Much Just Nora. Has. Posted. Ever.

You don't need more than that.

- -

He pulled into the park entrance. Not a single car or person in sight.

At least that's something, he thought, unable to remember being physically alone.

The last time he was in nature, truly in nature, not just by the trees in his backyard or the sad excuse of a park with a single bench in the middle of the city trying to provide an escape from the skyscrapers, was his hunting trip.

The crackle of the leaves under his boots. The chill he got under the tree canopies where the sun couldn't reach. The squish of accidentally stepping in animal excrement and the following tingle when his nose caught up with his feet. The whoosh of the leaves when a big gust of wind passed them. His soul settled with the stillness of the lake. It was a peace he was unable to find since.

But the moment he stepped out of the car, his mind came to a startling halt.

Alone.

He didn't know why, but it was like the grass, the mud, the creek… they had all the answers, beckoning to him, whispering to him, *We know why you're here. We're here to shelter you, to hug you, to pet your head and say get lost in me to find yourself in you.* And he just walked. He found what probably used to be a footpath, loved in a past life but overgrown with roots and fungus.

He placed his hand on an old cedar elm tree, or what he assumed was an old tree; he had no idea how to tell the age. He liked not knowing, just the roughness of the bark against his hand, the ants seeing his arm as an extension of the tree.

I wish this was my world, he thought.

We found:

- -

Map of the world

Buy World Maps

News: The World Has Attained a 99 Percent AIP Injection Rate

Blog: These Other Broods Are Making the World Go to Shit

New! Picture from Samantha: My. Whole.
World. —Tagged: Pavel

Would you like to see more?

Rory closed his eyes and shook his head, wishing again for the solitude.

He followed the path, which ended up taking him to the creek, and he made his way to the bridge that straddled it.

Silence.

He sat on the bridge, staring out onto the water, which was working harder than the algorithms in his AIP.

Silence.

No. The water rapped the rocks, a crescendo that eventually consumed Rory's soul and stilled once again.

Silence.

No. What was that? The heavy sighing, the grasping for air, the growing shrieks that could only have possibly come from a white lady who hadn't yet made her peace.

No. The tears running down his face awoke Rory to the reality that it was coming from him.

A catharsis. The realization that he needed to disassociate the fact that the Rory he was, or wanted to be, was so different than the Rory everyone saw and thought they knew. The understanding that he needed to start new, to let the creek wash away the Rory of the AIP and rebirth him completely blank, letting him figure out what or who the new Rory would... no, should... no, could be.

Once it seemed like all of the water from his body had exited through his eyes, he laid on the bridge, his mind never before so light, hoping that now that the grass, mud, and creek had shown him this much that they could also create a footpath in his mind showing him who he was, not just who he was not. But he was asking too much, grateful for all that he was already gifted.

Finding himself would be a trek, a rainy, muddy, lonely, cold trek. He didn't know how he knew that, but he just did. And although he hoped he would one day make it to the zenith and show everyone and not only himself who he was capable of being, he wasn't confident the journey wouldn't kill him.

A rumble startled him. He looked around, but a second rumble made him realize it was his stomach.

I wonder what time it is, he thought as he noticed that it was no longer as bright as when he arrived.

We found:
- -
The time is 5:42 p.m.

Shit. How had he managed to spend the entire day at the park?

"I guess it's not all that bad," he said as he picked himself up. The AIP did give him a lot of benefits. It allowed him to have access to knowledge, to be given exactly what he needed, like the time. "Or a new pair of boots," he said as he looked down at his shoes. He laughed as advertisements for boots popped up on his AIP.

His stomach rumbled again. He thought back on the peanut butter and jelly sandwich and followed the footpath back to his car. The second he shut the car door, he shut the door on the peace that so effortlessly found him when he arrived.

His drive to the house was flooded with thoughts, questions he didn't expect answers to but that the AIP provided nonetheless.

How do I actually do this?

Please refine thought search parameters.

One: The people in my brood or the broods at least sorta similar to mine are the only ones who will talk to me. And they'll only talk to me because they like what they see when they scan me. How do I say, "Forget that shit. That's not me!" And if they don't laugh in my face and actually believe me, won't they then hate the real me because the me they thought they'd like was the me they saw, which is not the me I want them to see...?

We found:

News: A Brood Different Than Your Own
Attacks Another Brood

Blog: Why Broods Work

Pictures: your brood members having fun

Pictures: you happy with your brood
members

Would you like to see more?

Two: And what about everyone else? What if I belong in a completely different brood...? But the people in the other broods won't even talk to me or give me a chance because they already hate the me they think I am... So how I do say, "Give me a chance"?

We found:

News: Interbrood Violence Declines for
the Third Year in a Row!

Blog: Why the AIP Makes Us Happier. Spoiler: It's Because We Avoid the People We'd Hate

Video: a brood different from yours being violent

Pictures: other broods causing problems

Would you like to see more?

And what if everyone then hates me? The brood that I'm in because I'm not who they want me to be and the broods that I'm not in because they won't let me prove to them I'm not who they see or think I am?

See prior results.

What if I just end up alone?

We found:

Alone—antonyms

Brood

Academic study: Broods correlate with higher levels of self-reported happiness

Would you like to see more?

What if it ends up being just me?

We found:

Rory Walsh

Every. Single. Fucking. Thing. ~~Anyone.~~
Pretty Much Just Nora. Has. Posted.
Ever.

You don't need more than that.

Is that so different than now?

Please refine thought search parameters.

Is that even so bad?

Please refine thought search parameters.

But I don't want to be alone... it's so lonely.

See prior results re: alone.

CHAPTER XIII

2128

___

RORY

The email finally came through. He was sitting in his room, watching the sun melt the snow in their front yard, when his device pinged.

> *Dear Rory,*
>
> *After evaluating numerous athletes from around the country, your exceptional athletic ability, leadership, character, and commitment to academics were highlighted for our coaching staff. Therefore, I am very excited to offer you a full athletic grant-in-aid for soccer to the University of Maryland.*

He didn't bother reading the rest of the email. The first section was enough to cause his legs to shake, his heartbeat to speed up, and his internal organs to flip in absolute celebration.

After his field trip to Cedar Creek a few months ago, Rory spent the next few days figuring out a way he could spend his life chasing the peace he found.

Okay, how can I just, like, chill in nature... all the time?

We found:

Parks near you

Blog: Our Economy Is More Important Than a Single Fish Species

Hunting clothing and accessories

News: Climate Terrorists Riot Near Corporate Council HQ

Would you like to see more?

He was aware the AIP worked on an algorithm. It showed people what it thought they wanted to see based on their holistic AIP profile. His profile was so established in his mother's image, he had no idea how to manipulate the algorithm.

Am I just asking the wrong question? How do I get information that's... well... not this?

Other information:

News: Amazon Rain Forest Officially Only 990,000 Square Miles (Down From 2.12 Million in 2020)

Academic Study: High Pollution Levels Continue to Correlate with Decreased Penile Size

News: International Environmental Court Suing American Corporate Council for All-Time High Deforestation Levels

Academic Study: Fertility Continues to Decrease by 1 Percent Per Year—Still Linked to Plastic Usage

Blog post: Why We Need to Revisit Climate Change as a Problem

Pictures: climate migrants and refugees

Videos: Time-lapse of the impacts of rising temperatures in the Sahel

Would you like to see more?

Wait, is that literally it? Just ask for other stuff that it doesn't usually show me? Okay. Let's go. Jobs that will let me work with nature.

We found:

Hunter

Builder

Professional soccer player

Soccer coach

Park ranger

Would you like to see more?

Jobs that you normally wouldn't show me that let me work with nature...

We found:

Climate activist

Climate scientist

Environmental researcher

Environmental engineer

Marine biologist

Conservationist

Would you like to see more?

Environmental engineer. That's what I want. Please show me more about this option. How do I do that? Well, also… what is that?

We found:

Definition: Environmental engineer

News: Environmental Engineer Creates Cost-Effective and Efficient Desalinization Process

Top Colleges for Environmental Engineering

Pictures: environmental engineers and what they do

Would you like to see more?

That's it. That's what I want to do. Top schools for environmental engineering.

We found:

Stanford University

University of California—Berkley

University of Maryland

Would you like to see more?

Wait, University of Maryland? They're one of the schools recruiting me for soccer. They're the best in the country...

He always told himself he didn't want to attend St. Theresa's, he wouldn't fit in, and he was scared of being stuck in his parents' shadow acquiring the life they had. But now he had a plan. He knew where he wanted to go, what he wanted to study. That one of the schools recruiting him was a top program in what felt like was his calling was fate. But University of Maryland... that had been taken over by a brood that couldn't be more different from his own.

To even get there, he had to be damn good at soccer.

So for the next few months, that's what he did. He received six other athletic scholarship letters, but University of Maryland was the one he wanted. The one he needed. He didn't just want to escape, running from the life he had, he wanted a destination. Something to run to. And this was it. It wasn't at his fingertips anymore; he reached and snatched it, crushing it in his hand with no intention of ever letting it fly away. It was his.

He didn't know the words to use to tell his parents he was denouncing everything they had ever wanted and planned for him.

So instead, he hit forward on the email and sent it to his mother and his father.

Not a full minute later, Rory's father bellowed, "Rory! Here! *Now!*"

Rory sharply inhaled. He stabilized himself on the bed, lightheaded both from the excitement of the email and the anxiety of the conversation he was about to have.

Following his father's voice, his legs felt both like bricks and feathers, the most uncomfortable combination, as he made his way to the living room. They were both looking right at him, his mother, he swore, for the first time since Maeve passed. Had her eyes always been wilting flowers? It may have been the first time he actually saw her and not her lens.

Was it thirty seconds or thirty minutes that passed before a word was spoken? Rory honestly didn't know.

"Is this about Samantha?" she asked.

"What?"

"You've been distant since your last date a few months ago. You disappeared the next day, and then you were just always running. Always playing soccer. I thought you were upset your date didn't go well."

Rory turned away.

"And then she got engaged to that boy…" she said and paused like she was searching for a name. Finally finding it, she said, "Pavel. I imagined it broke your heart."

"It has nothing to do with her," Rory said.

"But you can't throw your entire life away, push your entire brood aside, for some girl who you must've known it would never work with. You were too different. Different broods don't work."

"It's not about her!" Rory looked back at his mother.

How does she not understand that this is so much bigger, so much more important than a girl I went on a couple dates with?

"Don't yell at your mother," his father said, surprisingly composed.

"Well, how would I know?" she said, rising from her chair by the window. "You never tell us anything! You don't talk to us!"

His parents were encroaching, ready to pounce and tie him down so that he would never be able to leave the house. No, they were no longer his parents. No longer "Mom" and "Dad." Now they were just Nora and Finn, disconnected.

"I've tried!" Rory said. "I've tried to tell you so many times!"

"Now, let's hold on a moment," his father said, making his way to the couch. "Let's all take a breath, sit down, and talk this through."

Nora and Rory watched him but didn't move.

"I said *sit!*"

Nora turned around and went back to her chair. Rory plopped on the floor.

"Rory, I don't think you fully comprehend everything we have done for you. We put you in the best school, we live in the best neighborhood, we have the best brood. Your mother has spent your entire life preparing you, making sure that you are accepted, that you have a future here. You can't just throw all that away."

"How can I be accepted if no one even knows who I am?"

"What are you talking about?" Finn asked.

"My entire life you have made me out to be a version of yourselves. Everything people see when they look at me, every perception of me they have, everything they think they know is about someone who doesn't exist."

"Don't be ridiculous," Nora said.

"I'm not! It's true. You have shaped my identity, cultivated my profile, essentially created someone I can't even recognize."

"We did our best. We did what was best for you," Finn said.

"No, you did what you thought was best. You did what was best *for you*, not what was best for me and definitely not what was best for Maeve."

"Don't you dare bring up your sister," Finn said.

"Why not? You know I'm right. You know she couldn't handle it. I heard you fighting about the talent show when you signed her up. You knew she didn't want to do it. You knew how she was, hated being seen and in front of people. But you ignored her. You forced her to do it. You forced other people to see her, or a version of her you wanted them to see. I don't even know."

"What do you mean, 'you know I'm right'?" Nora asked.

"You think I can't hear you guys fighting? You think I haven't noticed that you've never hugged or kissed in front of me? You think I don't know Dad blames you for Maeve's death, 'it happened on your watch, Nora, how could you lose her,' and you blame him for never loving her enough, 'did you ever even tell her, Finn'? You think I haven't realized she was always your favorite and you wish it was her still here instead of me?" he said, running out of breath.

"You need to watch yourself, Rory," Finn said.

"No! You know I'm right. You know if it weren't for these stupid broods and if it wasn't for your crazy religion, you wouldn't even be together anymore. You care more about how getting divorced would look to other people than your own happiness, not loving each other but merely coexisting in the same space just trying not to get in each other's way. Tell me I'm wrong."

"You know if you go to this school, there's no way you could be in our brood anymore," Nora said. "You would be leaving us. You would be making sure we lost both of our children."

"I may not be in the brood, but that doesn't mean I won't be your son. I will always be your son if you let me. It doesn't have to be a choice between you and the brood or no you at all. I can still be here; I can still be your son even if I'm not in the brood."

"That's not how it works," Nora responded. "How would it look to the other brood members if we were complacent and allowed our own son to walk away from righteousness and into sinfulness?"

"How would it look if you disavowed your own son just because he was a little bit different from you?"

"Well, I guess you've made your decision," Finn said.

"If you leave this house in August," Nora said, "for any school but St. Theresa's, just know you won't be welcomed to return."

"Well, I guess I'll save my goodbyes until then and start packing now," Rory said holding back tears.

Nora pulled out her device, and Finn closed his eyes.

It's like nothing happened. The decision for them, so easy. At least I can finally say I saw my mother for the first time. Congratulations, Rory.

We found:
- -

Order your celebration cake!

Graduation announcements

Balloons and party accessories

Would you like to see more?
- -

* * *

One week. It only took one week for Nora and Finn to have the fight. How could neither one of them try harder? How was it so easy for them to just lose another child?

Their choice. That's what it was this time around.

"There's nothing to talk about, Finn!"

"He's our fucking son," his dad said from the couch. Rory heard his mom screeching from his room and made his way to the top of the steps. He leaned on the banister and sat down at the top of the landing.

"You supported me when we found out," she responded.

"Because we're supposed to be a unified front. But we need to talk about this."

"Talk about what? Rory spitting in our faces and disrespecting everything we've ever done for him? Him *abandoning* us?"

"I know we're upset he's making this choice, but we've already lost one child, I can't bear to lose another. It's not like we have a whole litter here!"

"Not again, Finn," his mother hissed. "We're not having this conversation. Me not being able to have kids wasn't a choice, and you know that."

"Clearly God has punished you for being such an awful mother, He couldn't bring Himself to see you plague the world with more screw-ups. What kind of family loses both of their children like this?" A moment of silence passed, and he continued. "I misspoke. An awful person. You push everyone away, ever since your sister disappeared. You couldn't protect her, and you couldn't protect your own children." His father started sobbing… he had never heard his father sob before. He was struggling to hold back his own tears at the sound. Disappeared? He thought his mother's sister had died.

"You are a monster! It's my fault for not realizing it soon enough, but you are a *monster*, Finn—" A crack shook the house, his mother breaking into sobs alongside his father.

"You're right about him. We should let him go, but only because he's better off without you in his life." Another crack, and his mother's sobs got louder. A few minutes passed. But as Rory stood to retreat to his room, his father collectedly said, "Help me understand you, Nora. How can you just forsake your own son, your flesh and blood... especially after Maeve?"

Rory leaned on the banister to better hear Nora.

"He's not my son. A son who would neglect us and everything we've done for him... If he says the person I 'created' isn't him, then I don't want to know him. I don't want to know someone who doesn't share our values, who doesn't belong in our brood. And I can't be ostracized from our brood and lose everyone we love for a complete stranger."

He couldn't take it anymore. He couldn't listen to his parents saying they didn't want him, and they couldn't love him unless he fit into their perfect little box. It broke his heart. How could he even consider staying when all his parents wanted were a carbon copy of themselves rather than... him, for all his faults and flaws?

After he made it clear to his parents he would be attending the University of Maryland, and they made it clear he had no option but to succeed there because he officially had no safety net, he channeled all of his energy into soccer, more so than he ever had.

He couldn't afford to lose that scholarship. The Corporate Council had made college consistently more expensive every year by reducing subsidization, driving down the quantity of students attending, and he would never be able to keep attending if he was forced to pay for it.

His time was easy to fill during the rest of the school year. Before class, he would go to the gym and lift weights. After class, he would go on a long run. By the time he ate dinner and did his homework, he needed to go to sleep to do it all over again the next day.

The summer was definitely more challenging. He had an extra eight hours during the day that he needed to fill up. He, like a victim of Stockholm syndrome, longed to spend that time with his mom and dad, soaking up every minute he could before leaving and possibly only ever being able to see them again through his AIP.

We found:

- -

```
Finn Walsh—updates and new photos

Nora Walsh—updates and new photos

Pictures of you and your parents

Relationship timeline of the Walsh
family
```

Would you like to see more?

- -

But for as much as he wanted to catch glimpses of his parents, they had no interest in that, it seemed. When he entered a room, they would leave. When they made eye contact, his parents would turn away. It may have never felt like a home, but at least he had always been welcomed there. Now he was a burden, ticking away time, money, and food for his few last months.

At least his dad let him keep his car. "It was a gift," Finn said, not looking up from his device at the beginning of the summer when Rory asked whether he would be able to use it to move. "It's yours."

Rory thought he would at least be able to spend some time with his dad moving or get to see his parents one last time when he dropped off the car before taking a train from Philly to DC. But it seemed not. It seemed like when Rory took his stuff and got in the car to Maryland that he would be saying goodbye to his parents forever.

That's it. Everything I own, fit in one carload, he thought while scanning his room to make sure he didn't forget anything.

We found:

- -

Buy Stuff Here!

And Here!

Or Here!

But Here!

Also Here!

Would you like to see more?

- -

He walked down the hall to Maeve's room. That door had been closed for eight years. He had never seen his mom or dad walk in or out of that room, and he certainly hadn't entered, either. It just hurt too much, knowing she wouldn't be in there, not waiting for him with a book and an empty spot on the bed next to her. It would be real. The irrational hope that she could just be hiding away from the world in there with her books would be shattered the second that door opened.

But this would be the last time he could get the essence of Maeve. He grabbed the handle and took a deep breath. He opened the door, and it was exactly what he expected. Nothing had changed. The books where she had left them, the half-open drawers. His memory hadn't faded or tricked him.

He sat on her bed. "I miss you," he said while smoothing out her sheets around him.

I wonder how different it would've been if you hadn't left, if somehow Dad's CPR worked. Would Mom have still been so crazy intense and protective with my profile? Would you and I have been even closer? Would I have had someone to talk to, or would we have grown apart? Would you have tried again, being miserable and heartbroken your entire life? I guess the what-ifs don't matter, do they? I just miss you so much.

He patted her pillow and noticed a corner of a book peeking out, *The Giver*, with notes in all the margins. He hugged the book and laid on the bed, his head resting where hers used to. He rolled onto his side, a piece of her hair on the pillow magically still there next to him. He picked it up and wrapped it, unwrapped it, and wrapped it again around his fingers until it broke. Flipping the book open, he stuffed the pieces of hair into it, wanting something that was truly hers, a part of her that he could keep with him. Something more real than fabricated pictures he could pull up on his AIP.

Closing his eyes, he thought back to when she would read to him, when they would lie in this bed together, his head on her arm while she flipped through the pages in her book, sharing her worlds with him. He sniffed the pillow, hoping to relive those moments, but her scent was no longer there, replaced with mustiness and dust.

He sneezed so loudly it brought him back into the present.

He lifted himself up and walked back to the door. Looking around one last time, he let a single tear escape before closing the door onto his past.

His body twitched, and he composed himself. He slowly walked down the steps, *The Giver* in one hand and the other tracing the banister. The wood smooth but chipped every so often. His dad was on the couch and his mom in her traditional chair by the window.

"I think it's time I start heading out so I don't get stuck driving in the dark," Rory said as he reached the bottom of the steps.

Silence, but not the peaceful kind he had found a few months earlier.

"Okay, well, I love you guys. I really do, and I'm going to miss you. A lot," Rory said, his voice wavering. "Please let me know if you change your minds. It's not too far a drive. I'd be happy to come see you over the holidays." He hoped once more that this wouldn't be the last time he would see them.

He longed to run to them, to throw his arms around each of them and kiss them, their cheeks, their hands, hell, their feet even. Any place they would let him.

But before he could let this need overtake him, the child-like need that screams *Mommy, I need you. Mommy, please just hold me. Mommy, I long for you*, and take a step toward them, Nora said, "I saw your name on the Maryland roster today when I scanned you. It seems like you made your decision," without even looking up from her device.

He couldn't hold back the tears any longer. He didn't get *goodbye or we love you too*. He didn't even get the decency of eye contact. He ran out the door and to his car, bracing himself, his breath unable to regulate. Through blurry eyes he made out the outline of the two story-house that he grew up in, that he lost himself in, and that he started to find himself in. He rubbed his eyes, wanting to make sure that if this was the last time he'd be seeing it with his own eyes and not through an AIP, the memory would be as clear as the cloudless summer sky above.

With one last glance, he stepped into the car that contained his entire life, his entire future, and started the drive to the next chapter of his life—in Maryland.

CHAPTER XIV

2128

———

RORY

"Rory Walsh," a girl in a red shirt with a turtle on it said after scanning him. Standing behind a table at Prince Frederick Hall, she fingered through little envelopes with keys inside of them. "Here you go. I know they're primitive, but ever since we lost all public stipends under the CC… well, and decreased enrollment, of course, the school can't afford to digitize the locks system. But there's a bar code on the back of your envelope that you can scan with your device, and it'll give your AIP access to the campus map, your registration packet, class list, emergency numbers, and everything else you might need!"

Wow, *she's polite*, Rory thought. He more than expected her to throw the key at him, give him no information, and tell him to figure it out. *Must be getting paid for this.*

Rory read about how colleges and universities had changed after the Corporate Council took over the US. Before the CC, when the US was a representative republic, universities were flooded with students, and the country was flooded with colleges and universities. At peak enrollment, the University of Maryland could see upward of forty thousand students on its campus; now it would be lucky to have five thousand.

The US had at one point approximately 4,300 post-secondary institutions, and now it flaunted just 250, with more shuttering their doors each year. The cost of education had become a luxury that very few could afford. Tuition rates continued to increase, and debt became much too expensive to hold, with those who needed it unable to ever pay it off.

The handful of institutions left became associated with collections of broods. Broods similar to his parents' attended St. Theresa's, finding schools that aligned directly with their values and would certainly impart the same lessons onto future generations of those brood members.

Attending a school not associated with one's brood was unheard of. "Why would you want to spend four years with people who you know will hate you?" Rory overheard his mom saying to his dad the day before he left. She had a point. There was no guarantee. Hell, there was less of a chance someone from UMD would talk to Rory willingly than there was for the Amazon Rainforest to grow back in the next five years.

It only took him three trips to unload his boxes from the car. He was in a double room, unsure whether he'd have a roommate. Two-thirds of the residence halls at UMD were permanently closed, and he wasn't sure if the ones open would be completely full this year.

The room was plain with white floors and walls, only a little bit bigger than the one in which he had spent the last eighteen years of his life. There were two beds, two closets, two dressers, two desks, and a small refrigerator.

"No complaints if I get all this to myself," he said, throwing his last box of clothes on the floor and opening the closet closest to him.

He was itching to see the A. James Clark Hall, which housed the school of engineering, more or less his home for the next four years, really the first place he would ever call home. But he would kick himself later if he didn't unpack his stuff now, and so he made his bed, threw his clothes in the dresser, and set up his desk with school supplies.

He opened the refrigerator, and it was completely empty. "Why am I surprised? I should've expected that," he said looking around his room. He completely forgot to bring food with him.

We found:
- -

Food near me

Order Food Here! We Deliver!

Best food at the University of Maryland

Blog: The Best Brain Food

Would you like to see more?
- -

Please pull up food near me at UMD.

The AIP pulled up the campus map and overlaid restaurants on top of it.

Zoom in near Clark Hall.

The AIP zoomed into that portion of UMD's campus and expanded the restaurant selection. He found an Italian restaurant not too far from Clark Hall.

"Fantastic," he said as he grabbed his vaccine card and device and locked the door behind him. His AIP provided directions to the restaurant, allowing him to marvel at the campus.

The buildings were on complete opposite sides of the campus. If he followed his instructions at a quick pace, he could make it in fifteen to twenty minutes. Good to know so he could budget the time to get there for his classes.

But at that moment, he wasn't rushing to class. He was enjoying the breezy summer day, not too humid, not too hot. He walked along the drive, passing the other residence halls. The first, Caroline, was shuttered, the windows completely boarded. The second, Wicomico, seemed open, a student lounging on the steps with a book in hand. The last, Carroll, not shuttered but also not open at the moment, probably for the years where student enrollment was a little higher, catching the overflow from Prince Frederick and Wicomico.

The Georgian style residence halls with their large white columns, symmetrical windows, and ornate exterior molding reminded him of a house he played at as a child. When he and Maeve would retreat together, reading or telling stories, and his mother inevitably getting angry and pulling them apart, forcing them to play with the other kids.

He passed Morrill Hall and found himself on the quad, a beautiful tree-filled space, completely empty with paths coming to and from seemingly unplanned directions. A recluse so close to his residence hall. He imagined himself camping out under a tree, books surrounding him, or doing some type of experiment… or just lying on his back, looking up at the sky and the trees above him.

I'm going to be here a lot, he thought as a breeze ruffled the tree branches, birds chirping in delight, or maybe annoyance; he wasn't sure whether birds liked breezes as much as he did.

Turning away from the quad, he walked past another huge Georgian building. Many of them looked so similar he couldn't tell them apart from his first exploration of the campus.

What's there? His AIP pulled up the campus map.

We found:
--- --- --- --- --- --- --- --- --- --- --- --- --- --- ---

Francis Scott Key Hall

College of Arts and Humanities

Would you like to see more?
--- --- --- --- --- --- --- --- --- --- --- --- --- --- ---

He walked around the building and came out on the other end.
"Over here!" a voice called as he stumbled upon a huge
open clearing, McKeldin Mall.

"What?" he said noticing a group of young men staring
at him.

"The frisbee."

"Oh!" There was a frisbee maybe a foot in front of him. He
picked it up and tossed it toward the group. "Need another?"

"Nah, we're good," another said as the guys ran in different
directions and tossed the frisbee back and forth.

McKeldin Mall was full of students, playing frisbee, reading, picnicking, lounging around... and tanning. The women
wore bikinis, some even topless, laying on the grass and soaking in the sun. He blushed.

Looking around, none of the men or other women even
paid attention, which embarrassed him that he was so shaken
by the sight, his thighs beginning to throb. But to everyone
else, it seemed like no one even noticed there were scantily
clad women just a few feet away from them. As though this
happened every day. Besides Samantha at a single gymnastics practice, he had never seen so much of a woman's body.
His brood was modest, with women rarely in anything that
showed cleavage, even while swimming, instead wearing
one-piece bathing suits, similar to Samantha's leotard, that
left much to the imagination.

He quickly acknowledged himself objectifying the women in front of him, while it seemed like no one else on the mall did. Was he so distracted because of how his brood treated sexuality? Did pushing abstinence and modesty cause him to see women as something to be protected, shielded, or even conquered rather than just letting them live peacefully in their own skin?

Shaking his head, he noticed one of the women looking at him inquisitively.

He scanned the mall. Could these people be his friends? Could he join them and eat with them? Maybe joke and run around on brooms with them, like the group at the far end by the library, the largest and most beautiful building he had passed thus far? He hoped... maybe one day.

But the smiles that quickly turned to scowls once they scanned him told him that this would not be that day.

Disappointed, hungry, yet excited to see Clark, he continued on, passing the recreation field and turning a bit away from his final destination onto Baltimore Avenue to grab his dinner.

Ding, the bell above the door sounded when Rory walked in.

"Vaccine card," the man behind the counter in the empty restaurant said without looking up from his device.

Rory pulled out the card from his back pocket and held it up.

The man looked up at Rory, scowled, and said, "What do you want?"

"What?" Rory said.

"You want food, yes?"

"Oh, yeah, I do."

"So? What the hell do you want?"

"I'll… um… just take an eggplant sub, I guess."

"Okay. Fine," the man said and entered something into his device, probably Rory's order because then a smaller man scurried to make the sandwich.

He turned away and leaned against the counter.

"Off!" the man yelled.

"What?"

"Don't touch my counter!" he said, glaring.

"Oh, sorry. My bad," Rory said, backing away.

He crossed his arms, trying to make himself smaller.

"Here," the man said, tossing the sub at Rory. "Twenty-two dollars and fifty cents."

Rory pulled out his device to scan. He was given a stipend with his scholarship, but he was going to burn through it quick and needed to find a job.

"Hey, are you guys hiring?" Rory said.

"I assumed you were dumb, but seriously? Does it look like I need help, jackass?" the man said, pointing to the empty restaurant.

"Oh, sorry. I guess not," Rory said and scurried out the door.

He wanted to sit and enjoy his sub, but there was no way he was going to stay in that restaurant with that man watching him, judging him, counting the seconds until he left. Would he have even let him stay and sit in there? Or would he have kicked him out and told him to go somewhere else? He didn't want to wait around and find out.

He started walking down the street toward Clark Hall, peeling away the wrapper from his sub and taking a bite. He became uncomfortably aware of his presence. Every single person he walked by would smirk, point, or look away in… *shame? Is that disgust?* He inhaled his sub, hoping not to draw so much attention to himself.

His AIP told him the walk only took four minutes. *How is it even possible that I passed that many people in four minutes? What is that? Like, five a minute?* Coming from his little Allentown neighborhood, that was a high rate.

He was going to need to get comfortable with living in a bigger city.

Looking up at Clark Hall, with its huge glass windows and stunning architecture, he completely forgot about the judgment he faced, the people who stared. So different from the rest of the Georgian campus he passed, it was fitting. It stood out, just like he did.

This is it. Is this it? Is this where I'm going to find, no, create myself? Is this the place that's going to change everything?

* * *

"We didn't originally plan on this, but I feel like you all need a break," Rory's soccer coach said to the team on the Friday before classes. They huddled in a circle, some standing and using their practice jerseys to wipe the sweat off their faces, some laying on the ground and catching their breath, some sitting and unlacing their cleats. "You guys have put in a ton of great work over the past three weeks, and so you should take the weekend off."

"Yes..."

"Phew."

"Thanks, coach!"

"By that I mean, you should still make it to the gym, or do some recovery, or go on a run the next two days. I don't mean just sit on your asses and eat a shit ton of food. Your break is from team workouts and scrimmages, not from being athletes," the coach said. "You guys are free to go. Enjoy your weekend. See you at five-thirty bright and early Monday morning. Hey, Rory—can you hang back a minute?"

Panicking, Rory walked up to his coach. "Is everything okay, coach? Am I doing okay? Should I be working harder; are you not happy with my performance? I can do more!" He was nervous that before he even started the semester, the coach second guessed putting him on the team. Would he pull the scholarship money?

"Whoa, whoa, chill," the coach said, putting a hand on Rory's shoulder. "I just want to check up on you."

"How come?"

"I just know there have been quite a few team bonding events and you haven't been invited to any of them."

"Yeah, it's totally fine. I didn't come in with some unreasonable expectations that I was going to be best friends with these guys. You know?" Rory said, immediately regretting sharing his thoughts when seeing coach's brow furrow. "I mean, unless that's what you want or what you need me to do, then I guess I can totally try... something."

"I'm just worried about you," the coach said.

"My performance?"

"No, you. I can't imagine what you're going through. It must be really hard being here all alone from a different brood. To be completely honest, I'm still pretty shocked you accepted our offer. Grateful, but shocked. I just want to make sure you're adjusting okay."

"Yeah, I'm okay," Rory lied. "Thanks for checking in."

"Let me know if there's anything I can do. You're a valued member of this team, and I want you to enjoy... well, at least not hate your time here."

Rory nodded. The coach dropped his hand from his shoulder, and Rory turned and walked toward the locker rooms. By the time he arrived, the rest of his teammates were gone. He changed his shoes, tossed his cleats in his bag, and started walking to his residence.

It turned out that all of the first years from the soccer team were placed in Prince Frederick, so it wasn't uncommon for Rory to hear the team or pass open doors with members talking, eating, and laughing.

Walking up to Prince Frederick, there were more cars, more people, and much more stuff than when he had left for practice. He passed other first-years and their parents moving boxes into the residence hall. This must've been the move-in day for everyone else, those who weren't athletes.

He opened the door to his room and let out a shriek. He shouldn't have been surprised seeing all the people moving in and out of the hall, but he grew accustomed to living alone, his stuff wherever he pleased, and no one greeting him upon arrival.

But now, another teenager was looking back at him from the bed opposite his. His clothes a European style, well-fitting slacks and a sport coat on his thin frame. His hair was short with a trendy cut. *Who the hell sits on their bed in that?* Unlike Rory, he was relaxed, smiling, as though he waited for Rory's return.

>>>>>>>>SCAN>>>>>>>>IN>>>>>>>>PROGRESS>>>>>>>>
- -
Name: Sebastian Desjardins
- -
Nickname: Bash
- -

Born in: Portland, Maine

Most recently lived in: Portland, Maine

Father: Lucas Desjardins

Mother: Olive Pelletier

Heir to the Pelletier Lobster Company

Net worth: $212 million

Pictures:

```
Bash on a yacht with his friends

Bash on a yacht by himself

Bash crashing a yacht

Bash water skiing

Bash playing hockey

Bash throwing money into the water

Bash in Italy

Bash in Greece

Bash in France

Bash in England

Bash in South Africa

Bash in Morocco

Bash in Japan
```

Bash with a woman on his lap

Bash with a different woman kissing his cheek

Bash with a different woman's breast in his face

Bash in a tuxedo at a restaurant

Bash with his parents at a fundraiser

Bash drinking Dom Perignon

Bash...

Bash...

Bash...

"Hi there, Mr. hunting-religious-CC-loving-future-trophy-husband-dead-sister-finding-soccer star," Bash said with a smirk on his face that read, *You don't belong here.*

Fuck. He hates me. Shit. I hate him. What a rich, privileged jerk.

"No disrespect, but why the fuck are you here?" Bash asked, raising an eyebrow.

"What? That didn't come up on your scan? Soccer," Rory said, throwing his soccer bag on the floor by his bed.

"No need for the hostilities. I get that you play soccer. But why are you playing *here*?"

"You started it."

"That's an immature way to avoid my question."

"Why bother? You're going to ask for a different roommate… or never be here when I'm here… or pay off the residence hall to give you, like, a four-person suite to yourself… or whatever the hell rich guys like you can do," Rory said, grabbing his soap and towel.

"Intriguing,"

"What?"

"You," Bash said, sitting up in his bed.

"Why?"

"Inconsistency. There's a gap. It's like you turned eighteen and *poof*, all gone. Even a few weeks before then, the only thing I can find is your signed athletic contract from UMD. Why the disappearing act?"

"Why do you care?"

"Huh," Bash said, tilting his head to the side.

"*What?*"

"Why does nothing originate from you? Like, 90 percent of everything here is originated from your mom." He paused a moment, probably searching for her on his AIP, and said, "Nora?"

"Listen, I gotta shower," Rory said. "If you're still here when I get back, well, I guess we'll see if that even happens."

Bash smiled, put his hands behind his head, and leaned back against the wall.

Rory walked to the shower, unable to shake the conversation.

He couldn't help but wonder if this was some game Bash was playing. They were clearly from different broods. Maybe Bash hated his brood so much that he would play a strategic game, pulling him in with friendship and a false sense of security to break him in the long run. No one had noticed any of that about him before, or never cared to ask.

Would that be so bad? Would the possibility of getting hurt in the future be better or worse than not letting someone at least get to know him? Because isn't that what he wanted? Isn't that why he was here? To have someone take a risk, to take a chance on him.

But this is the closest I've ever gotten…

He found Bash exactly how he had left him, smile and all, as though he was chiseled on that spot.

"So, tell me something," Bash said.

"Okay. Fine. What do you want to know first?" Rory sighed and plopped onto his bed. This was fast, and he knew it. He hadn't ever opened up to anyone, let alone someone outside of his brood. He should be more cautious, but this could be his only chance. Everyone he had passed while at UMD so far refused to approach him, scowling, judging, but not Bash.

This guy could turn around and leave at any moment, probably paying for a better room or roommate, so he had to act fast. He didn't have time to build rapport. They didn't live in that kind of world. Decisions were made in seconds, and he hoped Bash would make the decision to stay.

How he got so invested in Bash so fast, he couldn't say, but he had gotten so lonely. He could use someone other than his AIP to talk to.

"When I described you, you didn't own up to it. Usually, we're all so *proud* of our broods and shit, but you didn't say anything."

"Oh, you mean when you called me hunting-religious-sister-finder or some shit?"

"Yes. None of that was offensive, though. The first thing that came up was that you found your dead sister. You hunt. You're hella religious. I don't even know how you have so many pictures at CCHQ, let alone all the 'all hail the CC' propaganda type shit you wore as a kid. And this caption, right here—'I'm going to make some girl the happiest wife,' blah blah blah," Bash explained. "I literally just described you, and you got super defensive."

"Well…" Rory started.

"Hold up. So then I got to thinking…" Bash stood up and started pacing up and down the room. "The origination. Nora… Nora… so then I scanned her. And your profiles are exactly the same. You are literally her. So then I thought… maybe that's not *really you*. Maybe that's her…"

"Perceptive," Rory said, genuinely amazed at watching Bash think. This man may have been the most intelligent person he'd met so far, a modern-day Sherlock Holmes.

"But if it's not you," Bash stopped, "why do you not originate any content?"

"Parental controls," Rory responded. "My mom put a child control on my device and profile that everything needed to be approved by her before it could be posted… that just expired when I turned eighteen."

"Shit… yours *just* expired? I didn't know parents could have them that long. I mean, I knew they were mandatory until, like, thirteen, but I assumed they all expired after that."

"Nope," Rory said. "Nora found a way."

"Fuck."

Shit. Is this really happening?

"So then, Rory Walsh, where does Nora end and Rory begin?" Bash said, sitting back down on his bed.

"Well, Bash, I'm still trying to figure that out, I guess," Rory said and smiled. "So is it my turn to ask a question yet?"

Bash crossed his arms and nodded.

"How did you get there?"

"Get where?"

"Like, how did you figure it out?" Rory paused. "And I guess, why did you care?"

"We're not that different, you and I," Bash said, not skipping a beat.

Is he saying what I think he's saying? This spoiled rich kid…

We found:
- -

Picture of Sebastian Desjardins

Learn How to Make Money—Fast!

News: Lucas Desjardins and Olive
Pelletier Inherit Pelletier Lobster
Company

Blog: Bash Desjardins Is Why We Need
Wealth Redistribution

Would you like to see more?
- -

Who got everything he's always wanted...

We found:
- -

Pictures: Sebastian Desjardins at
boarding school

Pictures: Sebastian Desjardins
traveling

Want Bash Desjardins Fashion? Buy Here!

Video: Sebastian Desjardins crashing
Daddy's yacht

News: Sebastian Desjardins Crashes His
Father's Yacht

Buy a new yacht near you

Would you like to see more?
- -

No way. I mean, his content pretty much all came from him... What does he *have to hide? Wait, maybe that's it... there's something about him that he's been hiding... that he doesn't want anyone to know... or that he can't let anyone know? Who is this guy...?*

We found:

- -

Name: Sebastian Desjardins

Nickname: Bash

Born in: Portland, Maine

Most recently lived in: Portland, Maine

Father: Lucas Desjardins

Mother: Olive Pelletier

Heir to the Pelletier Lobster Company

Net Worth: $212 million

Would you like to see more?

- -

Bash cocked his head. "You all right there?"

Rory didn't realize how long the room had been quiet. "Yeah, sorry. I just can't imagine how 'we're not that different.' Honestly, I feel like we couldn't be more different." The tension in the air had lifted. The hostility had all but disappeared between them.

If I'm like him... then he knows he's not the only one... he's not alone.

We found:

Alone—antonyms

Brood

Academic study: Broods Correlate
with Higher Levels of Self-Reported
Happiness

Would you like to see more?

Bash walked over to Rory and held out his hand, "It's a pleasure to meet you, Mr. Walsh."

Rory stood and shook Bash's hand.

I wonder if this is what friendship feels like.

We found:

Academic study: Oxytocin Levels
Heightened When Shown Pictures of Brood
Members

Blog: Brood Members Are More Than
Friends—They're Family

News: Interbrood Violence Continues to
Decrease—Is Segregation the Answer?

Video: your brood members at church

Would you like to see more?

CHAPTER XV

2128

―――

RORY

"Did I ever tell you about my first time ever coming in here?" Rory said. He had become fond of the Italian restaurant, but his first experience still bothered him. He wondered if he shocked Manny, the owner, not only by coming back every Friday afternoon after class but by also bringing a friend with him every time. A friend from a different brood, for that matter.

"No," Bash replied.

"It was early August, the day I moved in. There was literally no one else in here." Rory took a breath. "Manny was such an ass."

"And that surprises you?"

"No, but it surprises me that he's not anymore." He had a feeling Bash's presence restrained Manny from the outward hostility he showed during their first encounter, but he knew better than to ask.

"He's not? He's glaring at you right now," Bash said, looking over his shoulder.

"Yeah, but before he was actually mean. Called me dumb and shit."

"It must really bug you," Bash said.

"I mean, I kind of expected it… but it still sucked."

"Not just Manny. But, like, everyone. Your teammates, your teachers, your classmates, random people on the street."

Rory reflected on his experience thus far. He had prepared himself for the hateful remarks and the judgmental looks, but each one still hurt, their frequency not making the emotional toll any lighter.

"The coach is nice to me. I still have no idea why," Rory said.

"Seriously?"

"Seriously what?"

"You don't know why the coach is nice to you?"

"Should I?"

"Maybe you are dumb," Bash said and chuckled.

Rory's face got hot. Bash had a habit of belittling him, his words insinuating that he was better than Rory.

Was it the boarding school?

The "cultural understanding" from his travels?

Maybe just Bash's continued assumption that he was better than Rory because of the brood Rory was raised in. Which, in his defense, did have a penchant for peddling alternative information that never quite aligned with fact…

Bash tended to walk around with an intellectual crown on his head, treating Rory as his own personal jester, providing him with an insight into the fact that broods like his were bred to presume certain incorrect information as accurate. It was insulting. But to have a friend in Bash was more rewarding than the insults were painful.

"Sorry, I didn't mean it like that," Bash said. "The school, like every school, is in a budget crisis since so few people can afford to go anymore. Sports are the only thing that even make money anymore, and you're good. Like, *really* good.

So he doesn't see 'Rory Walsh' when he scans you. He just sees dollar bills."

"Oh, and I thought it was my radiant personality," Rory said and laughed. He found comfort in the coach's ability to overlook his profile, even if it was for his own personal gain.

"But seriously, how do you do it?"

"Do what?"

"Exist in a place where everyone hates you," Bash replied casually.

"It sucks. And it gets really lonely. Like, before you came around, it was just me... I had no one to talk to... no one to hang out with..." Rory dropped his voice. "And what I really can't figure out is: is it better or worse that it's not even me they hate?"

"What do you mean, 'better or worse'?"

"Well, on the one hand, I think, *But it's not me they hate.* You know, like, I can't take it personally? It's someone who, honestly, isn't even real, so it doesn't feel so bad. But on the other hand, it's like, 'Hey! The person you hate isn't me! Get to know me before you decide you hate me!' But I know they won't, so other days it hits harder... Does that make sense?"

"Yeah, but you don't even know *you* yet."

"But *you* gave me a chance."

"Did you ever figure out what type of environmental work you want to do when you graduate?"

"Not exactly, but I've decided I want to work with trees for sure."

"Okay, Lorax," Bash said and laughed.

"What?"

"Really? *The Lorax?*" Bash said and waved a fist in the air like he was scolding some neighborhood kids.

The hell is the lorax?

We found:

The Lorax by Dr. Seuss

Would you like to see more?

Rory skimmed the book on his AIP. "Oh, yeah. I guess like the Lorax," Rory said and laughed.

"How have you never heard of *The Lorax* before?"

"I guess it's because my parents' values probably align more with the Once-ler. They just want trees so they can kill the birds that nest in them."

"I never understood hunting. Or more so the psychology of hunting. You know? Like, all hunters today do it because they like it. There's, like, 1 percent of the world that actually needs to do it. So if a kid kills an animal without adult supervision, they're deranged. But as long as Daddy is watching, it's fine? Under what conditions is it no longer a sign of psychopathy to not only want to watch a living creature die but then to want the power of being able to do it yourself?"

That's a good point... I wonder what kind of people throughout the US even hunt anymore... Is there an overlap with modern hunting and psychopathy?

We found:

Study: A History of Hunting in the United States

Buy a Hunting Rifle in Less Than Five Minutes or It's Free!

Article: Profile of a Hunter

New photos of Finn Walsh

```
Updated list of game illegal to hunt

News: Increased Rates of Hunting in
Particular Brood Territories Amplify
Environmental Degradation


Would you like to see more?
```
- -

He wanted to read through the study his AIP provided, but he couldn't help himself from looking at the new pictures of his dad. Finn hadn't changed. Not a hint of sadness or regret. His profile was exactly the same as the day Rory left home, as though nothing had even happened, as though he hadn't lost a son.

"Rory?" Bash cocked his head.

He pushed the pictures out of his head and said, "Yeah, clearly I never got it either." He scrunched his nose at Bash squishing a piece of chicken between his fingers.

Bash always had a way of pivoting the conversation away from him. They saw each other every single day over the past thirty, but he still felt like he hadn't learned anything about the guy sitting across from him. Most of their conversations were superficial, and he wanted to break through Bash's defenses.

"I didn't mean to zone out on you. Sorry. I just saw some new pictures of my dad." His voice began to shake. "You know what still hurts the most?" He wanted to let Bash in, part the Red Sea of his insecurities and anxieties, allowing Bash to cross into the depths of his memories.

But what if Bash wasn't his Moses? What if Bash was the Egyptian army set to destroy him?

"What's that?"

"I never realized how lonely I was before until I truly lost everyone."

We found:

Lost, the television series

Update AIP directional services

Blog: Lost Souls from Other Broods Are
Going Straight to Hell!

Would you like to see more?

His attempts at manipulating his algorithm seemed to only confuse his AIP, if that was even possible. The results it provided him were rarely ever helpful or the ones he looked for, a portion still reminding him of his past life. But that portion of his results continued to shrink, him hoping that meant his efforts, although slow, were working.

"Who's 'everyone'? You mean like your sister?"

"Yes, but also no," Rory responded.

"You're losing me."

"Of course I miss Maeve. I loved her. If anyone would've been able to know what I was feeling or going through, it was her. But I mean after that. After she died it was just me, my mom, and my dad. I didn't have anyone else. Everyone else was too scared to talk to me. I was always lonely, but I thought to myself, *At least I have them. At least I'm not really alone.*"

Bash leaned back in his chair, his eyes on Rory.

"But then, when I left for UMD, my parents told me I'd never be welcomed in their house again. That I could never see them. And that destroyed me. I officially had no one. I really was alone."

"That's fucked up. I'm so sorry," Bash said.

"Being alone, truly alone for that month before you moved in, wasn't the loneliest I had ever felt, though. I realized it was more lonely living a life with Finn and Nora, a life that wasn't mine with a son they fabricated rather than the one they actually had, was so much more lonely than just... being alone." Rory's eyes started to burn, like they had been open a little too long without blinking.

Bash watched him for a moment.

Please say something. Please say something that matters.

We found:

Updates! New posts from Nora and Finn Walsh

"Matter" v. "Mass"—the definition of "matter" in the discipline of physics

States of matter

Family Matters, the television series.

Would you like to see more?

"I understand what you're feeling," Bash said after a few beats of silence.

"What? Your parents disowned you too?"

"Not that. The idea of being lonely because you can't show them who you really are."

"What do you mean?"

"Can I tell you a story?" Bash asked.

"Of course."

"Look, I know we have, like, an unspoken rule that everything we talk about stays between us, but I need to hear you say it. That it stays between us."

"Okay. It stays between us," Rory said, confused but also relieved.

"When I was six, I was walking with my mom to the docks. She needed to check on a lobster shipment that someone had called and told her there was a problem with, and because Dad was always working, she always took me along whenever she had errands. At the time, he was working with Grandpa at the lobster company. Grandpa was grooming him to take over, so he was pulling some late nights.

"There was a little doll store just a few blocks away from the docks, and my mom had gotten really close with the owner. The owner had a son, just a year older than me, and so my mom would drop me off so I could play with him while she did whatever it was she needed to. Usually, we would run around outside, play tag, or watch the boats come in and out of the dock from the store's roof. But that day it was raining, and his mom didn't want us to play outside so we wouldn't get the store all muddy or wet. So we grabbed some dolls and started playing in the back room. I'm sure a therapist would say I had my first crush, but I just remember wanting to hold his hand, so I did. He looked at me and grabbed my face, planting a huge, sloppy kiss on me."

Bash chuckled.

"He gave me his doll and told me to hide it under my shirt so his mom wouldn't take it away. And that's exactly what I did. My mom picked me up, and we went home, me so proud of sneaking the doll away. I pulled it out later that evening to play with it, to remember how much fun I had that afternoon.

"My dad came home from work and walked in to me playing with the doll on the living room floor. He walked in the door and before saying hi, or picking me up, or kissing mom, he walked over to me, grabbed the doll, and with what seemed like total ease, ripped off the head. He tossed both pieces of the doll on the floor at my feet and told me that boys didn't play with dolls."

"What?" Rory said. "Why?" He couldn't tell if the story was about Bash or about his dad.

Bash, no doubt seeing the confusion on his face, said, "Let me tell you another story. When I was nine, my mom was getting ready to go to a gala. It was the night my dad was being honored as the new CEO of Pelletier Lobster. She was in the shower, and I sneaked into her room. Her blue sparkly Vera Wang was laying across the bed and her white Manolos placed neatly on the floor below it. That dress was a work of art. At first, I just touched it, ran my fingers over it, but then my arms had a plan of their own.

"I undressed, threw my clothes on the floor, and slipped the dress on. I walked over to the mirror and admired the craftsmanship. The picture was incomplete, though. So I walked back and slid my feet into the white high heels. I heard my father's patent shoes on the marble staircase leading to the landing in front of their bedroom. I threw off the shoes, but didn't have time to take off the dress.

"He saw me and grabbed my arm, slapped me across the face, removed the dress so aggressively I was only scared that he would rip it. 'Men don't wear dresses,' he said, so close I could feel the spit on my lip. He threw me out of the room. Literally, threw me. Two days later he signed me up for hockey."

Rory's fingers started to tap in anxiety. A shiver ran up his spine as his mother's voice rang, telling Rory his friend was going straight to hell.

"Are you…" he started, but Bash ignored him and continued on.

"It wasn't that I wanted to wear the dress. It was that I wanted to see the dress, admire it like it was supposed to be admired, draped across a body, any body, and mine was closest. And you should've seen it… It was a thing to be appreciated."

"Oh," Rory said, moving his arms under his legs to stop the involuntary tapping of his fingers.

"I've got one last one for you," Bash said.

"Okay," Rory said, wishing Bash would just be honest with him. He was done with the stories; he needed Bash to tell him straight what was going on, but he could tell this was the way Bash needed to do it.

"I played hockey from the day my dad signed me up until last year, which I'm sure you already know. When I was fifteen, we had a player transfer to our boarding school and join our team. His name isn't important because this is my story, not his, but I'm sure you could find it if you try hard enough."

Rory didn't care to look for the name. He was focused on the uncommon sadness that overtook Bash and the way he avoided Rory's gaze with this last story. *This must be the important one.*

We found:

-- --

Impor—

Oh, just shut up already.

"He was perfect. He was sweet, attractive, an incredible hockey player, and we could talk for hours. The details don't matter. But I fell in love with him."

Nora's voice pierced through Rory's skull.

Sinner! Hell-bound! Ungodly!

"He didn't love me back. Or at least, I didn't think he did. I never told him I loved him, but he made me realize I was never going to be the man my father wanted. I would never be the face he showed to the world as the heir to Pelletier Lobster."

Repent! Repent! Repent!

"And I couldn't tell anyone. Our brood, my dad, wouldn't accept me."

You don't deserve acceptance!

Stop! Rory pushed back at Nora's voice, crushing it as he saw the pain in Bash's face.

We found:

Images of stop signs

Stop—definition

News: Corporate Council Stops Mandatory Voting Feature

Would you like to see more?

"Our brood spews their tolerance of other broods. *'It's okay if they're gay. Good for them,'* the broodmates would say. But not our brood. So I hid it. I became what I knew I wasn't. I slept with women. I spent my money. I treated people like they were peasants so they knew how powerful I was. I became who my dad expected and wanted me to be. To me, there was no other choice. Repress that shit, right?"

"But..." Rory started, hoping Bash would interrupt him because he honestly had no idea what to say next.

"And it wasn't some religious stuff like yours, which I can tell is what you're thinking because your face looks like I stepped in dog shit. No, it's just tradition... men are men and they like women. Women are women and they like men. And that's just how it is."

"So now what?" Rory asked, finally muting his mother's voice.

"Nothing."

"What do you mean?"

"I'm not as brave as you. I'm not willing to risk it all. I never was, and I don't think I ever will be. I'm not willing to lose everything: my family, my friends, my inheritance, Pelletier Lobster."

Rory's hands had lost all feeling. He pulled them out from beneath his legs and began to wiggle his fingers under the table.

"And that's why I'm grateful I got stuck with you as my roommate. I know you're figuring yourself out right now, but I've never said any of that to another person. Hell, I don't think I've ever even said it out loud to myself. I never realized how much I needed to convince myself it's okay being different from what others expect of me. You and I want different things. We trade one happiness for another. You the happiness of community for the happiness of self-actualization, me the happiness of love for the happiness of wealth and fame, figuring out and understanding which happiness is more important to us."

The doll store, Bash playing hockey, Bash's father. The stories ran on an endless loop in Rory's head. Bash in a dress. Bash with another man. The ideas still made him cringe. But *why* did they make him cringe? Years of conditioning had forced him to look at Bash with disgust, an irrational anger he couldn't substantiate.

But why did it matter? In the grandness of the world, why did it matter that Bash was different? Bash was one of the most genuine, accepting, and friendly people he had ever met. If people like Bash went to hell because of who they were born to be then he didn't want to spend eternity with the righteous pricks who would undoubtedly be in heaven condemning people like them.

If he would go to hell for choosing to show kindness and love to someone like Bash, then he'd charge the motorcycle himself and grab some heavy sunscreen on the way. He didn't want to believe in a God who would condemn him for loving his neighbor, the neighbor He Himself created.

"So," Rory said, "I guess we're two sides of the same coin. Some weird test groups in an identity experiment."

"I guess so," Bash said and laughed. "I wonder how long it'll take for us to figure out which strategy wins."

"I don't think you can win in an experiment," Rory said. "But who says we can't both win in our own different ways?"

"So how are you taking all this? I know this must be screwing with your brain right now. Are we still friends or am I tainted, the dirt you need to wipe off your shoe?"

Rory liked the way his stomach jumped when Bash said the word "friend."

"I think I figured out where Nora ends and where Rory begins."

It was no small feat to quiet the voices of his parents. Who knew how long it would take to destroy eighteen years' worth of conditioned ideals and to create his own. But Bash was good, and he was good for Rory. Bash wasn't his Moses, but he also wasn't the Egyptian army.

They were the same but in such different ways, walking side by side on the same footpath searching for their own creeks.

Bash was there when no one else was, not Samantha, not Finn, not Nora, not Maeve. He satisfied Rory's fundamental need for companionship, for friendship, and there was no way Rory was willing to sacrifice that. He couldn't imagine navigating this new life and the search for his own identity alone anymore.

He needed Bash, and Bash needed him too.

Rory stood up and held out his hand. "It's a pleasure to meet you, Mr. Desjardins."

Bash laughed. He got up and smacked Rory's hand.

CHAPTER XVI

2130

———

BASH

His fingers tapped the sides of his spiked coffee in agitation.

It's cold as shit, Bash thought as his legs trembled against the bleachers. The game should've ended, but they were in extra time. A few more minutes on the clock.

He'd gotten up three times to leave, pissed that Rory didn't seem to care. He never missed a single game. But Rory was a good player, and if he was honest with himself, he liked watching him play. It was really the only time he even saw his friend anymore, unless quick chats in passing in the kitchen or while they brushed their teeth counted.

Bash missed him.

The crisp October air woke him up more than his coffee, but he was still tired from the night before.

New! Photos of you!

- -

Oh, good. I miss the days when parental approvals existed. You turn thirteen and it's open season. No hiding anything anymore.

Without Rory around so much, especially during soccer season, he went out with his broodmates more than he should, and it was catching up with him. He could even convince them to come to the soccer games every once in a while, but now they were off either sleeping in or studying for midterms.

Reminder! Finance exam this week!
- -
Would you like to set an alarm?

The stands were empty, unusual for the height of the season but typical anytime exams were around the corner. Bash didn't have other bodies to shield him from the cold; students were scarce, and only parents watched the team play this morning. He moved closer to the team bench, hoping the breeze wouldn't catch him as much.

Current temperature is: partly cloudy and 48°F.
- -
The referee called the game, the University of Maryland losing by one. He stood and waved to Rory, who saluted him back. The lack of enthusiasm for his presence made his blood boil. Walking right up to the railing that overlooked the bench, Bash straightened his suit pants and brushed off his trench coat.

After congratulating the opponents, the team walked back to the bench, Rory seemingly avoiding his glance. His friend always walked alone; although a good player, not a true part of the team.

Does Rory have any friends on the team?

We found:

No

Photos of the University of Maryland
Soccer team

Article: University of Maryland
Entering Students Belong to Less, But
Bigger, Broods Compared to Prior Years

Brood—definition

Would you like to see more?

----

*Having no other friends, you'd think he'd be thrilled I
showed up.*

He grasped his coffee cup. His hands took on a life of their
own, taking the lid off and throwing the half-full cup directly
at Rory. A smirk creeped across his face as Rory, stunned,
threw his hands to his side and yelled, "What the hell?"

The rest of the team snickered, some players outright
laughing. Even the coach couldn't hide his amusement.

"Bash! What the hell, man?" Rory said approaching Bash
at the railing.

"Oh, now you see me."

"What are you talking about?"

"This is the most you've talked to me all season!"

"Hold on." Rory grabbed his stuff and motioned for Bash to
meet him by the exit. They walked in silence to the locker room.
Rory stripped off his clothes and walked into the showers.
Bash scanned the locker room, walked around, and knocked
Rory's clothes to the floor, taking their place on the bench.

He was acting childish, but his best friend was becoming more distant, spending less time with him, and he hated it. He had other friends, but all of them were in his brood, and they were friends with the persona he created. Rory, however, was friends with him, the him that he could be when no one else was around.

And… Rory's idealism excited him. Life was a little bland without him, his hopefulness providing the perfect dash of color. Rory gave him an outlet, a chance to be himself. But also, being friends with Rory was like watching a movie, wondering if the gutsy protagonist would prevail in the end.

At first, Bash definitely worried whether he could trust Rory. Maybe his news would make the poor boy's head explode. He was pleasantly surprised, though. It didn't take long for Rory to come to terms with what he heard, and it genuinely elated him that he wasn't treated any differently. Better, actually, after being honest. He'd made the right choice prodding him when they'd first met.

"Seriously?" Rory said walking out of the showers and noticing his clothes on the floor. Bash clasped his hands on his lap and grinned. Rory walked up to him, bent over toward the clothes, but then quickly slid him off the bench with a *thud*!

"Hey!" He stood up, rubbing his hip as Rory dropped his towel and threw on his clothes.

"What is your problem?"

"My problem? What is *your* problem?" They inched toward each other, and he poked Rory in the shoulder.

"You've got to be kidding me. I could destroy you," Rory said as he hovered over Bash.

"I'd like to see you try," Bash said taking off his trench, folding it in half, and gently placing it on the bench.

"We're not doing this. What is going on with you?"

"Nothing," he said as he put his hands in his pockets.

"You don't throw coffee at someone for no reason."

"Did you know I've never missed a home game?"

"Yeah," Rory said sheepishly.

"And where the fuck have you been?"

"Excuse me?"

He started to pace around the room. "I am always around for you. I come to every game, I wake up early to try and catch you before your crazy early classes, I invite you out, but you're never around! You barely acknowledge me when I'm here. I'm lucky if I get a grunt from you in the apartment. I swear I haven't seen you all season."

"You know I have two-a-days during season, plus games and scrimmages, and I'm a striker so I gotta stay in shape."

"I'm not an idiot. I know you're busy, but the past two years weren't nearly this bad. I at least felt like I had a friend."

"It's been… rough this year." Rory sat on the bench and rested his head in his hands.

He sat down next to Rory and lifted his arm wanting to place it on his shoulder but then changed his mind and dropped it in his lap.

"Everything… um… all right?"

"I'm screwed, and I don't know how to fix it."

Bash bit the side of his cheek, wondering whether he should listen, console him, or try and fix his problems.

Rory continued. "I got a job."

"And that's a bad thing?"

"Well, no, but yes."

"I need more to go on. Just tell me."

Rory sat up and sighed. "My stipend ran out. I'm fine on tuition, but I can't afford to live in the apartment or eat, so I got a job at Manny's after more groveling than I'm proud to share. Problem is, when I'm not at practice, I'm at work. So my money problem is solved, but now I have no time. I'm barely passing my classes." He tilted his head back and rolled his eyes. "And now, I have no chance in hell in getting the internship I need this summer."

"What? Why?"

"They found a new striker, an amazing recruit out of Ohio. So I've been spending even more time trying to make sure I don't get benched or replaced."

"The school will still cover your tuition even if they pull in someone better, though. Right?"

"It depends. It's all based on how many games I play or if I start. The percent covered goes down. Regardless, I haven't spent any time on my profile."

Bash quickly scanned Rory, content originating from Nora still overshadowing his time at UMD. "Yeah, I've been meaning to talk to you about that…"

"So I'm killing myself trying to stay here, either at practice or working so that I can afford to be here, and in the process, I'm screwing myself out of any chance to even do what I want to do. Without working on my profile at all I have no chance in hell in showing people who I actually am." Rory stood and rubbed his eyes in exhaustion.

"You don't need to work. I can cover the expenses," he said grabbing his friend's hand.

"I can't live off of you, Bash. It doesn't feel right."

He tried to cover Rory's expenses before, but he was stubborn and wouldn't take anything from him.

"We can fix this."

"I don't know if we can. I can't hide anything about my past, and I didn't do enough to try and change my profile.

There's just too much information. People see me, and they pry inside me. They tug, and they tear, and they uncover every little thing that's out there. There's no escaping it."

"Maybe it won't matter as much as you think."

"Growing up, my mom told me people from other broods were evil. We were literally bred to hate each other. If I can't show the world I've changed…. no, I didn't change. I've always been me, but what they see isn't. But if I can't make them see that, see past everything that's out there, I have no chance."

That was the world. The brood system did create unbreakable familial bonds, but it also bred hate, more hate than could be imaginable.

From the time they were kids, they were immediately taught to hate those who weren't like them, who weren't in their broods.

Hostility was the norm.

Maybe Rory was right. Maybe everything he was trying to do was for nothing. Why did it matter if he came to the university, if he worked to stay, if after leaving nothing that he did in his time would help him? If he left and was lost, alone, broodless, what then?

"Well, what if I took you with me?"

Rory stepped back inquisitively.

"To Pelletier… We've got plenty of people who work on the environment… sustainable fishing and catching practices… boat and emissions efficiency… stuff like that. I'm sure we can find you something."

Saving the planet was all that Rory wanted to do. Bash knew that being around nature was the only time Rory felt like himself, free from the shackles of the world, wanting to make sure every single person today and forever in the future would have that same chance. If he could help him to do it, he would try.

"You would do that for me?"

"Why not? You're smart. I know you. I got your back."

"But what about everyone else? Everyone who works for Pelletier is in your brood. Your dad—"

"I'll handle him. I'm the heir; there's really not much I can't do," he said, but he knew it wasn't true. There was a lot that was out of his hands. "And you're my best friend, I'm happy to be your fallback if you need it." If the worst came about and his brood wouldn't allow Rory to join Pelletier, which was a very probable option, at least he could provide for Rory, know that his friend was safe with at least one person who believed him. Who knows, maybe that would be enough for him.

For a moment, Rory's eyes lit up before he dropped them, falling back down onto the bench.

"What's wrong now? Shouldn't you be happy or, I don't know… thanking me?"

"I'm so sorry. Yes, thank you so much," Rory said, a hint of sadness lingering in his voice.

"You need to pick yourself up. It's going to be fine."

"I don't know what I'm doing anymore."

Bash leaned against a locker and crossed his arms. He was growing tired of Rory's self-pity. This was not a good color on him.

"I just wonder what it was all for. Was it worth it? I wanted to find my own identity, find a way to override my profile and show the world, join a brood more like the one I feel I would belong in. But I can't create enough content to ever be reassigned. And there aren't enough people, not even in your brood, who would give me a chance to help me reclassify.

And even if I ever did reclassify, I'd still be judged for all of my mom's old content. It's starting to feel hopeless. I wonder if I would've just been happier living a lie."

"But then you wouldn't have met me." He meant it. His life would be just as empty as it used to be without Rory.

"You're right," Rory said. "And I don't deserve you. I've been an awful friend. You are the only person who's ever taken a chance on me, and I haven't been there for you. I'm sorry."

"I'm sorry for dumping coffee on you."

"I deserved it."

"You should keep trying, though. I envy you for going out there and finding a way to be yourself. I almost regret not trying myself."

"Not enough to actually do it?"

"No, not that much. But maybe if you can do it, that'll give me the push I need to try." He doubted Rory's attempts would succeed, but he wanted to give his friend hope. Hope that it would get better for him, that he would happy, that he made the right choices. He didn't. But maybe?

"Thanks for letting me be the guinea pig."

"Well, you *have* been a terrible friend lately. It's the least you can do," he said with a smile.

CHAPTER XVII

2131

RORY

"We need to find a new place," Rory said to Bash as the door to Manny's closed behind him.

Bash laughed. "It's been four years. And you literally work there. I think it's a little late at this point to find a new spot."

"Manny has always looked at me weird, and I think he put something in my sub today because my stomach is not at all happy," Rory said, clutching his stomach.

The combination of cool afternoon air and walking fought the nausea back. Rory loved when it rained because the few hours afterward provided sanctuary from the overwhelming humidity.

"Oh yeah, if he was going to poison your eggplant sub, he would've done it already. I mean, if I was him and I hated you, I would've done it the first time you walked into my store, especially if you were alone."

Rory laughed, straightening up.

"No way. Then people would know it's him. Bitter man poisons member of a different brood. It would be obvious. No, he needed to play the slow game. Build up rapport. Feed me for years with no problem, get to know my best friend who eats with me every day, take me onto his own staff even. Then *bam*, I randomly drop dead and no one's the wiser."

"You've had too much time to think about this," Bash said and smacked him across the shoulders.

"Hey! Get your hands off of him!" a man yelled.

"Is he talking to me?" Bash asked.

"I don't know." Rory didn't see anyone else around them. Odd for a Friday afternoon after lunchtime.

A group of three men were walking directly toward them. They were large and wearing tank tops that showed off sleeves of tattoos, Corporate Council symbols if he was seeing correctly.

Rory quickly scanned them, focusing on the leader of the pack.

>>>>>>>>SCAN>>>>>>>>IN>>>>>>>>PROGRESS>>>>>>>>
- -
Name: Richard Bluman
- -
Nickname: Dick
- -
Born in: Celina, Ohio
- -
Most recently lived in: Celina, Ohio
- -
Occupation: unemployed, previously tile and floor installer
- -
Brood Name: Vigil Servant
- -
Photos:
- -

Nick at tailgate

Nick graduating local high school

Nick at Corporate Council rally

Nick drinking beer

Nick volunteering at hospice center

Rory's scan was interrupted by Bash saying, "Shit," and scooting behind Rory.

Brood name? He had been more accustomed to a color classification, not a brood name appearing in his scans.

But Bash was right to hide. The Vigil Servants were a brood similar to the one Rory came from but much more violent, and their crusade was to eliminate anyone they thought stood in the way of the CC's mission.

"Why you hiding?" said Dick.

They were like a flock of birds, a triangle with him leading the other two.

"I don't want any trouble," Bash said, stepping out a little from behind Rory.

"Yeah, well, you shouldn't have attacked this Servant. This country needs more people in broods like his. Broods that support the freedoms in this country and promote the CC values. Not scum like you who benefit from the CC but do nothing to fight and protect our way of life." The other two were silent, letting the one in the middle lead them forward.

"Guys, listen—" Rory started but Dick cut him off, lifting his arm.

"No, we got this. We take care of our own." The three approached, circling Bash and Rory. One of the silent men pushed Rory aside, staring directly at Bash with sharp eyes.

"No! Wait!" Rory yelled, trying to get back in the circle, back to Bash. He should've yelled something more helpful, but his brain wasn't working, the fear paralyzing him.

"Guys, fellas, you don't understand," Bash said and put his hands up by his face in a motion of submission. Bash had always been composed, but now his face was full of fear.

"We understand just fine. You think you're a tough guy because you're rich? You think you can pick on him because he's different? Huh? Is that what you think?" Dick now hovered over Bash, so close he could've kissed him, face fuming and fists clenched.

One of the others grabbed the back of Bash's neck, holding him in place, a smirk across the assailant's face. Dick pulled back his arm like an arrow in a bow and released it straight across Bash's face.

"No! Stop!" Rory ran toward them, but the final silent crony wrapped his arm around Rory's neck and pulled him back.

There was no one on the street. Where was everyone? They hadn't made it very far from Manny's, the restaurant just a block away.

"It's okay," he whispered to Rory, tightening his grip. "We've got this. He won't give you any more trouble."

Bash was in the fetal position with his arms wrapped around his head, trying to protect himself from the kicks and blows that kept coming.

"No! Please!" Rory said trying to get free. "You're going to kill him!" Tears flowed freely as he lashed out, completely ineffectively. It was like punching a brick wall, his captor completely unphased.

"Stop! Why do you care so much?" he asked and grabbed Rory's shoulders to stop the swinging.

"He's my friend! He wasn't doing anything wrong!"

The men attacking Bash stopped. Rory was released. Dick's face turned red, his mouth a straight line across his face.

Had he done it? Had he stopped the blows? He breathed a sigh of relief and closed his eyes when a fist flew across his face with a *crack*. He lost his balance, the trees around him now blurry as he fell onto the pavement, facing Bash, who was silent with eyes shut, barely breathing.

No, Rory thought, unsure of how to help his friend and utterly confused as to why he was now their target.

"What did you say?" Dick crouched down next to him and grabbed Rory's chin in his hand.

"He's my friend..." he whispered.

"How could you..." Dick said, pushing Rory's face into the pavement, seemingly angrier with him than with Bash. "How could you ever be friends with someone like him?" He uppercut Rory in the side. "Filthy." He spit in Rory's face and stood up.

Rory closed his eyes, waiting for a kick or another blow, but it never came.

He opened his eyes, and the men were gone, Bash still laying across from him, his breathing more shallow. The trees around him were still blurry and wouldn't stop moving. The nausea made everything sway around him, forcing him to close his eyes to help it subside.

"Bash, please..." he whispered as he tried to shimmy his body closer to his friend's, but with every movement a sharp pain shot across his side. "Ugh," he moaned and rolled onto his back.

Manny appeared above him with a bottle of water. "I called for help. Medics should be here soon. I'm sorry I couldn't help, but there was nothing I could do." He shrugged and moved over to Bash. He poured the water over his face, blotted it with a towel. His gentleness was surprising.

"Is he okay?" Rory asked, but Manny didn't respond, just kept blotting and wiping away the blood.

Sirens in the distance got louder and louder until the sound deafened him.

"Manny!" he coughed, but the sirens drowned him out. Footsteps all around him. It must've been two, maybe three medics.

"Stop fidgeting," Rory heard from above him. He hadn't realized he was. "I'm going to move you onto this stretcher. We don't know the damage, so try to hold as still as you can."

"Bash…" he said and tried to point at his friend.

"We've got him. You just worry about yourself," the medic said. Two other medics ran over to Bash and pushed Manny out of the way. They examined him and rolled him onto a stretcher, placing him into an emergency vehicle.

"Let me go with him," Rory said.

"You will. You think we have the budget for multiple vehicles?" the medic asked with a twinge of anger that seemed directed at him.

He was lifted into the air on a stretcher, and the medics slid him into the emergency vehicle, close enough to Bash that he touched his best friend's shoulder. His breathing continued to slow.

His profile put his only friend's life at risk. The identity he was given hurt the only person to have ever taken a chance on him. It was all his fault.

"I'm so sorry…" Rory whispered.

The drive to the hospital only took a few minutes. The boys were poked, their clothes shredded, then hooked up to some kind of machine. Rory had no idea how any of this equipment worked.

Please, oh please, let him be okay. I don't know if you're out there or if you can hear me or if you're even real, but please, please take care of him.

The emergency vehicle halted, and the medics jumped out, pulling the stretchers with them and carrying them like caskets through the hospital doors.

The hospital lights were blinding. Because of the hits to his face and from the brightness of the hospital lights, Rory couldn't manage to keep his eyes open; every time he tried, a spike of light burned his irises.

Plop.

They dropped him onto a bed, sliding the stretcher out from beneath him like a party trick where a table cloth is pulled out from below a fully set table.

He fluttered his eyes, getting them acquainted with the white aggressive hospital lights. The ceiling above him was white. He tried to sit up, but he couldn't. He was tied down. *When did they even do that?* To his right was an empty bed. To his left, his best friend was lying, his breathing a little less shallow, his eyes closed and face directly pointed toward the ceiling.

"Bash," he said, but there was no effort behind the word, only a whisper.

Bash didn't move.

The medics marched out of the room, and a line of doctors passed them.

Three doctors went straight to Bash while only one came to him.

"Doctor, is he okay?"

"I'm a physician's assistant, but we need to confirm the medics' analyses. Just relax and let me examine you."

"But Bash…"

"There's nothing you can do for him, just help me now and stay still." Rory looked back up at the ceiling. The PA pulled out his device and ran it across his body.

"You look worse than you are. Broken rib, sprained wrist, and broken orbital bone. Those won't be hard to set."

Rory inhaled sharply and looked back over at Bash. Two of the doctors had their devices pulled out, and one was running it across Bash's body and the other was typing.

"What are they doing?" Rory asked.

"The physician running his device across your friend's body is taking a fully composed picture of his insides."

"How does that work?" Rory asked the PA trying to distract himself from the pain of his best friend.

"Our devices are embedded with a software that allows us to see what is happening for much quicker diagnostic work. We can see your bones, ligaments, organs… pretty much everything. It gives us a full picture of what is happening with a patient so we can provide the best and most comprehensive care."

Bash whimpered.

Rory closed his eyes and asked, "What about that other guy typing?"

"The other physician is submitting the work that needs to be done." As though expecting Rory's next question, he continued. "His device is connected to the other doctor's. So if the scan shows a broken femur, the other doctor sees that and can automatically request the necessary care without having to interrupt the other doctor's scan."

"Can you show me what's wrong with him?" His body began to numb, the pain disappearing, his mind all-consumed with thoughts of Bash.

"Unfortunately, I'm not allowed to tell you what I see."

The other doctors rolled Bash away.

"Where are they taking him?"

His PA looked at his device. "Looks like he's going to rapid surgery. It shouldn't take too long."

"What about me?"

"What about you?"

"You said you need to set some stuff."

"Oh, I've already done that."

The PA held up a clear tube filled with an orange liquid that was connected to his arm. "This is... for lack of a better way to explain it... like a paralyzing agent. While it runs through your body, it completely paralyzes you so you don't feel anything. Then I took this machine," the PA wheeled a machine closer that looked like a claw with needles attached to each finger to Rory's face so he could see it, "and programmed it to 'Bone Repair.' Then it concocted the proper agent and injected that bone to set and repair. Kind of like extra strong glue."

"That's it?"

"That's it. There's only a little bit of the paralyzing agent left. I'm going to let it run for a few more minutes until the bone repair has completed, but then you're fine to walk, run, instigate more fights, whatever you want."

"What?"

"I saw it when I scanned you. Someone uploaded a video of the fight. Seems like your buddies weren't happy you were friends with the other guy."

"Oh good. Another thing I want people to know about me." He rolled his eyes.

He was frustrated he couldn't scan the doctors, the PAs, or the medics. It wasn't fair they could see him while he couldn't see him, so he asked, "Why do you guys wear masks? All of you? Even the medics?" Rory didn't know much about the medical profession, even though his father was a PA. But... he and his father never really talked anyway, so he wasn't surprised this was all new to him.

"A lot of us wore masks after all the recent pandemics. But there were quite a few who stopped wearing them because they found them a nuisance or simply wanted a different interaction with patients. But it became mandatory after the AIPs because once patients were able to scan us, many began to refuse treatment. Patients only wanted professionals from broods similar to theirs, and in all honesty, some broods just don't feed into the healthcare profession as much as others. And now, I can't explain to you how many people died because they refused care."

The PA rubbed his eyes and crossed his arms.

He continued, "Seriously, people thought professionals from other broods would purposefully hurt or poison them, would even kill them. It was insane. Thought they were better off just dying on their own terms rather than being 'murdered.'" The judgment became stronger with each word, seemingly pointed at him just like the medic's.

"So, the masks are just to keep patients from scanning you?"

"Now? Pretty much. We can't have any connections with patients anymore. The anonymity is necessary to protect patients, so they don't die waiting for someone who's just exactly like them to help them."

Face coverings were illegal outside of the hospital doors as a safety precaution. If interbrood violence happened, like what they went through today, it would be impossible to find their aggressors if they were hidden from being scanned.

But couldn't professionals also decide who to treat based on brood affiliation?

"But then, why don't we have to have masks? Can't you refuse to help me because of who I am?"

"No. We take an oath to help people. To help all people, regardless of who they are or what they believe. I think we're the only profession in the world that can't allow the brood system to get in the way. Plus, if we did ever refuse treatment, we'd be sentenced to life in labor for interbrood violence. Withholding lifesaving treatment to certain people is a form of violence... no different from taking this scalpel and running it across your wrists." The PA seemed to revel in the idea for a moment.

The thought and the PA's tone made Rory shiver, but it made sense. Was condemning someone to death any different than being the one to pull the trigger? He didn't think so.

The sound of wheels caused Rory to turn to the door. Bash was awake, sitting up, being wheeled back into the room.

"You are free to leave whenever you're ready. But you must be gone within two hours because we'll need your beds." The PA placed his device in the pocket of his white coat and walked out the door.

"Well, that was an adventure," Bash said and raised an eyebrow.

Rory wiggled his toes and began to sit up. He wasn't sore or in pain. He was shocked at how quickly he was able to go from agony to being able to go play a game of soccer.

"Bash, I'm so sorry. I just don't know what to say. This is all my fault."

"It's not your fault. Don't *beat* yourself up about it," Bash said and laughed.

"Come on, man."

"Hey, I got it worse than you, and if I can laugh about it then so can you." Bash crossed his arms.

"Listen, I just… I'm so sorry. You got beat up because you were with me. Because of who I am. I'm a danger to you."

"You didn't know those guys. They didn't know you or me. It's no one's fault but theirs."

"I don't even know why there were there. That brood never comes around here."

"Turns out there's some CC rally or something going on this week. We should've checked out the news before leaving the dorm. The empty streets should've warned us off. But it's okay. I'm okay. You're okay."

"I just think… maybe we should reconsider me moving in with you after school… You'll be busy working at the bank, making all those connections for Pelletier. Maybe it's better if I just disappear or something."

"Listen, Rory. You are my best friend. I am not going to let you go out into the world with monsters like them trying to 'protect you' when you don't even want to be protected. We will find something for you, a job that you like… a girl… something or someone." Bash was too good to him. He didn't deserve someone like Bash, someone who cared for him so much, even at his own expense.

"There's a video."

"There is?"

"Yeah, scan me. The PA says it comes up pretty early."

"Shit…"

"I know."

"There's no way my parents won't see this. They'll think you're trouble. That you're… putting a target on my back… on the company's back because of your brood affiliation… that there will be more people like them coming after people like us. Especially if this video goes viral. I'd already need to convince them to take you on solely because you're in a different brood, but if they think that me being around you will put me... or us... in danger..." He paused and looked away.

"You sure you're okay with me moving in after we graduate?"

Bash frowned. "Of course. I've got three years at the bank before I go back to Maine. That should be plenty of time for you to get on your feet after graduation, but I don't think I can be your fallback plan anymore. When I leave for Pelletier—"

"I completely understand."

"I mean, I want to be. I want to help... There's no way the board will approve you, which sucks so much more since you were attacked too. But I just know they'll say if it weren't for you, I wouldn't have been targeted." He cringed as he said the last sentence, as though he believed it himself.

Hearing him say it aloud broke his heart, but he couldn't expect Bash to give up anything for him. Hell, Bash couldn't even give up anything for his own happiness. But he was grateful he could still at least live with Bash for a few years while he figured out how to make his way, hopefully find a single employer to take a chance on him.

"I know. It's okay," Rory said.

"What? You look like you're holding back tears." He was. His one and only friendship was going to end one day. How could he possibly hold it together?

"This just means that our friendship has an expiration date. You can't take me to Pelletier and you're... only in DC for three years before then. I'm just not going to be ready to lose my best friend."

Bash's eyes began to water, and he put his face in his hands.

"But it's okay," Rory said. "We'll just make the next few years count. I'm just... going to miss you so much."

"Let's not… let's not think about that right now. We've got years until then, and we'll make sure you get the life of your dreams so you won't even miss me when I go."

Rory stood and walked over to his best friend. Bash moved over to make room on the bed.

"You know that I'm so grateful we randomly got stuck rooming together, right?" Rory asked.

Bash smiled back at him. "Yeah, you're pretty lucky."

Rory laughed and wrapped his arms around him.

"I'm pretty lucky too. But I'll definitely feel luckier once the paralyzing agent works its way out of my legs," Bash said and chuckled, leaning his head on Rory's shoulder.

CHAPTER XVIII

2131

DAVINA

"I think I'm ready for something else," Davina said to Leah as the two weeded the garden. She just recently turned fifteen, now spending more time supporting the colony and learning practical skills than in the classroom. Leah and Nora were great mentors, but she couldn't help but feel like her calling was in a different role.

"What do you mean?"

"I've learned a lot tending the garden and cooking with you, but I'd really like to help out with some of the younger kids," she said, clapping the dirt off her hands. "Besides Nora and Amos, I'm really the only other person born and raised here, and now that there are more and more families joining, I want to help guide the kids and teach them how to coexist with the jungle."

The colony had continued to grow, doubling in size since Davina's birth. Originally stumbling upon the colony as a means to escape, some new members now searched for the colony, excited when they found the little oasis. Jonathan's departure must have sparked rumors, a land without AIPs where people harmoniously lived, causing individuals and families to now seek it out. Like every society, members had their arguments, but in a place where every individual agreed to contribute to the growth of the community and each individual upon arrival, they were pretty quickly resolved.

No one had left the colony since Jonathan and his wife's departure. There was a handful of kids who had made the trek to the colony with their parents, and one additional baby had been born. With the arrival of new families was the arrival of new skills: teachers, seamstresses, bankers, a plumber, two doctors who were married to one another and parents of the beautiful new baby, and the list went on.

At the entrance to the colony, everyone left their old lives.

Davina may have had two parents, but dozens of family members raised her. Once she became old enough, she joined Leah and Nora in the garden and in the kitchen. She was probably qualified for other positions, but she liked the shared responsibility of the garden. If she made a mistake, the other two would be right there to fix it. She was never alone and appreciated working in a supporting role.

But she missed her time with the children. After gardening and cooking, she was too tired to play with them. There was one teacher, which was enough for the few children, but it put a strain on the only educator and also left a gap in the colony's needs if the teacher was ever to leave the colony in any way.

"I think that's a wonderful idea," Leah replied. "We can manage here, and I'm sure if we need help we'd be able to easily find it."

"I'm more than happy to help whenever you guys are in a bind, but I just miss getting to be around the little ones and in nature. I know their academic curriculum is pretty covered, which I'd also be happy to help with, but I want to teach them more like the stuff that Amos taught me. Take them out a little farther, show them the terrain, teach them how to protect themselves and to live on and off the land."

"I know Amos would really appreciate that. He's getting a little older, and it's been harder for him to keep up with the children like he did with you and Nora."

"Do you think he'd mentor me?"

Leah cocked her head.

"Teach me everything he knows. He's lived here his entire life and knows every single thing about the jungle."

"You'd have to ask him. We're almost done here. You're welcome to head over to the dwelling," Leah said with a smile.

She kissed Leah on the cheek and walked over, passing the seamstress making clothes for the baby and waving to a doctor patching up a child's knee. Hearing her parents mention their past lives, she couldn't imagine living in a place where people didn't support one another. Where someone was driven from their home, from their family, for who they loved. That her parents couldn't be together and were forced to flee broke her heart.

But that was all she knew. Her parents didn't reminisce on their history. They only focused on the new life they built together. That was the motto of the colony.

But it was hard for Davina to grasp what the rest of the world was like because no one ever talked about it. She struggled to understand the concepts of hate because she had never seen it and the concepts of loss because she had never experienced it.

She struggled to fully connect with some of the others because she had been born in a bubble, and although she appreciated her life and community more than anything, she wondered if it was a bit of a disservice to only feel the good things and be shielded from all the bad. How would her first taste of anything less than great feel?

And did Nora feel the same way? Did she also long to see what existed outside the colony but fear it deeply at the same time?

Davina wanted to ask her, to connect with her, because they were the same. Right? They both lived their entire lives in the colony, but the two were disconnected. It may have been the age—Nora was probably a decade older than her—or maybe it was just that their personalities were so different.

She admired Nora, her strength, her stoicism, her complete confidence in who she was and the work she did. Nora's personality seemed to take after Amos's. She would probably be the matriarch of the colony after Amos inevitably passed, her mother willingly passing off the responsibility, content with the roles of chef and agriculturalist.

But Davina only speculated. She didn't know Nora well enough to do anything but speculate.

Davina still felt like a child, unqualified to make decisions, skeptical of her ability to take responsibility for anyone or anything but herself. She was sweet and fun, and maybe with Amos's help she could channel that into being a teacher who could connect with the same kids with whom she used to play.

She tapped on the dwelling door and said, "Amos! It's Davina. Can I come in?"

His response met her through the window, "Of course."

He was laying on the floor, his fingers massaging his temples. No one, including Amos, knew how old he was, but the wrinkles defined him. He reached out his hands, and she pulled him up, his bones cracking with every movement.

"I wanted to ask you something," she said, sitting next to him.

"I figured as much." He smiled at her.

"Well, I am so grateful for everything you taught me growing up here, about which plants we can grow and eat, what feces belong to which animal, when to stand still and when to run." She laughed and poked him with her elbow. "And with all the new kids coming and growing, I want to help them the same way you helped me."

"I am happy to hand my torch to you. My hips can't keep up with these kids anymore."

"But... I don't know if I'm quite ready yet. You've had... well... many more years getting to learn this jungle than I have, and I was hoping that you could teach me. Maybe I could be an apprentice for a little while?"

"You're not confident in what you know?" He tilted his head to the side and smiled out of the corner of his mouth, as though testing not only her but her perception of his past lessons.

"It's not that... It's that I'm not confident I know everything I need to know."

He grabbed her hands. They were soft, not rough like she expected. Maybe the wrinkles were just from the sun. Maybe he was younger than any of them actually thought. "None of us know everything we need to know. We are learning every day, from the jungle, from each other."

"So... is that a no?"

"I am happy to have you as an apprentice, but your knowledge is not your problem."

"It's not?"

"No. It's your faith in yourself. And today, you will not believe me when I say you are ready. And, if in a few days or weeks or however long it takes for me to tell you that you are ready, what I need is for you yourself to believe it."

"Amos, I don't think I'll ever be able to fill your shoes."
She dropped his hands and turned back toward the window.

"It's okay. The seamstresses will put yarn in them for you
to make them snug." He laughed. She turned to him and
smiled back.

She wasn't sure what the joke meant, but he found it
funny, so she laughed along with him.

"When can we start?"

"Come with me," he said and led her into the jungle. "We
start with the sunset."

"The sunset?"

"Yes."

She had explored with Amos before, but they had never
come out this far. The path was anything but straight. It was
uphill, steep, and a bit treacherous as she stumbled over a
few vines. They walked until they were met with a clearing,
opening the cloud forest to them. She leaned over, caught her
breath, and looked up at Amos, unwavering. He didn't seem
tired in the slightest.

"Watch," Amos said, staring across the clearing.

The two stood in silence and watched the sunset. The
cloud forest merged together all the colors of purple, orange,
and pink in a hazy way. She had never seen the sunset so
clearly from their colony or Monteverde in general.

"Now, take me home."

"But I've never been here, and it's dark…" She was so
focused on keeping up with Amos that she barely paid attention to the route they took.

"Think, look, and listen."

She closed her eyes and took a breath. They had to go
downhill first and foremost. The direction of the sunset in
the colony was behind the large dining hall; she'd use moss

growth and the stars to lead her directionally. She stopped every so often to listen. The big cats came out at night, and they were all but silent.

She found her way, Amos slowly behind, providing no help except the repetition of that same phrase. Every day afterward, she met him in the morning, and they ended each day watching the sunset. Because no matter what or how much she learned, the most important thing he would impart on her was to slow down and watch the beauty of the earth before her.

Amos told her she was ready, every day. He reminded her that she knew enough and needed to trust her instincts, but for weeks she ended the day asking for another.

He was right. It wasn't about what she knew or how much she knew because even if he taught her everything he knew, she'd still have more to learn.

It was about her believing in herself, in her ability to continue to learn and to convey what she had already learned, to admit when she was wrong, and to correct others when she knew she was right. And it took Amos being wrong to show her that. Picking up a toxic plant and smelling it, handing it to her to eat, and turning away from her while she did so, she realized that anyone, even Amos, could mess up.

Whether he had just made a mistake when he handed her the wrong plant or pretended to make one to test her, it was the confidence she needed to know that she could trust herself.

She took that confidence, like a burning fire, and ensured to both never let it die out or fan too large to be controlled. With it, she took the hands of the children and walked them out to watch the sunset, her first lesson she received from Amos being the most important one.

CHAPTER XIX

2132

RORY

"Listen," Bash said to Rory as he put on his cap in front of the bathroom mirror in their two-bedroom apartment off-campus on graduation day. "I still want you to come live with me. I have a nice place in Logan Circle and a couple of weeks before I start at the bank, so we can move your stuff in, no problem."

"I have no way to pay rent. Manny barely paid me enough to eat every week, so I have nothing saved."

"You think I care about that? What are you going to do? Be homeless while going on hundreds of job interviews, praying that someone takes a chance on you?"

He has a point.

"And I know you'd rather be in the woods planting trees, but your best chance to find a job is DC, and it's way easier to do that when you don't need to worry about where you're going to sleep or what restaurant dumpster you're going to raid. So push your pride aside and come with me."

"Okay," Rory said. "Hey, can I ask you for something?"

"What?"

He knew what Bash's answer would be, but he had to try one last time. "If I don't get a job, are you sure you can't take me to Pelletier with you? I'm scared no one's going to give me a shot. When people scan me, I don't fit anywhere."

His profile had become inconsistent. He had so much data from his first eighteen years that it was impossible to dilute it. But he still tried, though not as hard as he probably should have. Now his brood would question everything about him. Why did he go to UMD? Why did he no longer post anything positive about the CC? Why did he completely change the moment he left home?

They wouldn't have him anymore.

And anyone else would question the inconsistency. Why did he change? Did he change? Posting was his mother's full-time job, but he had class, interviews, and soccer. He couldn't commit to it as much as she had.

They wouldn't accept him.

He didn't have an unwavering narrative that fit within one brood. And no one would care enough to ever find out why.

We found:
- -

Blog: Getting Along with Your Brood

News: Broods Continue to Claim Territory, Checkpoints Decrease Inter-Brood Violence

Study: Suicide Rates 100 Percent for Self-Proclaimed "Broodless"

Article: Be a Better Broodmate

"You know I can't do that," Bash said. "How's it going to look to my family, my board, and my brood if I bring you on? I know you, but they're not going to see everything I know when they scan you."

Rory sighed. He hated that he agreed, that their run-in with the Servants had ruined any chance of him finding a future at Pelletier Lobster.

"But hey, I'm sure you'll find something in the next few years."

Three years. That's how long Bash needed to work at the bank to get the experience, financing options, and CC connections his father wanted before he could join Pelletier Lobster, which meant that Rory had a deadline.

* * *

I probably just got the interview because they interview everyone. There's no way I'm a good candidate, Rory thought. With so few university graduates, every applicant was granted an interview for positions that required a degree.

As Rory sat in the lobby of the top environmental engineering firm in Washington, DC, the sun shone brightly through the floor-to-ceiling windows, providing light to the plants scattered around the room. The minimalist white walls gleamed, and a single painting of the Potomac distracted him from the otherwise empty waiting area. He tried to loosen the tie Bash had tied a little too tightly around his neck, but he only made it crooked. He was starting to sweat through Bash's sport coat.

"Mr. Walsh, Ms. Moulin will see you now," an administrative assistant said. She led the way to an office at the far end of the hallway, also completely encapsulated by windows. There wasn't a single light fixture in the entire office that he could see.

A woman in a red jacket with lipstick that matched perfectly sat behind a glass desk, hands clasped, staring directly at him.

"Good morning, Mr. Walsh," Ms. Moulin said coldly.

"Rory, please," he responded.

"That's inappropriate. Please take a seat, Mr. Walsh." She sat so still that if her lips hadn't moved, he would have been convinced she wasn't real.

"This is a lovely—"

"Let's get started. I don't anticipate this being a lengthy interview."

"Oh," Rory said, not at all surprised. He had heard a version of that same line in past interviews.

"After years of being in a brood that does not believe in the advancement of environmental protection and wholeheartedly continues to support the CC, which continually passes policies that hasten environmental degradation, why should we hire you?"

"The past four years and my experiences at UMD are more telling of my character than the prior eighteen. I am passionate about environmental protection—"

"So passionate that you graduated in the bottom half of your program, clearly spent more time playing soccer than studying, and did not volunteer with any environmental organizations. Am I at all mistaken, Mr. Walsh?"

"No, but I attended UMD on a soccer scholarship." He raised his voice, talking over her attempts at interruption again.

"I can see that, Mr. Walsh. Do you think I am unable to read a scan?"

"No, I was just trying to explain the reasoning behind my investment in soccer while at—" His words hastened, as he tried to give himself the opportunity to explain.

She raised her hand, motioning for him to stop speaking. "Tell me, Mr. Walsh, why is it that I should take a chance on hiring you, someone with complete inconsistencies in his record, years of supporting a council who did nothing to promote environmental sustainability, no participation in any activity that would show commitment to our values and mission, and who did not fully dedicate and apply himself at university?"

Rory had no answer and no energy left in him. He had fought in prior interviews, argued, yelled, but he was exhausted. If the lesser firms wouldn't give him a chance, he couldn't expect this one to. The competition was tougher, Ms. Moulin was much more stubborn than his prior interviewers, and he was ready to leave her office and never come back.

He had also never been able to find a way to convey that his mother had manipulated his profile, that he was just a child when he and his family visited CCHQ, that he had spent the past four years working to get into this office, to have this interview, that his attempts to change his identity to those who scanned him were futile because of how hard his mother worked to groom him for his brood. He couldn't expect anyone to understand.

The only thing he could say was, "Should I show myself out?"

"That would be best," Ms. Moulin said. "But let me give you some advice before you leave. Go back to your brood. Go back to your family and your people. You will not succeed here or in this industry."

Rory looked at her. "I have no brood," he said and left the office.

He tried to rip off his tie, but it only choked him further. He grabbed his hair and pulled, a few pieces disconnecting from his head. His fingers finally made their way to the knot. He clumsily loosened it, pulled the tie over his head, and shoved it in his pocket.

Unbelievable, he thought as he made his way to the metro. There was not a single soul in that city that belonged to a brood even similar to the one from which Rory had come. The brood he wished he could be a part of had commandeered the city, but members avoided him more than the last pandemic. As he walked onto a train car, people moved to another, looked away, or said in hushed tones, "Broods like his want all other broods to disappear," or similar phrases.

Rory avoided eye contact and stood in the back of the metro car until his stop at DuPont Circle, from where he would walk to the apartment at Logan Circle.

It took him two years to become immune to the judgment of passersby during his time at the University of Maryland, but today, after his seventeenth failed job interview in two months after graduating, he couldn't take the staring, the street crossing when he approached someone, the hiding of children behind parent legs so they wouldn't be able to scan him.

He got to the apartment, slammed the door behind him, and collapsed onto the couch with his arms covering his head.

Why does it matter if I know what I want, if I know who I am but I can't live it out? No one will give me the chance. If I can't get anyone else to see me, what good is it being me?

Laying on the couch with Bash's sport coat on the floor next to him, Rory appreciated what Bash had done, giving him a place to live, putting food on their table, but he was lost. Just like when he had told his parents he was leaving, he was killing the days and sucking up Bash's resources in the process.

He felt guilty.

Alone.

Wondered whether anyone would miss him if he ended it all. Maeve was loved; she had Mom, Dad, and him. All missing her after she left. He, though, had Bash now but would have no one in just a few years.

He could disappear off the face of the earth and no one would come looking for him.

Why not do it early and save Bash the extra bedroom and a few thousand dollars?

But he couldn't. His heart ached when he thought of Maeve, and the nightmares hadn't stopped.

Bash couldn't find him like that. He wouldn't forgive himself for shitting on all of Bash's help, even if it was temporary. He was grateful for it all, and it was selfish of him to ask for it to begin with. His entitlement of relying on Bash after the past few years was showing.

It would be hours before he got home from the bank. He got up and grabbed a bottle of gin from the liquor cabinet and poured himself a drink.

Different broods don't work, Nora's voice permeated him.

He poured himself another drink.

You would be making sure that we lost both of our children, Nora's voice haunted.

He poured himself another drink.

It seems like you made your decision.

He poured himself another drink.

Silence.

He had found the answer to silencing her: the bottom of a bottle of gin.

CHAPTER XX

2133

——

BASH

She looked at Bash from across the table... again. He wasn't even directly across from her. She had to crane her neck to meet his eyes, directly picking him out from the other seven people around that table.

She looked at him more than anyone else, and he couldn't read her expression. What did she want? An analyst, that's all he was, so she couldn't be looking for power. And the financials were right in front of her, not written across his face.

Her job as a Corporate Council business liaison brought her to the bank frequently, and even more so now that they were declared the financial powerhouse of the country. The CC was always looking for loans or investments in their new technologies, but the returns had gotten shoddier, making the bank less willing to invest.

It also meant she just worked harder for the CC to get what they wanted, which they inevitably would.

He packed up his stuff and started walking out the door to his office. "Bash." She was quick, still sitting when he passed the doorframe but now right behind him not ten steps later.

"Eleanor." They hadn't talked frequently, but the formalities disappeared quickly. That was natural. There was no rule of business etiquette or time passed or number of conversations had that dictated when the address changed, but at some point, he went from "Mr. Desjardins" to "Bash," and there was no rhyme or reason for it.

"What sounds good to you for dinner?" Her face was unsmiling, but gentle.

"Excuse me?" Had he zoned out during the meeting? He was ready to go home. Were they working through dinner?

"Well, you hadn't asked yet, so I figured I'd take the leap." She took a step closer to him.

"Ask what?"

"For a date." A smirk creeped across her lips.

"Is that allowed?"

"We don't work for the same people. I don't see why it would be a problem."

"What made you think I should ask? You were the one who kept looking at me."

"You're right, but you looked back."

She was clever. He liked that. He had no interest in her, but dinner couldn't hurt. Rory would be in the same place he left him, passed out on the couch, so he could use the company.

"Let me grab my jacket," he said, and they walked to a small Middle Eastern restaurant a block away.

They talked mostly about work. That's where their relationship had started, so it only made sense. He about his deal with his father and her about her start at the CC.

"It was a good job when I got it, but to be candid, I'm not being paid enough for my skills," she said straightly and shifted her weight to cross her legs under the table.

Her honesty invigorated him.

"How did you come to that conclusion?"

She placed her forearms on the table, clasping her expressive hands. "I see the deals I package for them. The caliber of clients I present. The public opinion in the business community that I narrate. They pay back to me less than 1 percent of everything I bring them."

Was it his net worth? Was that why she set her sights on him? He scanned her again. No ex-boyfriends, which was curious for an attractive woman in her mid-twenties in DC.

"Seems like you need a new job," he casually remarked.

"Or a new partnership," she said with a chuckle and straightened her back.

Partnership? Was she talking about him or Pelletier? Maybe both. Before tonight, he'd never noticed Eleanor, or anyone for that matter. He would never be able to have who he wanted, so he assumed he would be single—forever. But a partnership. That was an interesting proposal.

"The CC has been trying to *catch* Pelletier for quite some time now." She raised her eyebrow, clearly proud of her lobster pun. "But your father seems to evade what I would consider even the most generous proposals."

"So you want me to grease him up for you?"

"No, I have my sights set more long-term." She sat back and released her hands.

"On me."

"That's right."

"Are you speaking on behalf of Eleanor or the Corporate Council?"

"I'm not sure. I guess that depends on how well this date progresses." She took a sip of her drink.

"So now it's a date?"

"It always was." She was striking. Every response calculated. Her intelligence was unmatched, and he appreciated it. As a representative of the CC, she would get a commission of any future partnership with Pelletier, possibly even being able to leverage it for a salary bump. As Eleanor, though, she would be able to share in his net worth, not having to worry about whether she could splurge on a two-bedroom in Navy Yard.

But what would he get out of it? With just Eleanor, nothing. Or, not necessarily.

She was beautiful, had public experience, could hold her own, and was in his brood. Automatically, their lives were intertwined. The board would love her. His father would envy him. Pelletier Lobster Company would have a legacy.

As a representative of the CC, he would get favorable trading terms, low fees, exceptional reach. His father was a fool for not even taking a meeting. Pelletier was overpaying for its position, particularly for being a top-ten exporter.

He wanted her in both respects. She, Eleanor, would be a perfect personal partner, and she, a representative of the CC, would be a perfect business partner. No partnership would be more strategic for him.

But what type of partnership did she want?

There were some things he knew he would never be able to provide her. And he couldn't be honest with her about who he was. Would he be morally all right with lying to someone he would be so personally and professionally intertwined with?

He was getting ahead of himself.

They hadn't even gotten to dessert.

For all he knew, they'd show up at work the next day, and she'd pretend their date never even happened. He hoped not. He liked her. Unlike most people he'd met, she didn't bother him. She intellectually fueled him. He didn't know in what capacity he could truly be with her, but he could see himself living and reigning beside her.

She raised her old-fashioned and said, "To us."

He raised his and responded, "To you."

* * *

2134

"Bash, you can't live like this," Eleanor whispered as they ate dinner in the kitchen while Rory slept on the couch hugging a bottle of gin two-thirds empty.

"He's my best friend, Elle, and I told him he could stay here until I moved back to Portland."

"On the contingency that he looks for work, not drink through a pint of gin a day... one that you buy him, by the way. When's the last time he went on a job interview? Two years ago? That couch has a permanent imprint of his body on it."

He and Eleanor were inseparable. Their relationship was beautiful, but he didn't know how to describe it. They told the world they had been together for over a year, and that was true in the sense that every day in the past year was spent together. They intellectually sparred. She challenged him and never held back. They planned a life and future together. He enjoyed her company without question, and it seemed like she felt the same.

But their kisses were platonic. The bed they shared was like siblings rather than lovers, and she never complained.

To him, it was perfect. He felt guilty for even thinking it, but Eleanor had slowly come to take Rory's spot. Whether he was scared for the inevitable loss of his best friend or seeking to replace him with someone who could accompany him to Maine, or whether Rory's conscious disappearance created a void in him, Eleanor had provided exactly what he needed at that moment in his life.

"Yeah, I think it was like three months after we moved here," Bash said. "I don't know what happened. He just told me it didn't go well. That he had tried and given it his best shot, but that he just couldn't make it work. And I didn't know what to say after that. He just looks so small and helpless on that couch... I don't even get how that's possible since his appendages hang off both sides."

After his last interview, Rory became distant. They no longer talked, no longer spent time together, Rory just waking up and falling asleep in the exact same position with his new best friend constantly in his hand. Bash wanted to do *something,* anything he reasonably could, to take away Rory's pain, or at least help numb it.

"I don't even get why you're friends, Bash. He has nothing in common with you. What, did you just feel bad so you took in a stray who ran away from his brood?"

They had had this argument multiple times, each time Bash just saying they grew close when they roomed together at UMD freshman year. He didn't have the energy to fight her, worried that her constant prodding might tear down his walls and spoil their perfect alliance.

"I know this is hard to hear," Eleanor said, "but you're not helping him."

"Yes, I am. I'm giving him a place to live, food to eat, a friend to spend his days with so he's not so damn alone."

"A friend... Are you talking about yourself or the gin?"

"*Me,* Eleanor!"

Rory stirred, sat up, burped, and laid back down.

Bash put his head in his hands.

"Look at him," she said, reaching over and rubbing his back. "You need to cut him loose. You need to give him the chance to learn how to function on his own. You need to dry him out because this is killing him in so many ways."

"Can't I just wait out the last year? I promised him."

"This isn't going to be any easier a year from now. If anything, it'll be so much harder because you'll be leaving without a trace. At least while you're still here, you can check up on him, invite him over every once in a while, something to help transition him. You know?"

He couldn't disagree with her. He knew she was right, but it was too hard to admit.

"Can I be honest for a moment?"

"Of course," Eleanor replied, moving her hand from his back into his hands.

"I think that regardless of when he needs to leave, he's not going to make it."

"Oh, sure he will! He just needs to get back out there and interview again." But her face showed him that she couldn't even convince herself of what she had just said.

"That's not what I mean. I think this society, the AIPs, something, everything... it's going to kill him." Bash croaked out each word as his throat dried out.

"We won't let that happen. I know how important he is to you. I'll never know why, but I know he is." Eleanor wrapped her hands around his face.

He pushed her away. "How are we going to stop it? He has no one. He has nothing. I thought he had himself at one point, but it seems like he even lost that."

Eleanor sat back in her chair and tapped her fingers on the table. "We'll figure it out. We'll talk to people. Maybe we can set him up in a program of some sort," she said with a look of determination.

"Yeah, a program for homeless, broodless alcoholics. That totally seems like that exists." Bash pushed his chair back and grabbed the plates off the table.

No results found.

- -

"Bash, I know this is hard on you, and I know if we don't figure this out for him, you won't have a clear head to run Pelletier." Her voice had shifted tone from concern to rebuke. "I don't mean to sound insensitive because I know he's your best friend, but we can't let him ruin your future. It's in our best interest to get him some help, to get him set up, for you to know he's okay. Your dad hasn't had the best track record the past year, and you know how tough it's going to be to ramp up Pelletier to get it back in the top ten."

"You're right, but I don't know how to do that. He's in my head."

"We're partners in this. My future at Pelletier, at the CC, as your probable future life partner is wrapped up in you. I'm just as invested as you are in making sure that he's going to make it." Under her breath she continued, "And that he's just out of our lives and doesn't screw up these next steps for us."

He may not have agreed with her motivations, but he appreciated her help. She was set on making sure their future wouldn't be upset, and if that meant creating opportunity for Rory, no one would be more successful at the job than she. When Eleanor put her mind to something, nothing and no one would stand in her way.

"Listen, just for the next few weeks, we'll ask around, talk to our broodmates, maybe see if there's anything that can save him, give him new life or something," she said to his back as he started loading the dishwasher. "Should we tell him? Maybe the prospect of this would give him the hope he needs to get off the couch and do something, help us…"

"No, I know Rory. If we don't find something, it'll kill him faster than the gin."

"Okay, boots to the ground. Let's see what we can find."

And that's what they did while Rory withered away on the couch.

* * *

Eleanor worked harder on figuring something out for Rory than she did at her CC job. Her constant updates and minutes of the day put his own effort to shame.

Bash started buying gin every other day. After Eleanor and his conversation, he talked to his broodmates at the bank, asking what they would do or if they had any ideas or suggestions.

"I'd cut him loose, man," one of them would say.

"Don't bother yourself with that."

"He's not in your brood? What are you doing?"

One week passed.

"It's useless," he told Eleanor. "I feel like I'm running around in circles asking the same people the same questions."

"We can't give up. We'll find something." Each day with no progress diminished his energy, but it only seemed to fuel Eleanor's. She was more motivated and working harder with each dead end. He was ready to quit, over and over, but her ambition provided enough gas for the two of them.

Bash started buying a pint every third day, weaning his best friend from the gin like a baby off the breast.

Two weeks passed.

"I'm losing steam here, Elle."

"I know, I know."

Three weeks passed.

"Bash! Bash, Bash, Bash!" Eleanor ran into the apartment, grabbed Bash's shoulders, and gave him a huge kiss. "Ah!" she shrieked and kissed each of his cheeks.

"What is it? What's happening?"

"Okay, so, it's just a lead… a single, tiny theory, but it's something."

"Tell me," Bash said.

"No," Rory moaned from the couch and wrapped his arms around his head.

Eleanor grabbed Bash's hands and led him to the kitchen.

"So I was leaving CC liaison offices when a businessman from Peru walked in. He was talking to a colleague of mine when he said something like, 'Do you ever wonder why they've never been able to get more than a 99 percent global AIP injection rate?' Have you ever thought about that?"

He hadn't thought about it. He now wondered if it was an accessibility problem. Were there people on the planet who weren't able to get injected? Was the CC not as successful at providing AIPs as they portrayed?

Eleanor continued, "Because honestly, I haven't. But he made a good point, so I walked over and said, 'That's so interesting! Have you thought about it?' And he goes, 'Yes, I think about it quite often.' So then I say, 'Come up with anything?' and he goes, 'Well, stick with me, but what if there are people or groups of people out there that, like, don't want the AIP?'"

No way, Bash thought. Why wouldn't someone want the AIP? The AIP was incredible. It provided all the information available in the entire world in response to a single, simple thought.

She sped up as her excitement grew. "At that point, my colleague goes, 'No way. Everyone would get the AIP if they could.' And then the businessman goes, 'But would they? There's no way there are still people in our world who can't be reached *if they want to be reached.*' And Bash! You know what? I think he's right!" Eleanor placed her hand under her chest to catch her breath.

"Elle, what are you saying? Are there people out there *choosing* to live without AIPs?"

No results found.
- -

"Well, so, it's just a theory. But yes. What if, like how we have broods, there are people out there in their own non- or anti-AIP brood? I mean, the businessman makes a point; that 99 percent number has been stagnant for *years.*"

"Okay, even *if* you're right and there are some weird barbarians choosing to live in broods without AIPs, and that is a *huge* if, how the hell would we go about even finding them if they don't want to be found?"

No results found.
- -

Bash continued, "I keep trying to search for something, anything, on my AIP, but there's nothing. Someone would've shared something about this. Right?"

"I thought about that," Elle said. "But you know, that's the weird part. There's *nothing*. No legends, no blogs, no online rumors. Nothing. You'd think that if they didn't exist there would still be something like mermaid lore or whatever."

"Okay. I see where you're going, but the CC doesn't regulate anything on the AIPs. I could post anything, even trying to overthrow them, and it would be up there forever for anyone to find."

She handed him her device. *Posting temporarily unavailable*, it read.

"That happens every once in a while. Maybe you're just overloaded, too much activity."

Eleanor smiled.

"What?"

"I ran with my theory. The conversation you and I are having right now, I had with myself already. So I posted a blog post saying there were people somewhere like this. Within one minute of posting, it disappeared. Completely. Without a trace. So I tried again. But this time I got an error saying, 'Posting unavailable.' And then my account got temporarily suspended. It's been suspended for, like, an hour. I think they're waiting until my thought algorithm stops taking me there, and then they'll unsuspend me or something."

"What?" Bash ran his fingers through his hair, pacing around the kitchen. "But why? What's the point? Why does it matter that no one knows about this?"

"Think about it. Really think about it. People... without AIPs... willingly..."

"I'm sorry, I'm not registering," Bash said. "We technically all have a choice whether or not we get them."

"But do we? Like, they say we do, but we've been so conditioned that it's really only a choice in name itself. Have you ever heard of anyone in our society refusing one since their rollout? The CC makes so much money for every AIP injected in the world. Advertising money, consumerism, materialism constantly in our heads, constantly behind our eyes screaming, *'Buy this! Get that! Go here!'* If people stopped getting AIPs, the CC would have nothing to prop up their empire. They can't afford for anyone to know about… what are you calling them? Barbarians?"

"This is incredible. You are incredible," Bash said, completely in awe.

"But I told you, it's just a small lead, a tiny theory. But it's something. I have a really good feeling about this. I think I'm onto something. I think this is the answer for Rory. I don't know how or when, but I'm going to figure this out. So now the question is, do we tell him yet?"

"Not yet. Like you said, it's a theory. I have full faith in you to figure it out, but I can't risk destroying him over a rumor."

"I understand that," she said without a beat, shaking her head after peeking over at Rory.

"I know you don't get why Rory is so important to me, but I'm so grateful for all of your help." He looked over at Rory and smiled, the first twinge of hope he felt for his friend since seeing him melt into the couch with his gin.

"Of course. I'm really excited that I actually found something… or, I mean.. *thought* something, I guess. I don't know, but I'm going to keep digging." Her eyes sparkled, not fading the entire time she spoke.

"Have I told you recently that I love you? That I truly love you?" And Bash meant it. Not a romantic love, but a love stronger than he had ever felt for anyone.

"I know," Elle said. She put her hands on his cheeks and gave him a kiss on the forehead, as though she understood exactly what he meant.

CHAPTER XXI

2135

BASH

"We're cutting it so close," Bash said to Elle as he packed up another box in their bedroom. He grabbed a marker and wrote *Extra sheets.* They were two months away from picking up their life in Logan Circle and moving across the Northeast to Maine.

"I know. But I wanted to make sure that I had absolutely everything. You know this is going to be impossible for him, so I want to give him as much as I can find," Elle responded, taking the marker and writing *Blouses* on her box.

Eleanor had spent months chasing leads, talking to individuals, keeping her ears perked for rumors. Barbarians lived in what were called "colonies." From her research, which was all orally relayed to her and could be nothing but story, there were four established colonies around the world, the closest being somewhere in Central America.

There were possibly unofficial colonies that hadn't made it to her ears, Bash thought, but these would be even more impossible to find.

"You're right," Bash said, mostly to himself. "I'm just scared for him. What if he doesn't go for it? What if he starts drinking again?"

"I know you're scared." Elle turned away and stacked the boxes in the corner of the room.

Rory had sobered. Most of his day was still spent on the couch, but Bash motivated him to channel his addictive energy into exercise. Although they didn't tell Rory about their plans or their theory because they didn't want to get his hopes up, they wanted to prepare Rory emotionally and physically, in case something came of their research.

"I know I always ask this," he told Eleanor, lowering his voice, "but what if they don't exist? What if the people you talked to are like the people who believe that… I don't know… like we never went to the moon or something?"

"I know. I'm scared of that too. But what's worse? That he dies alone, scared, hopeless, cold, hungry, in a city full of people who hate him, or that he spends the rest of his life searching, probably still alone, cold, scared, and hungry but at least full of hope that the people he may one day meet give him the chance to truly show himself?"

"But what if they end up hating that person?" Bash asked.

"They won't," Elle said, but she didn't convince him, almost like she actually said, *That's his problem.*

"Are you ready?" He sighed and took her hand.

"As ready as I think I'll ever be." Her voice was excited, not fearful like the way he felt.

"Hey, Rory," Bash said. "Can you come into the kitchen? There's something we need to tell you."

"What? I still have two more months!" Rory pushed himself to a sitting position, eyes wide.

"It's not that," Eleanor said. "There's something we need you to know."

Rory joined them at the kitchen table. He had cleaned up and shaved, and his athletic build was visible again.

"You hate it here," Bash said. It wasn't a question.

Rory lifted his head up and then dropped it, clasping his hands in his lap.

"What if I told you it didn't have to be like this?" Bash said.

"Sure," Rory responded, not looking up, twiddling his thumbs.

Bash took a deep breath.

Eleanor placed her hand on his shoulder, squeezed, and said, "Rory, I've been doing a lot of research the past few months."

Rory looked up at her. He and Eleanor hadn't spent any time together; she had only seen him sprawled across the couch. His brow furrowed, probably surprised that she took over since the two of them never spoke, his confused expression not a shock to Bash. "What kind of research?"

"I'm about to tell you something. Something... a little bit crazy. Okay, a lot crazy. But I need you not to interrupt me. I need you to listen, to chew and swallow every single word. Okay?"

Rory looked at Bash, and Bash smiled at his friend, hoping to convince him to listen to Eleanor. "Okay," Rory replied hesitantly.

"Close to the past decade or so, the AIP injection rate has been stagnant at 99 percent. It has not wavered. I have spent the past half of a year trying to understand where that other 1 percent is. That other 1 percent is scattered in what I think to be four broods—er, I'm sorry, they're called colonies—around the world. These colonies are groups of like-minded individuals who live together in harmony and refuse to be injected with the AIP."

Rory's lips parted and he breathed out audibly. He looked at Bash again, putting his arms on the table and leaning forward.

Eleanor continued. "This is pretty much all I've been able to deduce about the composition of the colonies themselves. There is one colony in Eastern Africa, somewhere within the territories of Kenya, Ethiopia, or Tanzania. There is one colony in Siberia, somewhere between the East Siberian Sea, the Bering Sea, and the Sea of Okhotsk. I think that one is the biggest.

"The third colony has been the most elusive. I've heard stories that it either exists in the territories of Georgia or Armenia. I've heard almost as many people say that there are no colonies in Georgia or Armenia and that the colony I am speaking of is somewhere in the Hindu Kush Mountain Range, maybe on the Pakistani side, maybe on the side of Afghanistan.

"However, the last colony resides much closer, somewhere in between Costa Rica and Panama. I know this is still a vast amount of territory to search, but it's much smaller than that of the other three colonies. Do you have any questions so far?" As Eleanor spoke, Rory seemed to grow and get taller, the color back in his face.

"How did you find this out?" Rory asked. "How have these people been able to stay hidden? How do I find them?" He stopped for a moment, his eyes no longer focused on them. "There's nothing on my AIP about this. How do I get there? Can they remove my AIP? Do they accept outsiders? Do they accept people with AIPs?"

"Hold on," Eleanor said. "That's a lot of questions. We know there is nothing on the AIP about these colonies.

We believe this is possibly the only thing being regulated by the CC. It is in their best interest that these colonies are never discovered, that individuals do not adopt the values of the colonies and start refusing the AIP. The AIP is how the CC is able to be so powerful. I forgot your other questions," Eleanor said and looked at Bash out of the corner of her eyes.

The light returned to Rory's eyes. Bash couldn't remember the last time he had seen his friend so hopeful. The past few years had been full of ebbs and flows for him. He had loved having Rory live with him, his only true friend, even if he had spent much of that time in pain, different than their first four years together. The only person to know his darkest spaces. It was a war between deep sadness for his friend's suffering and satisfaction for being significant and needed.

He liked taking care of Rory, blotting the sweat from his forehead, cooking him meals, and holding his hand when he would cry in his sleep. But Rory wouldn't need him anymore, and that was a beautiful yet depressing thought. Like a child leaving home, his best friend would find his own way making new memories, but would be leaving him behind.

He never imagined sending his best friend into the unknown would be the only way to save him. He considered, many times over, to take Rory with him. He would be in charge, and he could possibly protect Rory—well, probably not, but even if he could, that wouldn't give him the fulfillment he needed. His friend would be continuously judged, mistrusted, and mostly alone. Bash saw how the job affected his father; it would be demanding, taking all of his time and energy, and he wouldn't be able to be with Rory in the way that was needed.

This was the only way his friend could seize the life he so wanted.

"So how did you find out about this?" Rory asked, looking from Bash to Eleanor and back again.

"It all started with a rumor that a Peruvian businessman told me," Eleanor said. "But then, I dug deeper. I talked to people. I investigated, and eventually I found enough people telling me the same stories, from different broods even, that I felt like it had to have some semblance of truth."

"How did you get these people to talk to you?" His voice pointed, jealous almost.

"Elle has a pretty powerful position in the liaison's office," Bash said. "She has access to individuals across the world in various business communities. They all want to stay in the good graces of the CC, so it wasn't challenging to convince them to speak with her."

Rory seemed to consider what the two had told him and asked, "Is it possible they accept outsiders, or is it like a brood I have to be born and bred into?"

"Quite honestly, I don't know that," Eleanor said. "But then again, if they don't have AIPs or know anything about you, I guess... how would they know you're so different from them?"

Rory smiled at the thought. "Do you think they could remove my AIP?"

"I don't think anyone but the CC has access to that technology," Bash replied. "But even if they can't get yours out, that shouldn't matter, right? Because you don't want them to scan you, not the other way around."

Rory nodded. "How have they been able to hide?"

"Well, I have a theory that the CC may know where they are," Eleanor said. "It's just that we don't. That they're doing a really, really good job to make sure we don't. I've been scanning and searching for ways to get to where the colonies are rumored to be. There are none. There are no planes that fly into any of these territories. There are no ports for boats to arrive at. Even when I search directions for cars or by foot, they are completely unavailable."

Rory rested his arms on the table and his head on his arms in a sign of resignation.

"If there was a way to get to these colonies, would you take it?" Bash asked, reaching across the table and placing his hand on Rory's head.

He looked up. "Of course. Without any hesitation."

"There is a way," Eleanor said, "but it's not going to be easy. In fact, it's going to be the hardest journey you will ever take, mentally, emotionally, but most of all physically."

Rory sat back in his chair and bit his cheek. He looked at his legs. "That's why you've been so intent on me exercising every single day."

"Yes. Believe me, I wanted to tell you, but I needed to make sure this was more than just... a theory."

Rory stood and walked to Bash. He looked away, bracing for impact for manipulating his friend, but it didn't come.

Rory embraced him. "Thank you," he said, not letting go.

Bash turned into the hug, his shoulder becoming damp.

"You should wait to thank me until you hear the rest of what Eleanor has to say."

Rory peeled away and went back to his chair and sat down.

Eleanor pulled out a piece of folded paper, a marker, and a compass.

"If you check your AIP, you will see there is a plane ticket in your name from Dulles International Airport to Port-au-Prince. There were no planes that would land further south than Mexico until Bogota. However, the border between Colombia and Panama is completely closed, and the closest port is Caracas, but boats will not take you west from that port. So, you have a boat that will take you from Port-au-Prince to Puerto Cabezas.

"From Puerto Cabezas to Managua, there is a train ticket in your name. A business colleague of mine will greet you at the train station in Managua and drive you as close to the Costa Rican border as she can—about five miles, give or take—from the old Migration Point in Peñas Blancas. She is unable to take you further. There are guards who protect that border. You should wait until nightfall, and then cross that border into Costa Rica.

"Now this," she said and passed Rory the piece of paper, "is a map of Costa Rica and Panama. I do not believe that the AIP will give you any directions or help once you have crossed that border. You need to work your way across and through both countries because we have no idea where that colony is located.

"Use the marker to cross out the places you have been so you do not forget. This is a compass. There are instructions on how to use it on the other side of your map. It was given to me by a friend who had saved it from an earlier time. It was her great-great-great grandfather's. Do you understand everything I have told you?"

Rory looked at her, almost through her, completely still.

"Did you hear what I told you?" Eleanor said.

Eyes, red still from his hug with Bash, flooded as he mouthed, *Yes.* His chest rose; his breathing sped up.

Bash bent down and wrapped his arms around his best friend, overwhelmingly happy Rory would be able to create the new life he so wanted and needed, yet devastated they were parting, probably never to see each other again.

They cried together.

Bash released him, put his hands on Rory's shoulders, and said, "You... you are my everything. You are my best friend. You are the only person in this entire world to have even known me, who will ever know me."

Rory responded, "I owe you everything. I owe you my entire life. You were the first... no, the only person to have ever given me a chance, to have really believed in me. To have given me the freedom and the space to create myself but not to force me to do it alone. And now, you've truly saved me for a second time."

"I'm sorry I couldn't have done more. I'm sorry that saving you means sending you away. I'm sorry that I don't have the strength to take you with me." Bash grabbed his heart and began gasping, heaving, unable to control the waterfall of tears.

"You have nothing to ever apologize for. You have given me more than anyone else in this world. You have given me more than I could have ever expected someone to give."

Wrapped around each other, they just sobbed. Sobbed for the beginning of their friendship. Sobbed for the end of their friendship.

CHAPTER XXII

2135

———

RORY

The airport was quiet. Only a few cars idled in the drop-off area, Eleanor waiting for Bash in one of them as he and Rory parted.

"Okay, are you sure you don't have any questions?" Bash asked.

"We've gone over it so many times, I've got it memorized," Rory responded.

Bash grabbed his shoulders and without blinking said, "Promise me that no matter who you meet or fall in love with that you'll never forget me."

Rory had judged Bash's role in his life too soon that one day at Manny's. He had saved him, saved his soul, saved his body, saved his mind. There was no question that Bash really was his Moses now sending him off to his own personal promised land.

"I could never forget you," Rory said, pulling him into a hug.

"I don't know how your device will work, but if you can, let me know, somehow, that you're safe, that you made it, something. Okay?"

"I will. I'll do everything I can."

"You better get going," Bash said, releasing him and smiling.

Rory smiled, turned around, and walked into the airport.

"Vaccine card," the officer behind the door said.

"Oh yeah, sorry." Rory grabbed his card out of his backpack and handed it to the officer. He examined it to make sure it was fully filled out.

They're a lot more thorough here, Rory thought as he waited for the officer to return the card.

"Have a safe flight," the officer said and handed it back.

"Thanks," Rory said.

Where's my terminal?

We found:

Your plane ticket

A map of Dulles International Airport

Food at Dulles

Directions to your terminal

Would you like to see more?

Rory hadn't realized that the AIP would provide him instructions on how to get to his specific terminal, since he had never used it to navigate within a particular building.

He used the directions feature attached to his plane ticket to tell him exactly where to turn, what escalators to use, and even what side of the airport to walk on to get to his terminal.

Once he passed through security, he realized he hadn't eaten in about three hours. He had his lunch box from Bash but wanted to save that for the plane—or for Port-au-Prince because he didn't actually know where his future meals would be coming from.

Rory had been so caught up in his goodbyes with Bash that he hadn't bothered to think through how he would sustain himself during the trip. He wrote off hunting with his father, but now he wasn't sure how he would be able to eat in Costa Rica. But then again, he had no rifle, no knife, no anything to even use to kill whatever he could find in the jungle. There was no way he would have been able to even bring something like that on the flight.

But even if he had the resources and knowledge, would he be able to morally eat his prey? The thought caused him to cringe. If he was desperate and starving, his moral superiority would probably wash away with the first jungle rainfall.

Maybe some berries or something, he thought trying to get rid of the pictures of dead animals his AIP kept providing.

We found:
- -

Edible plants of Central America

Reptiles of Central America

Birdlife of Central America

How to cook agoutis

Would you like to see more?
- -

The AIP was only supposed to provide feedback with purposeful thought, thought that specifically asked the AIP for help, but Rory never felt it worked that way. It always seemed to interrupt him, to provide him with feedback regardless of whether his thoughts were directed to the AIP or not. Was there something particularly wrong with his brain that caused the AIP not to be able to differentiate between purposeful or passive thought? Or maybe, in a way, all his thoughts were purposeful...

The smell of cinnamon hit his nostrils.

Mmmm, what is that and where is it coming from?

We found:

- -

Bakery

Bar

Steakhouse

Coffee

Would you like to see more?

- -

He let his AIP take him to the bakery where he bought two sandwiches, a cinnamon roll, and four bottles of water, not knowing where or when he'd able to replenish his stock. He used about a third of the money that Bash had given him for his trek on that transaction alone, but he hoped that it, along with his lunch box, would last him at least through the boat ride to Puerto Cabezas. Bash offered more, but he put up a fight to even take what he was given. His friend had done enough for him. He ate one of the sandwiches, drank some water, and put everything else in his backpack. He found a water station and refilled the bottle to take onto the plane with him.

Alert! flashed across his AIP as he put the cap back onto his water bottle.

```
Your flight is now boarding. Please
exit the bakery, turn right, and
walk approximately 55 meters to your
terminal.
```

He appreciated how helpful the AIP could be and how easy it was to connect actions between it and his device. Emails? Only notified on the device. Video calls? Notifications on device and AIP. Alarms? The flashing in his head always kept him from running late. It was harder to miss or ignore something popping up right in front of his eyes than in his pocket.

It felt selfish, but at moments like this, moments when the AIP could lead him to where he needed to go or scan some berries and tell him whether or not they were poisonous, he didn't want to lose it. The fear of being without it, the possibility that it could just disappear at a certain range, of feeling helpless, made him second guess whether he should keep heading to his terminal or leave the airport altogether.

He wanted the colonies to be real, the members to exist without AIPs, but he wanted his to stay. It was the only familiarity he would have in a completely new world.

But it was just a hypothesis. Bash didn't know what would happen to his AIP. No one would until he got there. It might work perfectly, without a glitch.

He walked with resolve and arrived to a line at his terminal. He pulled his vaccine card out of his pocket and slowly inched forward.

A man waiting in line behind him asked, "I don't get why we need these stupid physical cards. Can't they just find that information over the AIP?" to no one in particular, it seemed.

Rory looked around. He wasn't sure if the man was waiting on a response, but none was given so he turned around and said, "Medical information can't be shared for everyone to see. We have to give consent every time, which is why it can't come up in a scan."

He could tell the man scanned him because it took him a moment to respond, "I wasn't asking you."

"Sorry. I wasn't sure who you were asking, so I figured I'd help." He had learned from his father that medical information was still under strict laws and regulations.

Rory didn't wait for a response, made eye contact with the flight attendant at the stand, and walked onto the plane. About halfway down, he sat in his seat near the window.

"You're joking," he heard as the same man from the line walked up to his row. He sat next to Rory.

It was only a three-hour flight, and Rory was planning on sleeping the entire time to try and save his energy for the rest of his journey, so he paid no attention. But although his eyes were closed, he couldn't fall asleep.

The man next to him had no problem with that, though. Rory heard the shaking of a bottle *(Sleeping pills, maybe?)* and then snoring. He thought about asking Bash to get him some sleeping pills for the trip in case he couldn't settle his nerves enough to fall asleep, but he was worried he wouldn't wake up after taking them. Because his family was so against medication, even more so after Maeve's death, he never understood how taking it would impact the AIP. If the sleeping pills essentially affect the reflexes in his brain, would they somehow override the AIP? He truly had no idea. If alcohol could override his thoughts and drown out the AIP, could sleeping pills do the same thing?

We found:

```
Study: Brain-Altering Drugs and the AIP
Buy Sleeping Pills with One Click!
```

News: Scientists Continue to Study the
Impacts of Alcohol

Would you like to see more?

It had taken years, but his algorithm had updated. Back in high school, he may have seen blog posts talking about the conspiracy of sleeping pills or how medication would send him to hell, but now he saw news articles and studies. The feeling of realization gave him the same satisfaction as a win on the soccer pitch.

But as the plane took off, his contentment disappeared, replaced once again with paranoia.

What if the plane crashes? What if the boat sinks? What if the train runs off its tracks? What if I get attacked? What if I die? What if I'm kidnapped? What if the border guards shoot me? What if I survive but I never find the colony, stuck alone, lost in the jungles of Central America?

His mind bounced from one tragedy to the next, worried that a positive outcome was impossible.

Rory gripped the armrests as he realized he had no idea what he was doing. He was a kid, chasing a pipe dream of a place and a people that had no evidence of even existing. He trusted Eleanor and Bash and all the work and research they did, but he couldn't help wondering if a theory was all that it was.

Did that matter? Chasing hope had more meaning than living in emptiness.

Chasing... He was still chasing... He was on the run. Running toward something somewhere. And he really hadn't ever been anywhere before. He went from Pennsylvania to Maryland to DC. His entire life existed within a few hundred-mile radius.

He had never left the country. He had no idea what would happen, what it would be like, how he could prepare himself. And the question of whether or not his AIP would disappear continued to ring in the back of his mind, worried that by losing it he would lose a part of himself.

And where were his search results on that query? Why wouldn't the AIP tell him whether it would stand by him? Was that answer enough that it wouldn't?

He opened his eyes and stared out the window at the fluffy clouds. The sky was bright, the sun shining. For a moment the beauty distracted him, but that moment passed too quickly. The plane started descending, the emptiness of the sky interrupted by the ground below. Multicolored houses became bigger and bigger until they disappeared, revealing a stretch of concrete below them until *tap*, the plane gently landed and quickly decelerated to a stop.

The man next to him was still asleep as passengers stood and collected their belongings.

My worst nightmare.

Rory didn't know whether to try and wake the man up or to just crawl over him. Realizing that trying to crawl over him would probably wake him anyway, Rory nudged his neighbor, but he just flipped his head to the other side and kept on snoring.

I tried. Rory awkwardly crouched on his seat and holding his headrest straddled his way across. *Oh please, dear God, don't let him wake up now.*

He was deep asleep. Rory threw his other leg over and fell into the aisle. The rest of the passengers had already deplaned so there was no one to catch him—or more accurately, no one to watch and record his fall.

He popped up, grabbed his backpack and lunch box, and walked off the plane.

Rory whipped out his device. *Service update necessary due to out of range location. Please follow AIP directions to closest service center to update plan.*

The nearest service center wasn't in the airport. It was miles away. There was no way he could leave the airport and make his way to this service center to then come back and meet his contact. Not only did he not have the time, but he probably didn't have the money.

Well, that answers that, I guess.

Someone yelled behind him in a language he couldn't understand.

He walked to a trash can to toss his device. If he couldn't update it, he couldn't use it, so there was no point in just carrying it around.

The yelling hadn't stopped, but he assumed it was directed toward someone else until a woman ran up to him and grabbed his arm. "Ay! Vaccine card!"

"Oh, sorry." Rory grabbed the card out of his back pocket and handed it to the woman. She scanned it and threw it back at him, waving her arms in a way that he only assumed meant *ok now, you can go.*

"*Imbécile*," she said as he turned away.

I know what that one means.

His plane had landed a few minutes early. He wondered whether he should snack on the other sandwich he had purchased, but he wasn't hungry enough to tap into his supply yet. He could wait a few more hours until the hunger turned to nausea, and he really wanted to stretch how long his food would last.

Near the exit of the Port-Au-Prince airport was a bathroom next to a water station. He grabbed his bottle out of his bag and chugged the water. He wanted to make sure his bottle was always full, but he also wanted to keep hydrated.

After refilling his water and emptying his bladder, he left the airport, walked over to the airport park, and sat on the bench that Bash told him he needed to wait on for his contact.

"Rory," a woman's voice appeared behind him before he had even comfortably sat on the bench.

Rory jumped and turned toward the voice. The woman wore a mask that distorted her facial features. He had never seen anything like it before, wondering why she would need to hide herself from him... or from others.

"Uh... hi?"

"Come with me."

"Sorry, who are you?" He couldn't scan her because of the mask, surprised at how much it bothered him that he couldn't immediately know everything about her.

"I'm your contact. Eleanor informed me that I'm taking you to the docks."

"Okay." Rory grabbed his belongings and followed the woman. If someone had told him a few years ago that he would be blindly following a masked woman in a foreign country, he had no idea how he would respond with anything but laughter. But here he was.

She was a quick walker. Rory had to keep a consistent bounce in his step to keep up with her. They walked up to a small car, and the woman ushered Rory into the backseat, saying, "We'll be at the docks soon."

The car ride was silent. Rory couldn't understand how he wasn't even able to hear the other cars on the road near them. He tapped his thumbs, not knowing what to ask or say, worried that one of his paranoid thoughts was coming to fruition.

Too late to turn back now. He turned his head toward the window. The roads were lined with palm trees, the green in stark contrast to the light blue sky. The city was alive, there were people everywhere, walking, on two-wheelers, four-wheelers, in cars. *At least I get to see something like this before getting kidnapped or murdered or whatever.*

But the woman didn't lie. It did only take a few minutes to get to the docks. She brought the car to a screeching halt, ran around, and opened Rory's door. "Out. Your next contact will meet you here."

I guess I'm not dying just yet. He started to make his way out of the car.

"Okay, thank you," he said, trying to get a look at her but the mask still blocked his view.

She scurried back around the car, and before he had even shut the door behind him, she was back in the driver's seat and throwing the car into reverse.

"Dammit!" he yelled, jumping out of the car's way and falling onto the concrete. The docks were empty. As Rory sat where he fell, he quickly became aware that he had dressed for April DC weather and not Haiti weather. His back started to sweat where the backpack hit, and his sneakers began to tighten around his feet.

We found:

- -

88°F and 76 percent humidity in Port-Au-Prince

- -

It still works! There was a lag in the AIP's efficiency, results taking a few extra moments to appear and thoughts needing to be much more intentional, but he was excited he still generally had access to it.

An hour passed, and no one had appeared. Rory stood up and began to walk along the dock, worrying he was in the wrong location.

He reviewed the instructions Bash and Eleanor provided. A second hour passed. He reached into his bag and grabbed the other sandwich. He didn't notice a water filling station, but he needed something to chase the sandwich with so he took a swig.

It's so peaceful, he thought, wrapping his arms around his knees and watching the waves disappear under the dock. His AIP was silent.

Maybe this wouldn't be so bad. Even if there was no colony, he could see himself sitting out here forever, withering away in the sun and letting the waves wash him away.

Except he knew he couldn't. Not that he wouldn't be able to mentally take the solitude, but he had no way to fend for himself. He spent his entire life going to grocers and farmer's markets—not cultivating land and growing crops. He didn't know where to start.

How could I survive here? What do they even grow in Haiti?

We found:

- -

How to grow rice

Buy Plantains Here!

Farming, irrigation, and agriculture at
Haitian universities

Would you like to see more?
- -

The sun was beginning to set, causing Rory's eyes to get heavy. His back started to tense from sitting so long, and his legs cramped from his position on the floor. He extended his legs and laid back, placing his backpack under his head.

"Wow... I've never seen so many stars... are you supposed to count them to fall asleep or stay awake?" he asked himself.

He was in a foreign country, with a cinnamon roll, whatever Eleanor and Bash made him, and just two bottles of water left. His AIP lagged, and he had no device.

He tried to plan the possibility of heading to a hotel for the night, but with close to no money, not even knowing if the currency he had would be accepted, and with no understanding of the language, he had no idea how he could even get to a hotel. And what if his contact did come? Maybe he was just running really late. Would he miss his chance? Would the contact wait for him?

That would depend on how much Bash paid him, he thought and chuckled.

He wanted so badly to sleep but also shook with the thought of falling asleep alone, at night, and outside... especially in a strange place. But his worries exhausted him. As he counted his 284th star (or maybe it was 285), his eyes lost focus and closed on the Haitian night sky for just a moment.

"Hey, wake up."

Rory felt a sharp kick in his side. The star-illuminated black sky that Rory remembered had morphed into a blush pink.

"Let's go!" the person who kicked him said and hastily leaned over, grabbing Rory's arm to sit him up. Rory rubbed his eyes and stared into a young man's face.

"Sebastian Desjardins sent me. I'm taking you to Puerto Cabezas." The man grabbed Rory's bags and headed to a small fishing boat with Rory, half-awake, stumbling behind him.

CHAPTER XXIII

2135

___

RORY

"Why can't I scan you?" Rory analyzed the man's face. He thought about the weather, about Haiti, about Bash, about his parents. Something to trigger the AIP.

Nothing. No results.

"I dunno. I can scan you just fine." With one leg, he pushed the boat away from the dock.

There were AIPs all over Haiti... literally everywhere, for that matter. Why wasn't it working anymore? Did it have something to do with him tossing the device? Too far from his service location? For as much as Rory wanted the AIPs to disappear, he was lonely and naked without the constant pinging, longing for it to return.

Even more so, he had no idea who this man was. What if he was a murderer? A psychopath? What if he was going to take Rory out on the water and toss him overboard where he could never be found—not that anyone would look for him anyhow.

Rory's hands started sweating. Up until the day before, he had never been around someone he didn't know, someone he couldn't scan. The car ride was short, though. Now, he was stuck on some type of fishing vessel with a young, strong man whose name he didn't even know without the refuge of his AIP keeping him company or giving him a sense of security and safety.

"This is a pretty small boat to get us to Puerto Cabezas. Right?" Rory asked. He had no idea what to say or ask without having scanned him.

What was he allowed to ask? Was it considered rude to ask about him, his family, even his name? People didn't talk about these things anymore; it was just known. Rory couldn't foster conversation anymore. He didn't know what was off-limits or where to start. But the fisherman didn't seem phased, just kept preparing the boat to take them out to sea.

"So you're a nautical expert? Do you spend every day on the water for hours? Please enlighten me because that didn't come up in my scan," the fisherman responded.

Rory was taken aback by the hostility. Had the fisherman scanned him while he slept, hating him for what he saw? Was he simply frustrated that he needed to take the trip to Puerto Cabezas? Or, maybe, was this just his personality? Rory couldn't put it into context. He couldn't see anything about this man's history to answer the questions running through his mind.

"Sorry. Is there anywhere I should sit or go? Or is there something I should do or help with?" He shifted his weight from one leg to another, looking around the vessel.

"The sun's still pretty low, so you won't feel the heat as much for at least a few more hours. But if you get hot you can take that door," he pointed to the left of Rory, "into my quarters. You can sit wherever you want, but stay off my bed. If you wanna stay up here, just keep out of my way."

The fisherman had moved to the front of the boat, pressed some buttons, and the boat began to take off.

Is that the stern? No... starboard...

Rory was lost. He realized how little he truly knew, how much of a crutch the AIP had been, feeding him information that it seemed like his brain never truly retained because it didn't need to.

Is this how evolution works?

He wondered if the brain had evolved to adapt to the AIP. It was still being used, but more so to ask for something rather than to recall it. It had taken him years to modify his algorithms. How long would it take him to modify the way he used his brain to train it in a completely different way?

He walked to the opposite side of the boat and watched the island shrink. The trees and the docks were disappearing, overwhelmed by the water, and bluer and more mesmerizing than the Monet Bash purchased for Eleanor.

The boat glided across the water, barely making any ripples behind it, the water gently bubbling but only for a moment.

The boat itself was smaller than he imagined it would be, but deceptively large after walking across it. The front, where the fisherman lounged, met at a point, as though the boat wanted to cut through the water, splitting it and forcing it to part along the sides. There was a steering wheel and a host of buttons that the fisherman tinkered with and then walked away from, now relaxing on a stool and staring out at the sea in front of him.

The back was wider, flatter, sinking into the water far more than the front. In the center was the door that held the quarters.

Rory leaned his back against the boat, turning his attention from the water behind them to the fisherman.

He had to be younger than Rory, maybe even a teenager. His face still had a boyish charm to it, and his hair peeked out from under his tight hat. Rory couldn't help but notice the similarities between him and Bash. But the differences were much more stark. This man had seen work, his muscles defined through his torn and stained clothes, the soles of his boots beginning to peel.

I need to call him something... maybe River?

Rory rolled his eyes and shook his head. His lack of creativity was another aspect of himself that the AIP had shielded him from, but not knowing the man in front of him unsettled him. If he couldn't use his AIP to get to know him, he would at least create a persona to make himself more comfortable.

Is making something up really that different from seeing him across my AIP?

Rory's own profile wasn't reflective of him. Other people's assumptions of him were based on the narrative of someone else. Was looking at River and making assumptions based on his personality and physique really any worse?

He walked back to where River had dropped off his bags. He sat down and pulled out his lunch, but the second he opened it, rancidity smacked his nose. It must've been potent enough to reach River because he lifted his eyes toward Rory and crinkled his nose.

He didn't know what Bash and Eleanor gave him, but it must have spoiled in the hot sun. The cinnamon roll didn't look any better than the rest of his food smelled. He shoved the food into the lunch box and shut it.

"Are you hungry?" River asked.

He nodded.

"Bash told me to bring some food. Let me grab it." River walked into his quarters and came back out with a bag of food that he threw at Rory. "I set everything up and loaded the boat before I woke you."

That was nice of him.

"How long is it going to take to get there?" Rory asked looking through the bag of food. There was a fishy smelling rice dish, some warm sandwiches, what he assumed to be fruit though he had never seen anything like it before, and six bottles of water.

"This bugger is pretty fast. It should only take us a day and a half if the weather cooperates, but I'm going to stop in Kingston to top off my tank to be safe."

River must've noticed him rummaging through the bag because he said, "That's all for the boat and the train. Bash said the next contact in Managua should also be bringing you food, but maybe save some plantains just in case."

"What is this?" he said as he lifted the rice dish in the air and shook it so River could see.

"It's rice with rock lobster. That's what this boat is for."

"You... um... fish rock lobster?"

"I dive for it and catch it, yes. For the Pelletier Lobster Company."

"Oh! You work for Bash?"

"Technically I work for his dad, for now. But yeah." He smirked. "Your scan still not working?"

"No."

"That sucks."

River looked out at the water.

Rory opened the rice dish. He hadn't had fish since he was a kid and decided to become a vegetarian, and he had never had lobster before, but he didn't want to be rude. "Do you have a fork?"

"Oh yeah, let me grab one." He disappeared into his quarters.

This is going to be a long boat ride. Sitting in silence with this man would make the hours pass by slower. Rory wondered if he should just hide out in the quarters, but he was enjoying being on the deck and watching the gentle waves pass by.

River handed the fork to Rory and went back to his seat at the front of the boat, looking back out at the water.

Rory took another whiff of the rice dish. *Hmm, smells a little spicy.* He imagined the lobster being boiled alive and what sound a dying lobster made. He sighed, closing his eyes, and took a hesitant bite, swirling the food in his mouth before swallowing. "Whoa, this is really good!"

"Thanks. Family recipe," he said not breaking eye contact with the water.

Rory shoveled the rest of the rice dish into his mouth, instantly regretting how quickly he ate it, wishing he would've saved some for later in the trip. He placed the fork and empty bowl next to his bag and laid on his back, stretching his arms above his head.

"If you want to sleep, you're welcome to go to the quarters. I put out an extra mattress on the floor." It sounded as though River was trying to get rid of him.

"Oh, I can go into the quarters if I'm bothering you, but I was just stretching. The dish was just really good so I ate it a little too fast." Rory sat back up and crossed his legs to make himself as small as possible.

"I don't care. You're not in my way." He stood and grabbed some water. "So listen, how did you and Bash get connected? You guys are so... different. Or at least it seems like you're different. I've only ever talked to him one time, and that was when he told me I needed to transport you, but from what I've scanned of him and then you... I just don't get it."

Rory wasn't sure how honest he should be with River. He would never tell him any of Bash's secrets, but this could be one of the last people he would ever see. "Honestly, Bash saved me." He walked up to Rory and sat down next to him, his legs extended and his arms behind him, holding up his torso. "What do you mean he saved you?"

"Pretty much everything that you're seeing on your scan of me isn't real. It isn't me. And Bash saw through my profile and gave me the chance to be myself."

"Okay... this seems like a lot of baggage, and I don't know if I care enough." He leaned onto his elbows and stared up into the sky, seemingly unconvinced.

"My freshman year, Bash gave me a chance. No one else before him or since did. He's my best friend... my only friend."

"Okay."

He clearly doesn't care, but then why did he ask? Was he expecting some huge revelation?

"So, how long have you worked for Bash's family?"

"My entire life. My dad is his mom's brother."

That's why he reminded me of Bash...

"What? Why aren't you guys in Maine? How did you get to Haiti?"

"My dad always told me he was a screw up, but I never believed it. He was happy working for the family business, but he never wanted to run it. He wanted to travel, see the world. He likes being out on the water. I think he'd go insane sitting behind a desk, so when he heard that Pelletier Lobster was expanding its supply chain and needed more inventory, Dad volunteered to come down here and catch and provide rock lobster. Then he met my mom here, fell in love, and they had me, and now it's my job to catch the rock lobster. I catch some other things too."

Tuna, marlin, ya know. And then I sell it at the market for some extra cash."

"And you've only talked to Bash one time? He's your family…"

"Looks like you and your family aren't super close anymore, either." He looked at Rory while leaning on his elbow. "What's Bash really like? He seems like a rich prick from everything I've seen, but then he's helping someone like you."

"Bash is a really good guy. We lived together all four years at school, and he took care of me for close to three years after we graduated."

"Why'd he take care of you?"

"No one would hire me, and I was disowned by my brood when I went to school."

"No, sorry, why did he take care of you? Not why did he feel bad for you, but why did he actually help? I don't really care about your sob story is what I'm saying. People help other people when they get something out of it—money, in my case. Wouldn't even give you a second look if I wasn't getting paid to do it."

"What? I didn't pay Bash to help me."

"It doesn't have to be tangible. You filled some kind of need for him. Did you introduce him to a girl? Did he feel guilty about something he did to you and then needed to make it up to you? Did he need some deeper meaning in his life and take you on as a charity case? You see what I'm asking?"

"Yeah, I get it."

What was he insinuating? Couldn't Bash just want to help him or be friends with him because of companionship? Couldn't he just be so fun or such a good person that Bash just enjoyed spending time with him? Did this man really see him as so miserable of a person that he couldn't fathom someone like Bash just enjoying his presence?

River continued, "Sorry, I didn't mean to offend you. But you gotta admit that looking at the two of you, it doesn't make sense that you're friends. He parties on yachts and spends the family's money on alcohol and women. And you... go to church and play soccer..."

Rory shivered. It was too early for the sun to set, but dark clouds moved across the sky.

River followed Rory's gaze. "No..." he said and jumped up. "It's supposed to be clear for the next three days, I was going to be fine taking him and coming back," he mumbled to himself but loud enough for Rory to hear while walking into his quarters. "You should probably get inside the quarters. It looks like we're going to catch a mild storm. If you need them, there are some sleeping pills in the bathroom."

Rory started feeling a little queasy as the boat began to sway more, the sleeping pills enticing him. He was also starting to trust River more, convinced that he would be safe. Precedent also showed that he would be woken up, even if it was with a kick to the side.

"Okay. Thanks." He grabbed his stuff and made his way to the quarters.

Walking through the door, he came to an abrupt stop. Printouts of pictures of Bash hung on the walls, articles about Bash, an itinerary of a trip he took, even a map of Bash's whereabouts with his address circled in red marker. He walked around the small room, avoiding the bed and a floor mattress, squinting at all the information posted about Bash.

Why does he have these if he can scan Bash whenever he wants on his AIP? Unless these are particularly important...? Rory walked around the quarters, analyzing the printouts, like a how-to guide to find Bash and... become him?

None of this sat well with him. But what could he do? He was on the ocean, in a storm with this man, and no access to an AIP or device. What was this guy trying to do here?

He dropped his bag on the mattress on the floor. He opened one of the doors, and a line of suits stuffed in a small closet faced him. They were identical to the suits Bash wore in the photos. He shut the door and couldn't control his breathing. He wanted to forget everything he just saw, or maybe remember it and try to make sense of it. He had no idea. He opened the other door.

Oh good. He stepped into a small bathroom with a standing shower, a toilet, and a vanity. He relieved himself and washed his face. He grabbed the sleeping pills off the vanity and threw himself on the mattress on the floor.

The boat shook so violently it dizzied him. The nausea that subsided when he walked into the quarters, hiding his view of the water, came back in full force.

He didn't know the time, how long they had been on the water, or how far they were from Kingston or Puerto Cabezas.

"Take one only before a full seven or eight hours of sleep," he read and opened the bottle, reaching in and pulling out a single pill.

He wanted the nausea to subside and to forget about the suits, the pictures of Bash, the worry of the rest of the journey, the loss of his best friend.

He swallowed a pill, laid down, and shut his eyes.

* * *

The driveway to his parents' house appeared. He was ten years old in his soccer uniform.

The sky was dark, the sun being overtaken by the clouds. The air was salty. Rory puckered his lips when it hit him as he jumped out of his dad's truck. *That's not right.*

"Hold up, little man," his dad said, dropping the keys as he struggled to find the right one for the front door.

"But I really gotta go!" Rory said, shifting his weight back and forth and grabbing the sides of his soccer shorts.

"I know, I know," Finn said, finally turning the key and flinging the door open. "Don't forget to change and wash up! You're not eating dinner all grass-stained and sweaty!"

Rory walked to the bathroom but stopped short at Maeve's room. The door was closed. *That's not right.*

He placed his hand on the door, the door instantly turning into water, enveloping him for a moment, and running past him, down the stairs. Behind that door, Maeve's room was a jungle with monkeys swinging from tree to tree, snakes slithering across the dirt, grass, and fungus. A macaw flew directly toward him, forcing him to duck, losing his balance and falling onto all fours, causing him to drop his soccer bag. *That's. Not. Right!*

He looked a few feet in front of him where there was a hand, attached to an arm, attached to a body sprawled out on the jungle floor as though asleep, facing away from him.

"Maeve," he whispered and crawled toward the body. "Maeve," he said more confidently and touched the shoulder of the person laying in front of him.

No answer.

"Maeve!" he yelled, shaking the body and rolling it onto its back, making direct eye contact with his own open, glazed over eyes. *That's! Not! Right!*

He screamed, but no sound came from him. He tried to fall back, his body paralyzed. He shut his eyes, and when he opened them, he stared into the eyes of himself as a ten-year-old, on his butt and in a pool of his own urine. Behind his ten-year-old self, his father stood, arm around Bash, looking at the two Rorys on the floor, making no effort to help either one of them.

His father smiled at Bash, the type of son he probably wished he had. The son who wouldn't question his given identity. Who wouldn't leave his family, his life, 99 percent of the entire world for a life-threatening, lonely journey that might not even provide him with what he's looking for.

The room went black. Everything disappeared—the jungle, ten-year-old Rory, Finn, Bash, everything except immobile Rory, completely and utterly alone.

That... might be right.

* * *

He awoke violently with a shock of pain across his cheek.

"Dude! You've been out for, like, nine hours," River said hovering over Rory, massaging the palm of his hand. "You don't gotta get out, but we're in Kingston. I need to refuel and am going to get some food. You've got, like, an hour if you want to get off the boat."

Rory sat up, and as though the sleeping were only temporarily suppressing the nausea, vomited in the trash bag between River's bed and his mattress.

CHAPTER XXIV

2135

RORY

Rory ran into the quarters and slammed the door behind him. He rummaged through his belongings, his body only a little damp, either from the shower or the embarrassment, he wasn't sure. He threw on his clothes and sat on the mattress, his legs shaking.

There was a knock on the door before it opened. River walked in with a hand over his eyes. "You decent?"

"Yeah," Rory said, his face and body heating up so much he wondered if it was worth showering.

River peeked through his fingers and dropped his hand. "Listen, we're about fifteen hours from Puerto Cabezas. I think we passed through the only storm so it should be pretty smooth from here on out, but if you've gotta yak again, can you do it overboard? Because I do not want my quarters smelling up."

"Oh, yeah, sure. I'm really sorry about that."

"It happens. Now, I'm beat. The boat is hooked up to my device so there's nothing I need to steer. It's just going to take us where we need to go. I have my device alerted so that whenever anything unplanned for comes up or if we get close, my AIP will wake me up."

"Okay," Rory replied.

"So I'm going to go to sleep… in my bed… in here."

There was a silence between the two as he stared at Rory on the floor mattress.

"Well, I can help you move the mattress on deck, but I don't exactly want you in here while I'm sleeping."

What, too busy plotting against Bash?

"Oh," Rory said and jumped to his feet. "That's okay. I can grab it." He paused a moment.

"What?" River moved out of the doorway and further into the quarters.

"Well, what if I need to use the bathroom?"

"Piss overboard. If you need to shit, then wake me up, but I'd rather you hold it until I wake up."

Rory wasn't sure if he was kidding, but River wasn't smiling. "Got it."

He threw the rest of his belongings into his bag, grabbed the short side of the mattress, and dragged it backward through the door onto the deck. Once he had cleared the entrance to the quarters, the door closed and a second later there was a *click!*

The world around him was black, only illuminated by the moon and millions of stars.

It wasn't as dark as he'd expected, the world just so naturally… bright.

He laid down, his arms crossed under his head, and stared up at the sky. The stars danced, an intricate ballet of constellations and meteors with the orchestra of waves lightly crashing into the sides of the boat providing perfect accompaniment.

Silence.

Emptiness.

Peace.

He found it. Again. Finally.

There was not a worry tugging at his heart. His breathing slowed. It deepened. His body was completely weightless, the perfect temperature. Not too hot. Not too cold. He never believed in a soul, or at least that if anyone had one it would be humans of all species, but at that moment a part of him had left his body and joined the performance in the sky. He was lost in the encore of the night but also found by the calm and acceptance it provided him.

He wasn't tired so his eyes just traced the twinkling of the night sky.

For the first time in years, he thought of his parents. In college, he would pull them up on his AIP daily. He would check their updates, their new photos. It broke his heart their profiles hadn't changed.

They were still active, still smiling. He wondered if they missed him, like he missed them, but it never seemed that way.

Eventually, their happiness amplified his pain, and he couldn't bring himself to keep checking up on them. The last photo he remembered was them with the rest of their broodmates at some child's birthday party.

How, after losing Maeve, did they not want to hold on to him? Did they not feel the same pain he did when she left this world, joining the infinite stars above his head? Or did the pain of losing her supersede any other pain they would ever feel?

Maybe they never loved him like they loved Maeve. Or maybe their own need for acceptance would always outweigh anything they felt for him.

He thought he had grown out of the need for their love, but at that moment, all he wanted was a pat on the back from his dad or even a wink from his mom sitting in her chair by the window.

Hidden in the bottom of his bag, he had put his sister's copy of *The Giver*. He hadn't opened it since he had taken it from her room, but for the first time since he left home, he felt her presence. She was the lead ballerina in the sky, keeping the night clear.

He flipped through the pages until he found where he had placed the remnants of her hair. He plucked out the pieces and walked over to the edge of the boat.

"I hope you're happy. I hope that... you found the peace you needed," he said as he fingered the pieces of hair and looked up to the sky. "If you're out there, please don't leave me again. Help me find my way, and keep me safe. I miss you, Maeve." He extended his arm and dropped the hair into the sea below.

Smiling, he walked back to the mattress and picked up the book. He placed it next to him, protecting it like he would a baby.

The night moved quickly, even though he and his mind were still. The stars began to fade, and he heard a distant laughing.

"Maeve?" he said and sat up.

The laughing grew closer and louder.

A white bird flew toward him and pulled behind it the sky in colors of red, pink, and purple, shades that paint colors could never possibly capture.

The quarters' door reverberated against the frame. "Oh good, you're up too."

Rory sighed hearing River's voice, his moments of peace fading quicker than the sun rose.

"Beautiful, ain't she? Definitely my favorite part of being out on the water like this. You can search and scan for sunrises all you want, but the AIP just doesn't do a view like this justice."

That's something we agree on.

"I picked up some steamed cabbage and saltfish in Kingston. Do you want some?"

"I've never had it before," Rory responded. He quickly stuffed the book back into his bag.

"I didn't think so, but you've only got a few snacks left, so I figured I'd see if you wanted to save what you have. It's good stuff. It's homemade; my buddy's wife made it."

"Okay, sure." He had already eaten the lobster so he figured he would make a second exception to his staunch vegetarianism. He'd pick it back up once he had more of a choice of what to eat.

"I'll grab some plates and stuff. By that stool," he said and pointed to the spot he sat the prior day, "there's a board. You see it?"

Rory nodded.

"It's actually a table. Pull it out and unhook the legs."

He did as told. River came out with their food, silverware, and another stool. He handed Rory the stool and placed everything else on the table.

"How much longer?" Rory asked.

"Already sick of me?"

"Oh, no," Rory said and looked down at his hands.

"I'm just kidding. Plus, you've barely even seen me. How could you be done with me already?"

Rory thought back to the printouts of Bash and the suits in the closet and tried to crack a smile.

"Honestly, the boat made really good time last night. The wind must've been in our favor and the tide pretty mild because we only have about five hours to go."

He was right; it was an impeccable night.

"That's not bad," Rory replied.

"Yeah, I need to clean myself up after we eat, and then you're welcome to do the same. I assume after we're done with all that, we'll be just a couple of hours away."

Rory wanted to ask him about his obsession with Bash, but he couldn't gauge how River would respond. *Maybe I wait until after we're cleaned up. I mean, two hours is what? Like, sixty miles? I can probably swim that far if he decides to throw me overboard.*

The two ate in silence. The vegetables and fish were better than the rice and rock lobster. Over the past two days, he had eaten the most tasty and filling meals, unlike anything he had ever tried before.

Waves crashed as they cleaned the table and as Rory moved the mattress back into the quarters. As River cleaned himself up, Rory stood on the edge of the boat overlooking the water.

Why even bother with these colonies?

Maybe he could have this guy ask Bash to buy him a boat so he could live on the water.

He could overcome his aversion and eat fish every day. But he knew that wasn't possible. After all they'd gone though, Bash was still beholden to his family and investors. There's no way Bash could get away with helping the man who caused him to be hospitalized by a brood so similar to Rory's own, not even all the way down in Haiti.

After they took turns cleaning up and Rory walked back out onto the deck, River said, "I know you're wondering when you can get rid of me, so you've got two and a half hours until freedom."

"May I?" Rory said, pointing to the other stool.

"I guess," he said.

"Can I ask you a question?"

"What's that?"

"So you have all of these random printouts of Bash in your quarters."

"That's not a question."

"I mean, I guess I'm just wondering... Why?"

"Why do I have printouts of my cousin?"

"Yeah... and..."

"Spit it out, dude." River squinted at him.

"I saw the suits and maps too."

River looked away at the water.

Rory didn't have anything else to say, so he looked down at his hands.

"That doesn't concern you. Let's just say Pelletier needs a better figurehead than Bash."

"What?" His heart dropped. Did River want Bash's job? His position? Bash gave up himself and his own happiness for that purpose alone. No one could take it from him.

"He spends the company money on girls and yachts while his suppliers barely scrape by. They're not happy. My plan is to go have a chat with him now that we've... built some rapport."

Rory couldn't control the twitching of his muscles. Was his own cousin going to hurt Bash? What else would "have a chat" mean? What could he do? He could push him over-board. But they were still hours away. If he couldn't kill an animal, he wouldn't be able to hurt a person, even one after his best friend.

He had to tell someone, but how? He didn't have his AIP or his device. But he would have more contacts!

His best option was staying quiet and then telling every other person working to get him to the colony what was happening.

He looked back at River, his face red, the expression of anger and jealousy, but also something more recognizable to Rory—loneliness.

"You know what's not fair too?"

He shook his head. Where else could this conversation possibly go?

"I've worked my ass off since I was eight, manning this boat. And I've got nothing to show for it. Bash has everything, and what has he done? Partied it away? He doesn't deserve to run Pelletier."

"Uh-huh," he said avoiding River. He couldn't fuel this man's fire, not when Bash's life might be at stake.

"We're getting close. You should get your stuff together or relax or something."

This was River's way of telling him the conversation was over, and he was not at all upset about it. Rory was ready to get away from him. He grabbed his backpack and walked to the other side of the vessel to look out at the water. It was as though no time had passed before they approached on Puerto Cabezas.

River slowed the boat, Rory's energy waning, and pulled into a dock.

"Okay!" he yelled. "So the train station is literally right there. You see it?"

Rory nodded.

"Your AIP working yet?"

"No," Rory replied.

"Okay. I don't think that should be a problem because when I scan you, the train ticket comes up. It seems like this is one of those bullet trains, so you should be in Managua in no time. We made really good time so you have two hours until your train leaves... oh right, you can't tell the time because of the AIP. Well, I guess just go to the station now and wait for your train."

Rory started heading off the boat. Passing River, he stopped and said, "Thanks. I really appreciate you bringing me here."

"Don't thank me. Thank Bash."

Rory grimaced, knowing he wouldn't ever be able to do that, and walked toward the station, waiting to find someone who could relay his message to Bash.

Shit, I don't understand anything. AIP—translate... something... please... he thought in desperation.

Silence.

It was a good thing he had two hours to find his train because it took him almost that long. He wandered the station, stepping onto almost every platform, looking at the writing on the train.

Damn. The world really isn't built in a non-AIP way anymore.

AIP directional services replaced signage, no one learned other languages because the AIP could just translate, and he couldn't even show anyone a ticket stub because travel documents were just attached to the virtual profile.

That was the most exhausting two hours of my life... If that tired me out, what the hell am I going to do once I get to the jungle? I really am just walking into my death holding the scythe to hand over to the reaper when I see him.

The woman at the door scanned him and walked him to a first-class cabin. Rory sat on the luxurious seat, grabbed a blanket from a basket on the floor, and leaned his head against the window. The train began to roll and almost immediately gained enough speed that everything out the window blurred. The colors blended and painted the world around him, Matisse holding the brush, and it lulled Rory to sleep.

* * *

"*Señor! Ay! Managua! Señor!*"

The woman from the door poked Rory with a baton.

"Oh, sorry." Luckily, she hadn't left him on the train for its next destination.

He grabbed his bag and walked off the train. It was still bright in Managua. Understanding time without the AIP was a struggle. The sun was still high, but not too high. It was hot, but not as hot as it was in Port-au-Prince when he landed.

His breathing hastened when someone grabbed his shoulder.

"*Señor Rory?*" The woman scanned him. "Good! I was nervous I was grabbing the wrong shoulder, but you were the only one who got off the train and looked lost." Her accent was so thick he had trouble understanding her, but he was impressed that she spoke English. "*Señor*, I have your car."

"My car? I thought someone was driving me?"

"There is a directional system in the car that will take you to a very small house near the border. You can stay at that house until tomorrow morning. There is food, water, a bathroom, a bed. Everything you need for one night. *Señora* Eleanor told us this would be best." She handed him a key fob and pointed. "Your car is over there. Good luck." The woman scurried away.

"Wait! There's something I need to tell you!" She turned back toward him. "The man, on the boat. I think he's planning to hurt Bash. Can you get a message to him or Eleanor?"

"*Si*," she said hesitantly.

"Tell them, the man who took me on the boat is Bash's cousin. I don't know if he knows that. And, say he has plans for a coup or something. He had a ton of information about Bash, and it looked like he was taking steps to go to Maine. Please. Promise me you'll tell him. You're my last chance."

She nodded. He wasn't sure, but it looked genuine. There was nothing he could do but hope. He had no money, no AIP, no way of getting back. Even if he stole the car, it was preprogrammed, and it would run out of charge eventually anyway. He had no choice but to keep going to the colony and hope she would relay the message. With a rock in his gut, he sulked to the car, looking back toward the direction of the woman every few steps.

Rory walked over to the two-seater, threw his bag in the passenger seat, and turned on the car.

"Hello, Mr. Walsh. I will now take you to Casa Frontera. Please put me in auto-pilot by placing your foot on the brake and shifting into gear A."

He did as he was told.

"Thank you. Please stay awake during the entire trip. If a break is needed, please override the autopilot by placing your foot on the brake and shifting into manual gears."

The car lurched forward and made its way to the Costa Rican border.

Two and a half hours later, the car pulled onto a long path that led to a small one-story Spanish colonial.

He grabbed his bag and stepped out of the car. The stucco was a sort of yellowing color, probably white in a past life but showing its age now. The red barrel tile of the roof was missing in places, but the door, some type of light brown wood with a white rectangle in the middle, must have been recently replaced. As Rory approached, the rectangle, he realized, was a note with his name on it.

Rory—In case your AIP doesn't work as expected: this is a house owned by one of the business owners who I work with. He and his wife are meeting with the CC this week and will be back the day after you are set to arrive. You are able to stay for one night but must be gone before they arrive in the afternoon. There is a scanner next to the door—your face will be scanned and has been approved to open the door. You are welcome to the food and water. Inside, there is a machete next to the door. Take it with you. We don't know how treacherous those jungles will be. Relax, wash up, and chart out your next steps. Good luck.

—ELEANOR

If I was a face scanner, where would I be? Rory looked around the door until he found a black box about a foot away. He lifted the lid, meeting a buzzing noise. The buzzing noise lasted only a few seconds as it scanned him, and then the door clicked.

The door opened without resistance. The house was dark; very little natural sunlight peeked through the windows. *Click!* the door responded, closing behind him. He found another black box on the inside of the door, with the machete propped up underneath it.

"That's bigger than I expected it," he said.

A few steps inside led to a bedroom, bathroom, a tiny kitchen, and a modest living room that opened to a small porch.

He walked into the kitchen and opened his backpack to see what food he had left, none of it good anymore. *Damn. I swear I'm wasting more food than I'm eating.* He grabbed the bag with the leftover food from River and dropped his backpack on the floor.

He dumped the leftover food into a trash can and opened the refrigerator.

He grabbed a container with what looked like rice, beans, and vegetables. There didn't seem to be a microwave so he grabbed a pot, dumped the contents into it, and placed it on the stove to heat. *The sunset must be beautiful from out there,* he thought as he contemplated where to eat. He plated his food and headed for the porch, stopping when he reached the couch.

Tonight may be the last time I ever sit on a couch, sleep on a bed, use a stove, get a shower...

He melted onto the couch. *Oh, how I took you for granted.* The couch was a little lumpy, but it was the comfiest he knew he might ever feel again.

He admired the textures of the food, the spice, the fuller he felt with each bite.

What if this is the last time I get to eat anything but plants?
What if I eat a poisonous plant and this is my last meal ever?

He placed the empty plate and fork on the floor by his feet and rested his head on his knees.

Tears flowed differently this time. Not a feeling of catharsis like in the park or even disappointment tinged with hopefulness like when he saw his parents for the last time, but a combination of fear and grief. Fear for the unknown, the jungle, the possibility that what he searched for didn't exist. Grief for the life he was losing and everything it provided him, even if it was one he hated.

His sleep was so light the sunrise shone through his eyelids. His head pounded from the heaving and dehydration. The family would be back soon, and he needed to maximize his daylight. He didn't know these parts. There was no way he would kill time until nightfall to start trekking through the wilderness like Eleanor recommended back in DC. He needed the sun.

As he made his way back to the kitchen with his empty plate, he regretted not sleeping in the bed.

He filled his backpack with cheese, bread, jam, and fruit, and made some snacks and sandwiches for his journey. He took out the map, compass, and marker to start planning his route in search of the colonies.

He grabbed the marker and made a dotted line that zigzagged from his current position all the way to Zapzurro in Colombia.

He gripped the map and compass, put the marker in his pocket, took one last look around the colonial, picked up the machete, and looked into the face scanner. He breathed in the cool morning air as the door clicked behind him. An unjustified calmness settled him as he made his way toward the border, only a few hundred feet away from Casa Frontera. Much closer than the expected five miles or so.

There wasn't a single border guard. He tentatively hid behind a tree, counting to one thousand.

This is it. This must be a sign.

He didn't pass a single person as he ran across the border into Costa Rica.

No one shouting, no footsteps behind him.

But he was too scared to check whether anyone had followed him, so he kept running until he reached the Rio Sapoa, only slowing down to chop any obstacles out of his way. The thought of the river he needed to cross fueled his confidence.

The whooshing of the water greeted him before the river even came into sight.

He sighed a breath of relief as he approached it.

Just like intro to mechanical engineering, he thought as he scrounged around for everything he'd need to make a raft large and sturdy enough to carry him across.

CHAPTER XXV

2135

DAVINA

Davina walked through the jungle with a satchel on her back that contained the few belongings she owned, carving a path ahead of her with her machete. She didn't say goodbye to anyone; she couldn't. She just grabbed her stuff and left the colony. It hurt too much to stay.

I love them all so much; they're my family. But how can I keep facing them every single day?

She had been walking for a few hours, unsure of where she was headed, but she wanted to put some distance between her and the colony so they couldn't find her.

What is that?

She squinted. A figure laid on the jungle floor in the distance. Whether a large animal or a person, she couldn't quite make out. She gripped her machete tighter and held it out in front of her as she approached, taking cover among the foliage.

With each step, the outline of a man's body became clearer.

He was thin and bruised, and she couldn't tell if he was even breathing.

She walked closer but couldn't see his chest rise or fall. She searched for a pulse; it was faint, but she found one. He didn't stir to her touch. His muscles showed strength, definition after a long journey. But his cheeks were sunk in. He needed food. Just a few years older than herself, probably, his hair was long, covering his eyes and forehead.

How is he still alive? How has he not been eaten by something just laying here like this?

She placed her hand on him. *He's so warm. Feverish.* The backpack next to him was torn, belongings spilling out and most destroyed. She slowly pulled a machete out of his hand and placed it behind her in case he were to wake up.

She pulled off her own satchel and grabbed some water and a shirt. She wet the shirt and started to pat the man's face trying to cool him down.

She lifted his chin and opened his mouth slightly. She took the water and dribbled a few droplets. Tapping his face, she said, "*Señor... señor?*"

No response.

There's no way I can carry him, but I can't just leave him, either.

A gash on his leg had partially healed, and dried blood encrusted it. She crawled around his body to see if there were any other wounds. His clothes were soaking wet, and there was a rash on his stomach, probably from a lack of air as she had to peel the shirt off of his skin before ripping it. She tossed it near his ruined backpack. There were bug bites covering most of his body, ants crawling over him. She took the wet shirt she used on his face and cleaned the rest of him, working her way down from his neck, to his chest, to his legs. She tried to turn him to reach his back, but as she gripped his shoulder his eyes began to flutter.

She crouched back and put her hands in the air, giving him space to realize where he was and that he wasn't alone.

"*Señor. ¿Estás bien?*"

"What?"

"Oh, English, okay. I'm sorry. Are you okay?"

He wiggled his head from left to right and whispered, "Help," as he clutched his throat.

She grabbed her flask and lifted his head, resting it on her knee as she slowly poured water into his mouth.

He coughed, getting a little energy from the water. She waited a moment and lifted the flask to his lips again. Licking his lips, he opened and closed his mouth, like he was trying to create enough saliva to talk.

His voice was hoarse. "I'm lost," was all he could manage. She poured a little more water into his mouth. He began to sit up, one arm on the forest ground and the other placed onto his chest as though it hurt him to move it. He touched his chest, looked down, and widened his eyes as he noticed his shirt was missing. "What did you do to me?" His energy picked up, and he tried to push her away.

She slowly backed away, on all fours so as not to threaten him, and said, "My name is Davina. I found you lying here, and I tried to wake you up but was unable to. You looked thirsty and hurt so I gave you some water and cleaned off as much of the dirt and blood that I could."

He inspected his body and grazed his arms, stomach, and legs. "Thank you," he said and eyed her flask.

She handed it to him and said, "You said you were lost. What was your intended destination?"

He gulped the water and handed her the flask. "Honestly, I don't know. But I lost my map and compass so I don't know if I'll ever find it now," he said and put his head in his hands momentarily before smacking the bug bites on his legs.

Davina crouched back down and scooted closer.

"Maybe I can help. What's your name?"

He looked up at her. "What?" he asked.

"I asked what your name was."

His eyes began to water and his breathing became quick and shallow. He turned away from her and gripped his thighs.

"No one's ever asked me that before," he said with an unsteady voice. "My name is Rory Walsh." He laid back down on the jungle floor and began to laugh. The most genuine she had ever heard, and it made her laugh too. He screamed, "My name... is Rory Walsh!"

He sighed and grabbed his hair. She followed his gaze to the sky and looked back down at him. She had never seen anyone smile so big.

She thought he had forgotten she was there. "It's very nice to meet you, Rory Walsh," she whispered.

He popped up, eyes so bright he could burn down the entire jungle with just one glance, and grabbed her hands in his.

"It is so nice to meet you... er..."

"Davina," she said and smirked. She didn't know what he had gone through or was going through, but she could tell it was a lot, so she didn't blame him for forgetting her name.

"Can you tell me where I am?"

"You're a few miles outside of Monteverde. Is that where you were hoping to be?"

"I don't know." He pulled his hands back and scratched the bites on his chest.

She turned her head away.

How can I help him? He's giving me nothing.

"I think I was... looking for *you*."

"I'm sorry?" The man must've been delusional. She was no one—a mediocre teacher from a tiny colony who didn't deserve responsibility. There was no way *she* was who he searched for.

"You don't have an AIP. Or if you did, it's not working because you didn't know who I was."

"I don't have one."

"Are you..." A macaw squawked in the distance. He looked toward it, but she barely noticed the sounds of the jungle anymore.

"Am I what?" she asked after a moment.

"Are you the only one?"

"Without an AIP?"

He shook his head yes.

"No. There are a few of us."

"So they're *real*? The colonies are real!" He smiled and grabbed her hands. "Can I come with you?"

She pulled her hands away and looked down. She couldn't go back. "I was actually leaving..."

"What? Why?" His energy seemed to wane again, the initial adrenaline seeming to leave his system and the exhaustion of being alone in the jungle returning.

"I just need a fresh start." She thought back to the past year and how hard it was to stay involved, to look at all the children. She was helpless, unworthy to be a part of that family.

"I understand that," he said, disappointed.

That's it? No more questions?

"Can you at least show me how to get there?"

She looked away. There was no way he would make it by himself. She would be sending him to his death if she tried to give directions to someone who clearly wasn't from or didn't understand this jungle.

"You said you lost your map and compass. How do you expect to find your way in the jungle?" The jungle was already hard enough to walk through, only being able to see a few feet in the distance with the foliage blocking the view. Focusing on clearing a path and avoiding the fauna, he was bound to get even more lost, if not killed.

"I've found my way this far, haven't I?" He shrugged.

A spider monkey hopped from branch to branch in the tree canopy above them.

Maybe this is why I needed to leave today, why I took this exact route north.

His gaze still followed the monkey. His cheeks were so sunken the bones were completely visible. He was wet but his skin completely dry, the water evaporated by the sun. How he even had the energy to speak with her was unfathomable.

I was meant to find him and help him. This is how I'm supposed to make up for what happened. He needs me, and maybe this is what I need...

She stood up and gathered both of their things, throwing a dry shirt at him.

His face fell as he scrambled to put the shirt on. "What are you doing?"

She continued in silence. She placed the scattered belongings in her satchel and made her way directly in front of him. She smiled and extended her hand. Taking him to the colony, helping him—this was her penance.

"Let's go," she said.

"I thought you said you were leaving your colony? Needed a fresh start?"

"I think I found it."

"I don't understand."

"I just have this inexplicable feeling that *this*," she pointed back and forth from him to her, "was supposed to happen. Our meeting was written in the stars."

He squinted at her and tilted his head.

"I just think that everything we've been searching for, everything we've been running away from, everything we need... it's just all going to be okay."

He looked at her tentatively but reached out and grabbed her hand. She helped him up, but he was having a hard time placing one foot in front of the other, limping and using her as a crutch.

She stopped and grabbed his waist. "Do you think you'll be okay to walk?"

"Yeah, I just need to limber back up. I'm a little stiff." His stomach grumbled, and he blushed.

"Do you want some mango?" She didn't wait for a response as she reached into her satchel for the fruit. She peeled half of it in three swipes of her machete and handed it to him.

"Thank you." He reached for the mango and took a bite. "Mmm," he sighed as he chewed, his face almost orgasmic. She smiled and looked away, blushing.

The wind ruffled the leaves around them, bringing with it the mugginess and quick heat of impending rain.

He finished the mango and held the pit awkwardly in his hand. "You can just toss it. Maybe we'll get lucky and it'll turn into a mango tree," Davina said with a smile.

He took a step. Another. Each step took less effort than the last. He looked back at her. "Am I going in the right direction?"

She walked up to him and pointed. "Let's go this way."

"Can I ask you something?"

"You can ask me anything you want, Rory Walsh."

"How is your English so good? I assumed that everyone here would speak Spanish, that even if I got lucky enough to find a colony, that I'd have a hard time talking to anyone."

"We speak a few languages. My native language is English because of my parents, but I'm also fluent in Spanish. My Portuguese and French could use a little work, though." She smiled at Rory.

"I just thought that the AIP made learning languages irrelevant…"

"The colony is small, but the people in it are from all over. My parents joined a few years before I was born. They were originally from New York in the United States. I don't really understand the brood system, but they told me they were in different ones. They were taught to hate each other, so they never spoke.

"But one day, the two were caught in a storm and ran into the nearest shelter, where they became trapped for a few days. They started talking and told me that within a day, they fell madly in love. They hid their relationship for as long as they could, but eventually they were discovered, and it destroyed their broods. They knew if they wanted to be together, they had to leave. And so they did. I was born a few years later, here. I learned English from my parents but Spanish from Amos. Everyone has their own story."

His breath quickened, like he ran a kilometer in the last few seconds, but managed to say, "Who's Amos?"

"He's the father of our colony."

"Oh." He wheezed but continued, "So your colony isn't that old?"

"Well, the AIPs themselves aren't really that old."

"That's… true… I guess… like… only fifty years or… so." The pauses between the words growing. "They just… seem…

so much... older... since they've...... infected...... our entire...... world."

"Almost," she responded with a wink.

"What's it...... like? Living...... without one?"

"I don't know any differently."

He stopped and sat in the grass, catching his breath and looking at her apologetically as she handed him her flask again. He took a few sips and regulated his breathing.

"I guess that's true. I'm still getting used to it. I feel like I tried so hard to get away from it, but I just don't know what to do anymore... what to say... where to go. I've always been lost... but this is just a different kind of lost. And usually I feel like I 'find myself' in nature, but Costa Rica has done a number on me."

"It's a wonderful place, but it can also be dangerous." She helped him up as water droplets began to fall onto her head. She put the flask in her bag and kept walking. "It can be so unpredictable, hot and humid one moment and raining the next." She lifted her arms into the air as though saying, *As you can tell.*

She looked to her sides, but her companion had fallen behind. She faced him and reached out her arms.

"Can I help you?" she asked.

"I'm all right! Sorry, it's a little hard to keep up."

Thunder rang through the sky, causing him to jump. Davina stifled a laugh, but couldn't help finding his inexperience with the jungle a bit amusing.

"Shit!" he yelled as the rain picked up, soaking both of them. A complete downpour overcame them. She was used to the weather going from heat to sprinkles to downpour to sunny and dry, but he clearly hadn't become accustomed to it yet.

He covered his head with his arms and started limping faster toward her. "How do we get out of this?"

"We don't. We can stop and hide under the canopies, but the rain will find us, if not on its own, then using the wind as a guide." She expected a few rainstorms on her journey; they were frequent in the jungle. "Honestly, we should probably just keep moving. It will let up soon."

Before she had even finished speaking, the rain began to lessen. She didn't expect it to stop completely, but walking in a drizzle wasn't a problem.

"Agh!" Rory screamed, jumping in the air. The fear caused his limp to disappear as he ran toward her and grabbed her shoulder.

"What's wrong?" she asked him as she stabilized herself.

"I hate snakes!" She felt his whole body shiver. She walked a few steps away and wrapped herself with her arms. She thought back on that terrible day, and the shivers jumped from him to her.

Facing away, she said, "You don't need to worry! I know it's tricky, but that one's just a Coral Falsa. It can't really hurt you. There are only a few snakes in Costa Rica you really need to watch out for, actually. Although one looks a lot like this one." She bit her lip and rubbed her arms, needing to let the moment pass.

"Are you all right?" he asked.

"Oh, sure. I just remembered something."

"You seem to have gotten really upset... so fast."

"It's just been a hard year." She started walking away from him, but he grabbed her elbow and smiled reassuringly.

"I'm sorry. Do you want to talk about it? What happened?"

She didn't know whether to tell him, whether she could relive the pain. But maybe this was a part of her penance too. Acceptance.

"Well, at the colony, I'm a teacher. Or I was a teacher, I should say... for young kids, ages five to eleven. We don't have many children in the colony, so I only had nine to take care of. And I loved it. It was so rewarding teaching them about math, science, how to read." A butterfly had circled them before flying up into the canopy. "But mostly, about the world around us in all of its majesty." She tracked the butterfly until it flew out of sight.

"That seems really... nice?" he questioned. He kept jumping at movements in the grass around him. She realized that giving him his machete back wasn't the best idea. He wasn't very good at using it, and his swinging was dangerous, mostly just getting in the way of hers.

"It really was." She smiled and slowly reached for his machete, pulling it out of his hand.

"So why was it so bad?" Realizing what she wanted, he sheepishly grinned and handed it over to her.

The drizzling rain provided refuge from the heat, making their walk to the colony pleasant, at least for her. His feet kept slipping in the mud and sinking every few steps. She linked her arm through his to help him keep his balance.

"There's this beautiful waterfall not too far from where the colony dwellings are. It's a fun little watering hole to go swimming, relax, and learn about all the fun animals and foliage. I had finished my planned lessons for the day and I wanted to give the kids a treat, so I took them there. We walked around for a little while naming the plants, classifying the animal droppings...

"And then I let them just have fun and explore. Most of the kids went swimming and some of them just sat on the rocks by the water or walked around playing with frogs or whatever else they could find. The sun was starting to lower in the sky, and I wanted to get them back before it got dark." Her voice remained steady, but her eyes began to sting.

"Once the kids got all packed up, I put them in line to count off." She sighed. "But we were missing number five." She couldn't bring herself to say his name. "He was a seven-year-old boy, and I called out for him. I yelled for him. I made the other children pair up and wait while I ran around trying to find him but not so far that the rest would be out of sight.

"I just couldn't risk losing the rest of them," she whispered more to herself than to Rory. "So I took them back to the colony dwellings, and I ran to Amos. I told him, 'I lost one of the boys. I can't find him.' And Amos hit this huge drum that we have in the center of the dwellings that's used for big announcements or emergencies, and he created a search party. A few of us stayed back with the other kids, but almost everyone in the colony went to search for him."

Tears streamed down her face.

"But it was too dark. They were out almost all night, but they couldn't find him. So they came back, slept for a few hours, and all went out again at daybreak." Her voice began to quiver. "It only took a few hours at that point. They found him a little over two kilometers away from the waterfall, but in almost the complete opposite direction of the colony. It was as though he walked a little bit to explore and then got turned around in the jungle and couldn't find his way back." She stopped and took a few breaths.

"But they found him," Rory said.

"They did. They found him lying on the ground almost in the same way that I found you. But where you had a pulse, he had none. He had a bite on his hand. We talked about snakes that day, and about how some benign snakes can look like poisonous ones to protect themselves. We did an activity on how to spot the difference. He must have confused the two because it looked like he reached out for it, maybe he tried to pet it, and he was bit."

"That's why seeing me with the snake upset you so much?" he asked her. She shook her head and wiped her face with the back of her hand. Using her as a crutch helped keep his breathing steady, the words no longer a visible struggle for him.

"I was in the center of the dwellings next to the drum when I saw one of the men carrying him, holding him like he would hold a newborn child. I remember his mother who was next to me with his little sister. She ran toward her son with her arms stretched out and then collapsed to the ground when she realized her son was gone. The sounds that came from her were deafening."

She paused and motioned for him to stop walking while she expanded the path she originally made with her machete before finding him. She beckoned him to follow.

"They said it wasn't my fault. They said I did the right thing by bringing the other children back. But it was my fault. I brought them to the waterfall. I lost track of one of my kids, and he paid the ultimate price for it. I couldn't teach after that. I couldn't take on the responsibility of carrying someone's precious life in my hands. His parents even came to me and forgave me, asked me if I could come back to teach. His parents were comforting me. Every day, I saw his parents, and I thought about what I robbed them of. I look at those kids, and I only see his face. And the guilt, it was so heavy. I just couldn't carry it anymore. So I needed to leave."

He grabbed her hand. She pulled hers away immediately, unsure by the gesture. Turning to look at him, she realized the comfort in him, the way he was only hoping to relieve some of her pain.

She walked up to him and wrapped her arms around him.

"I'm sorry," he said.

"For what?"

"That you've been carrying that pain. That you're hurting." With the embrace, a weight was lifted off of her shoulders. Like he had shared in or taken away some of her suffering.

"Thank you." She released him and started walking, hooking her arm around his once again.

"Thank you for going back. I know it must be hard." She smiled at him. With each step, the thought of returning was easier, the right choice.

"What about you? What made you risk your life to come find us?"

"No one saw me for who I really was… who I really am. No one gave me the chance to really discover and be Rory Walsh. I was living a life that wasn't my own based on assumptions I just didn't fit into."

"And that was enough to leave everything behind?"

"Honestly, that is my everything. What do you have if you don't even have yourself?"

CHAPTER XXVI

2135

RORY

The dwellings appeared out of nowhere. A little oasis surrounded by jungle on all sides. Rory still didn't believe it. His mind must have been playing tricks on him, some sort of survival mechanism.

Barely making it through the jungle, this must have been heaven. There was no other explanation. He had to be dead because in what reality would someone like Davina find him and lead him to everything he'd ever been looking for?

Working his way through the jungle, he had meticulously checked off the places he passed, each stroke of the marker decrying the possibility of the colonies existing. His motivation waned as his legs tired.

The backpack, with only a book, some snacks, and a few sets of clothes, got heavier with each step, his back crying out to him to just get rid of it. He couldn't, his mind reminding him that it was not only the sole relic of his past life but also his only possibility for survival.

The air, always sticky, whispered to him to strip off his clothes, but the bugs, always biting and buzzing, reminded him to layer. And although his legs were scabbed and bleeding from his scratching, he had to thank those bugs because they protected his ankles from quite a few slithering pals and critters on more than one occasion.

His machete, short and ineffective, or maybe it was his skill at using it that was ineffective, he held tightly like a baseball bat, swinging it at everything and nothing at the same time, eventually trying to use it as a walking stick when his muscles struggled to hold his weight.

With no idea how long he'd been wandering, he only tapped into his food supply when his hunger reached his brain, making his eyes deceive him. He still ran out of food.

His water disappeared much more quickly than the food. After a bout of violent sickness after trying to sip some groundwater, he decided dehydration was the best option. But the jungle just saved him from that. And although he hated being constantly pummeled with unannounced rain storms, he held out his water bottle trying to catch the droplets, even using banana leaves as a funnel, the rain being the only thing that may have saved him.

The environment, nature, at one point his salvation, was now a constant terror. The sounds reverberating in his skull, louder than the AIP ever was. He didn't remember when it all became too much. When the hunger and the thirst and the fear and the debilitating fatigue made his body surrender. How he wasn't dead, he couldn't fathom.

Who the hell had been looking out for him? Who had protected him from the snakes, and the big cats, and the bugs? Who had shielded him from the elements? Who let him rest in the jungle floor in the exact spot that Davina would pass?

"Oh here, I found this on the jungle floor by you. I put it in my satchel so it wouldn't get ruined. Honestly, I'm surprised it's in better shape than your clothes," Davina said reaching into her bag and pulling out *The Giver*. She handed it to him with a smile.

Maeve... you didn't leave me.

He held the book in both hands, smiling. His backpack was tattered, and his clothes didn't resemble anything they meant to. But the book was just a little torn and wet, still the same book he took from Maeve's room all those years ago.

He looked around the little sliver of paradise and said, "This isn't at all what I expected."

The dwellings created a rectangle with three sides completed. Davina and Rory were on the fourth side, an opening with a line of traps. The traps must have been to protect the dwellings from the creatures with which they shared the jungle. On the sides were cement buildings that looked like little one-story cottages, one after another all facing the center, with the newest ones closest to where Davina and Rory entered. The roofs were covered in metal, a stark contrast to the light-colored walls. At the complete opposite end was a long cement building with a pair of doors in the middle and windows on both sides all the way across.

The center was a type of square. In the middle, the drum that Davina had mentioned stood, next to a huge garden with vegetables, fruits, and possibly even grains. Rory couldn't exactly tell. Children ran around, playing games and shouting at one another, while a few men and women sat off to the side knitting or spinning yarn, it seemed. Each person they passed on their way to the building all the way at the other end smiled or waved at Rory.

Their kindness melted his heart. They had no idea who he was. He could be anyone. He could be himself.

As they continued, a table of people laughing and playing some sort of game with sticks while eating a meal that smelled divine made Rory smile and his stomach grumble.

"What were you expecting?" Davina asked as they continued walking.

"I don't know, but definitely not this... Maybe something more primitive... thatched roofs and stuff."

She laughed.

"Hey, where are we going?" he asked her as they continued moving forward.

"We're going to meet Amos. He has to meet everyone who comes through here."

Rory thought they were heading to the long building at the end, but they stopped short. Davina grabbed his hand and tugged him toward the last little cement cottage.

Her touch radiated throughout his whole body, heating every part of him, his skin, his blood, his organs, as though giving him supernatural abilities. If he had thought he was dead, her touch told him otherwise, the only evidence that all of this was real. That she was real. Her hands were too soft for life in the jungle, but then again, how would he know? Her beauty hadn't faded since the first time he laid eyes on her.

Originally thinking he only found her perfect because she was the one to save him or because he was hurt, hungry, dehydrated, or possibly hallucinating, she only became more radiant to him.

Her heart was more beautiful than anything, which said a lot because he had never met a woman more breathtaking.

The confidence she had walking through the jungle, knowing where to step, where to turn, what to listen for, made him feel safe. The gentleness she used cleaning his wounds made him feel taken care of... protected. The openness of her words made him feel accepted. And the willingness to turn around and face her pain and fear to bring him here made him feel more loved than ever before.

People, like his mom and Bash, had done a lot for him. But until Davina, no one had truly ever sacrificed a piece of themselves for him. Nora created a profile in her image, prioritizing her place in the brood over him. Bash was so focused on public perception that Rory was forced to find embrace elsewhere.

He may have just met Davina, but he couldn't imagine a life without her. She intoxicated him, a siren singing out to him, and he willingly followed her, even if it led to his death. Because even if he did die, at least he would die happy.

"Amos!" She knocked on the door, the only wooden part of the little cottage, as far as he could tell.

She dropped his hand and walked over to the window, a square hole with only a mesh covering, and yelled through, "Amos!" A second later, she smiled and waved through the opening.

An older man opened the door and stepped out. Short silver hair on his head was almost unnoticeable with the silver beard that hit his mid-neck that was recently trimmed. His steps were heavy, slow, his body slightly succumbing to gravity as his posture leaned to one side, the side he held his hip with as he walked.

"Hello, Davina. Your parents were looking for you. Where have you been?"

"Can we come inside?" She slyly avoided his question.

"Of course." Amos ushered the two inside.

"It smells fantastic! Is Leah making something?"

"She is, and it seems like she's making enough to feed the entire colony if you'd like some. What do you think, young man? Would you like something to eat?"

Rory shook his head yes. He sheepishly walked toward the wall and leaned on it, looking up at the ceiling. The dwelling was larger on the inside than it looked from the outside, with the ceilings easily ten feet tall. The interior was open, a large living area with natural furniture, including a table and chairs atop a woven rug. Only a counter separated it from the kitchen where a woman, maybe a few years older than his own mother, fashioned together a meal. The opposite side of the cottage, with rebar windows across, provided natural light that illuminated the home.

"We haven't had a stray in quite a few years. Welcome."

Rory smiled. "Thank you. This is very nice of you. Both of you. All of you." He blushed and looked down at the floor.

Amos's attention shifted away from him as the older man looked at Davina with loving eyes, more emotion than he had ever seen from his own mother. "Davina, are you all right? It's not like you to disappear." He reached out and grabbed both of her hands. "We were worried."

"I'm okay. I was thinking about leaving the colony."

Amos didn't look surprised, but Rory was.

She's just telling him?

"I'm sorry to hear that. We would've missed you so much… but I see you've changed your mind?" A smile crept across his face, relief.

"I think so," she said.

"And this gentleman helped you make that decision?" Amos looked at him and winked, as though this was a plan the two had concocted together.

"He did. I think this is my redemption from what I let happen last year."

Amos kissed her hand. "Davina, you know it was not your fault. The jungle is a dangerous place, and all that happens is out of our control. What is meant to be *will be*, and we cannot stop it."

"You've said that before."

"And you still don't believe me."

She shook her head no.

"I hope one day you can forgive yourself."

She smiled and stepped back from Amos, extended her arm, and said, "Amos, this is Rory."

Amos dropped her other hand and motioned to the table. "Please, sit." He looked at Davina.

She smiled and sat.

"Thank you," Rory said and sat down.

"What would you like us to know?" Amos asked him.

"I'm sorry?"

"It is my experience that people come here to escape from somewhere, something, or someone. Which one is it for you?"

"I guess… all of it."

Rory didn't know where to start. Davina was so open with him and with Amos that he wondered if he should do the same. Should he tell this man about living a life that was crafted for him by his own parents, parents who wouldn't accept him and would rather see him leave than open their arms to him?

Should he talk about Maeve? His first friend and the first to ever break his heart, leaving him utterly alone but then watching over him in his most desperate times of need? Should he mention his best friend, so different from him yet so similar and so ready to help? What about how hard he worked to get here, to leave the notions of his old life behind so that he could carve a path for himself? An idea so important to him, he was willing to die for it.

Maybe he could talk about the AIP, how he spent so long hoping he could rid himself from it but how hard those first few days were without it, the loneliness unlike anything he had ever felt before.

He looked at Davina, who smiled back at him.

Or should he talk about this incredible woman who nursed his wounds, fed both his stomach and soul, and led him to his redemption?

Amos reached out and grabbed Rory's hand in his own as though he was reading the thoughts as Rory had them.

"We have all experienced loss. It is something that connects us all. But now, we welcome you here. It is nice to have you." Davina dropped her eyes.

"Thank you." He was unsure of what else to say or what to ask, Amos taking away all of his hesitation and fear.

"Would you like to tell him the rules or shall I?" Amos asked Davina.

"You can tell him."

Amos released his hands and took on a more formal tone.

"This is not only a colony but a family."

Oh no... Not like the broods, please.

"We take care of each other. We love each other. Everything we do is in support of each other. Do you understand?"

"I think so," Rory responded.

Amos quickly assuaged his worries by saying, "Everything you see here—the dwellings, the garden, the food, the clothes, the furniture—has all been created by the members of this colony. We work together to create a society that provides everything our fellow members need. Therefore, we require that everyone contribute to the colony. Davina was a teacher and hopefully will be again. Leah, along with some others, cooks. Her daughter tends to the garden and ensures that we have bountiful crops to feed the colony. Some build dwellings, some fashion textiles, some hunt or forage. Is there anything you are particularly suited to contribute?"

"I'm not sure... I was always really good at soccer, and I went to college for environmental engineering."

"I think you would be a very strong candidate for teaching, as well as providing some daily physical activity for the members. As you can see, a few of us are beginning to age, and we could use some physical... stimulation." He chuckled as he rubbed his hip. "We only have one other colony member who attended university, and she is the only one currently teaching any advanced level subjects. Would you be interested in taking these roles on?"

"I've never taught anything or really had anyone listen to me for any reason, but I guess so."

"That's okay. We are all learning every day, and I'm sure she would like any help you can provide."

"I almost went to university, in another life," a woman said and walked out of the kitchen balancing four plates of food, effortlessly. "I'm Leah. I overheard everything from the kitchen. Welcome, Rory." She placed a plate in front of everyone and sat down.

"Where's your daughter this evening?" Davina asked Leah.

"She wanted to show some of the younger children how to tend to the garden." Leah started eating, motioning for everyone else to join.

There was a sense of familiarity to the woman, something Rory couldn't put his finger on.

"Thank you. It smells delicious... Is there any meat in it? I'm a vegetarian."

"There's no meat, just vegetables from the garden and fresh grains from the baker." She smiled at Rory and moved her fork around her plate to show him.

"You said you almost went to university?" he asked.

"In another life. I don't like to talk about it. Like Amos said, we all ran away from something." She smiled and looked at Amos as the four continued to eat.

He took a bite of food and looked around the room.

Home.

He hadn't used that word in years, nothing living up to the name.

But around that table, nothing had ever felt more like family.

EPILOGUE: 2145

RORY

The mid-morning air was cool. The breeze was ruffling the papers on Rory's desk as he walked around the room handing out the homemade kits. "Now, before we make our thermometers, we need to review the history and usage of them. First, does anyone remember what liquid used to be in thermometers? We talked about this yesterday. Yes, Bash, go ahead."

"It used to be mercury." His son couldn't sit still for more than a few moments and popped out of his chair, reaching for his packet.

He smiled and pat his son on the shoulder, gently guiding him back into his seat. "Great, and why did mercury stop being used?" He looked around the room, but the answer came from right behind him.

"It's toxic."

"Good job, Bash, but next time wait for me to call on you. We want to give the other students a chance to answer too."

The four other children chuckled, and Rory walked back to his desk. He pushed a stray leaf onto the floor.

The kits he had created were for the students to make their own thermometers. He spent all night forging the materials and even had Davina work through the exercise with him to make sure it wasn't too challenging for the students.

He was teaching them about temperature and weather, and the next few lessons would be the introduction of climate, followed by how the concepts were different. He was excited to share his passion for the environment, something he didn't think he would ever be able to do a decade ago.

Since Rory landed ten years ago, Amos had passed, and Nora, Leah's daughter, became the matriarch of the colony. There had been a couple with an infant daughter who found their way about six years ago, but besides that, no one else had stumbled upon their little piece of heaven.

Three beautiful children had been born, one of his own: Bash, not short for Sebastian, just Bash. He rarely thought of his friend those days, but every once in a while, he looked into the canopies and hoped that he was all right, that he was happy, and that River never made his way to Maine.

He and Davina had fallen in love almost the moment they had met. After he had formally joined the colony, he moved into the dwelling that housed her and her parents. There wasn't exactly the concept of marriage in the traditional sense that he was accustomed to, but the two decided they would spend the rest of their lives together and made a commitment to each other in front of the rest of the colony.

It took a few years and a child of their own, but Davina found peace with the loss of the boy in the woods. She went back to teaching.

Rory's days were filled with tranquility, with contentment. That feeling he had at Cedar Creek State Park, on the boat to Puerto Cabezas, was no longer something that needed to be found. It never left him now. It was something he saw every time Davina smiled at him, every time Bash ran into his arms, every time the macaws flew above him, and every time he sat around the communal table with his colony, eating the most perfectly prepared meal by Leah.

"I'm done!" Bash ran up to Rory holding his crafted thermometer with a grin on his face.

"Good job! Now let's make sure it works. We're going to visit Leah, who is making some wonderful mango turnovers at the baker's dwelling. We're going to take all of your thermometers, as well as the one that I made here, and test the temperatures of the turnovers to make sure they're cool enough to eat. How does that sound?"

The children celebrated, grabbed their thermometers, and jumped out of their chairs to the door. Rory led the students out of the classroom, across the square, and to Amos's old dwelling, repurposed to house stoves for baking, always enticing and inviting colony members to snack and relax.

"Leah! We're here to test those turnovers of yours," he called as he pushed through the ajar door and guided the children inside to the large living room.

She stepped out with her daughter, each carrying a tray of turnovers, and they placed them on a table in front of the boys.

Rory leaned toward the students and put his hands on his knees. "All right, kids. Now be gentle, because if these turnovers are cool, we're going to eat them!"

"Yay!" A chorus of cheers melted into the stone walls.

The kids huddled around the turnovers and stuck their thermometers into them, comparing their temperatures.

Rory stepped back and joined Leah and Nora as the boys started tearing apart the desserts, laughing. "Hey, did I ever tell you that my mom's name was Nora?" he said to Leah's daughter, leaning against the wall.

"No, you didn't," Nora said to Rory, still watching the kids.

"In another life. I don't like to talk about it," he said shifting his gaze to Leah and smiling. "We all run from something, right?"

"Right," Leah responded and smiled back.

APPENDIX

Author's Note
Stanley, Scott M. and Galena K. Rhodes. "Before I Do." *The National Marriage Project at the University of Virginia.* 2014. Before-i-do.org.

ACKNOWLEDGMENTS

———

To think I wrote this book by myself is naive. Although an accomplishment of which I am proud, I could not have done it without the support, love, and help of those listed below. My gratitude in these next few pages is insufficient in recognizing their impact on both my life and journey as a writer. My husband, Ian Tvardovskaya, has not only supported my every crazy endeavor, from auditioning for MFA programs, to studying Lifespan Development for fun, to attending graduate programs in Foreign Service, to writing this book, to becoming parents, and everything in between, but has actively pushed me to do whatever it is I set my mind to. He has challenged me to reach for and attain goals I may have never thought possible for myself. Most importantly, he has helped me to do so by carrying so much weight in our family and household, giving me the space and opportunity to chase my dreams. I love you, Ian.

My mom, Irina Tvardovskaya, and dad, Bohdan Tvardovsky, have provided me with every opportunity to get me to where I am today. Arriving to the US as refugees, they studied, worked multiple jobs, and carved their way in a foreign land in hopes of providing us with a bright future. They spared no sacrifice for me, sending me to private schools, signing me up for sports, choir, piano lessons, acting classes, and so much more. Without their constant nudging to explore and create and their allowance to pursue my passions, I wouldn't have had the strength and courage to pursue the crazy endeavors of which Ian has been so supportive. They taught me to make living outside my comfort zone... my comfort zone.

My grandparents, Anna and Volodymyr Zahotynets, have supported generations of Tvardovskayas. They not only raised two incredible daughters, but they sacrificed the world they knew to come to the US temporarily to assist my mom in raising me, before eventually permanently resettling. The time they spent watching and helping me grow gave my parents the chance to work and support our family. Even now, their love permeates every room. Watching them chase our son, sing and read with him, provide him with a love that rivals our own, has created a foundation of familial kinship that I am so incredibly lucky to have and pass on to our children... and children's children... and children's children's children (if they so choose, of course), just like them.

I also want to thank a handful of teachers and mentors who lit a torch inside of me to be a lifelong learner.

To Mr. Overman, who made English fun and kept me challenged and engaged. Thank you for the feedback that was provided during the Trial of Socrates that equal parts highlighted my strengths and shared areas for opportunity, both of which motivated me to continue honing my skills.

To Gay Janis, who was nothing short of family, creating a community in the old Fine Arts Building that made students want to spend time both with her and each other, even if that meant hanging out in a dilapidated building for an upward of eight hours a day during tech week. Gay Janis supported me on the stage and in speech and debate and threw a flamethrower to my love for theatre and the arts. I am ever indebted to you.

To Eric Fleisch, who facilitated challenging conversations in the classroom in the most respectful way. To him who used accessible language and invited all students into the dialogue both in the classroom and outside of it. Thank you for fostering such a meaningful relationship with me that extended well past my Lehigh years.

Finally, to Derek Goldman, the only person within this sub-list who, although an educator, was not my teacher or professor within the classroom. Derek was and continues to be my mentor, the person who somehow found a way to overlap all of my passions, internationally, artistically, and through a business-oriented mindset. To the person who gave me the opportunity to work in theatre while at Georgetown, who always thought of and thinks of me for projects, and to whom I am grateful for continuously expanding my network.

I would also like to thank the Creator Institute; Eric Koester; my developmental editor, Michael Bailey; my acquiring editor, Alexa Tanen; my marketing and revisions editor, Jessica Drake-Thomas; and my layout editor Ruslan Nabiev for helping create this book with me, as well as my copyeditor, proofreader, and cover artist. Additionally, I'd like to thank Sarah Spech and Vinicius Aguiar, my "alpha" readers who took my messy first draft and trudged through it, providing me with invaluable feedback. Finally, I'd like to thank my beta readers, Elizabeth Colvin, Claudia Frantz, Solomiya Zborovska, and Hannah Halischak, for assisting with the finishing touches.

In addition to my parents, grandparents, and husband who all pre-ordered copies of *Identifiable*, I want to thank the following supporters who helped make this book a reality:

Solomiya Zborovska

Bohdana Zborovska

Claudia Frantz

Cynthia Giganti

Pathfinder Estates

Caroline Herron

Jessica Sterna

Elizabeth Colvin

Anndaria Jakyma

Samantha Robbins

Florin Economide

Sheldon Ruby

Damian Koester

Maria Redden

Markian Blazejowskyj

Michael Vanderkolk

Zoryana Donika

Talia Dunyak

Connor Moriarty

Edvin Berggren

Ann-Marie Camputaro

Rachael Martel

Hanna Berretz

Marissa Cangelosi

Oksana Rabosyuk

Natalie Sywyj

Marisa Thorne

Manuel Branco

Kristen Camputaro

Susan Camputaro

Eric Fasnacht

Justin Swain

Olena Firman

Laura Fasnacht

Olesya Rabosyuk

Katerina Arzhayev

The Casino Kombat Podcast

Kyoko Imai

Timothy Kasckow

Brooke Garee

Julie Lyden

Albert Hudson

Carol Casper

Benjamin Shaver

Benjamin Eneman

Jak Kramer

Kevin Goodwin

Luis M Garzon-Negreiros

Stefan Apostoluk

Razak Radityo

Rita Housseiny

Roksolana Balukh

Khrystyna Boyle

Parveen P. Gupta

Kirby Horvitz

Elizabeth Bubna

Cristina Spurlin
Marta Kotsubaev
Priti Sharma
Vinicius Aguiar
Olga Thomas
Sarah Spech
Chloe Diggs
George Salo
Ambar Chandra Sinha
Kimiya Sprengart
Riccardo Moauro
John Schultz
Amanda von Trapp
Celia Laskowski
Julia Pilla
Nicholas Deng
Marta Vilshanetska
Ru Story
Yuliya Vanchosovych
Esmeralda Begolli
Molly Fagan
Aaron Zacharia
Abigail M. Farrell
Abbey Patton
Breck Golden
Aleksei Klusov
Kristin Fasnacht
Yaryna Skabyk
Giancarlo Paternoster
Edward Offutt
Maria Krasniansky
Chloe Stein

Michael Brown
Hannah Halischak
Stephen Dubenko
Haider Naeem
Cheyenne Begley
Jessica J Borishchak
Muzna Abbas
JAV
Jeff Loeb
Benjamin Lillian
Daniela Cardenas
Aimee Slaughter
Derek Goldman
Andrew Schaus
Linda Lishchuk Hupert
Roman Drozd
Phil Burke
Samuel Boafo-Arko
Tomas Marambio
John Guido
Jamie Mindek
Kate Shafer
Michelle Christofferson
Joshua Caleb Parsons
Jamie Young
Daniel Heffernan
Santiago Zuniga
Celeen Hefele
Eric Koester
Mazahir Bootwala
Joe Rajka
Ievgeniia Olenych

Canan Ulu
Andrew Hart
Heather Smith
Logan Dopp
Evan Winterhalter
Stephanie Burns
Waleed Eliwat
Prathyusha Rainigari
Greer Garee
Marta Sydoryak
Aminat Yahaya
Eduardo Flores
Rishikesh Moharkar
Silas Humphries
Nadiya Balukh
Vasyl Rabosyuk
Leopold Wildenauer

Jennifer Biggin
Karen Garee
Layne Garee
Nicole Warner
Sean Felder
Richard Julian De La Paz
Nazar Kurdoba
Stefano Celle
Makala R Forster
Rachel Antoun
Austen Brower
Paul Doboszczak
Sonia Kostiw
Alexa Iwachiw
Michael Antonelli
Derick Schwedt